All in One Place

All in One Place

a Novel

CAROLYNE AARSEN

New York • Boston • Nashville

FaithWords
Hachette Book Group USA
237 Park Avenue
New York, NY 10017

Visit our Web site at www.faithwords.com.

Printed in the United States of America

First Edition: August 2007
10 9 8 7 6 5 4 3 2 1

The FaithWords name and logo are trademarks of Hachette Book Group USA.

Library of Congress Cataloging-in-Publication Data
Aarsen, Carolyne.
    All in one place : a novel / Carolyne Aarsen.—1st ed.
        p. cm.
    "Party-girl Terra Froese never expected to find herself stuck in small-town Montana, and Montana never bargained for Terra's antics"—Provided by the publisher.
    ISBN-13: 978-0-446-69682-1
    ISBN-10: 0-446-69682-X
1. Montana—Fiction. 2. Family—Fiction. I. Title.
PR9199.3.A14A79 2007
813'.6—dc22   2006100715

For my Mom.

Thanks for the home you made for us,
for the love you gave us, and for pointing us to Christ.

Acknowledgments

I want to thank my editor Anne Goldsmith and my agent Karen Solem, who both said I should tell Terra's story.

Thanks to Mark Mynhier and Sheriff Jim Cashell for their help with the police stuff. And thanks to Fern Aarsen for her help with the waitressing info. Diane, thanks for telling me what you liked and, probably more important, what you didn't like about the story.

Thanks to Heidi Nobles for keeping me on track, and thanks to all the good folks at FaithWords for their help in putting this story out into the world.

Where can I go from your Spirit? Where can I flee
from your presence?

—PSALM 139:7

All in One Place

Chapter One

By the time I left Idaho, I'd stopped looking over my shoulder. When I crossed the Continental Divide, my heart stopped jumping every time I heard a diesel pickup snarling up the highway behind me.

I was no detective, but near as I could tell, Eric didn't know where I was.

Four days ago, I'd waited until I knew without a doubt that he was at work, slipped out of the condo we shared, swiped his debit card, withdrew the maximum amount I could, rode the city bus as far as it would take me, and started hitchhiking. Phase one of my master plan could be summed up in three words: *Get outta town*. Okay, four words if you want to be precise about it.

Now, as I stood on the crest of a hill overlooking a large, open valley, I was on the cusp of phase two. Again, three words: *Connect with Leslie*.

I let the backpack slip off my shoulders onto the brown grass of the ditch and sank down beside it in an effort to rest my aching feet and still my fluttering nerves. I was leery of the reception I would get from my sister. Since August, nine months ago, I'd tapped out two long, rambling e-mails telling her what was happening. But each time I read the mess of my life laid out in black and white on a backlit screen, guilt and shame kept me from hitting the Send key.

The click of grasshoppers laid a gentle counterpoint to the sigh that I sucked deep into my chest. I slowly released my breath, searching for calm, reaching deep into a quiet place as my yoga instructor had taught me to do.

I pulled another breath in, tapping my fingers restlessly on my thigh, waiting.

Find the quiet place. Anytime now.

I reached deep, tried to picture myself mentally going deeper, deeper.

C'mon. C'mon.

The screech of a bird distracted me. Above, in the endless, cloudless sky, a hawk circled lazily, tucked its wings in, then swooped down across the field. With a few heavy beats of its wings, it lifted off again, a mouse hanging from its talons.

So much for inner peace. I guess there was a reason I dropped out of yoga class. That and the fact that my friend Amy and I kept chuckling over the intensity of the instructor as she droned on about *kleshas* and finding the state of non-ego.

The clothes were fun, though.

I dug into my backpack and pulled out my "visiting boots," remembering too well how I got them. Eric's remorse over yet another fight. He had come along, urging me to pick out whatever I wanted. I had thought spending over a thousand dollars would fix what was wrong between us, and, for a few weeks, it had.

I sighed as I stroked the leather. Sad that one of the best things that had come out of my relationship with Eric was a pair of Christian Louboutin boots with their signature red-leather soles. For now, the boots would give me that all important self-esteem edge I desperately needed to face Leslie.

As I toed off my worn Skechers and slipped on the boots, I did some reconnoitering before my final leg of the journey.

Beyond the bend and below me, the town of Harland waited, secure in the bowl of mountains surrounding the town. For the past three days, I'd been hitching rides from Seattle, headed toward this place, the place my sister now called home. For the past two hours those mountains—so high that they still had snow capping their peaks even though it was late May—had drawn me on, never getting closer.

I lifted my hair off the back of my neck. Surely it was too warm for May? I didn't expect Montana, home of mountains and rivers, to be this warm in spring.

My head felt like someone had been drizzling hot oil on it, basting the second thoughts scurrying through my brain.

I should have at least phoned. Would Leslie even want to see me after such a long silence? I knew Dan wouldn't be thrilled to see me come striding to his door, designer boots or not. Dan, who in his better moments laughed at my lame jokes, and in his worse ones fretted like a father with a teenage daughter about the negative influence he thought I exerted on my little sister. His wife.

The few times I checked my e-mail, I read about my little nephew Nicholas's stay in ICU and subsequent fight for his life. I knew I had messed up royally as an aunt and a sister. Leslie had sent a dozen e-mails pleading with me to connect. To call.

And I'd wanted to more than anything in the world. But at the time, I was holding on to my life with my fingertips and had no strength for anyone else.

You had your own problems. You didn't have time.

But I should have been there for my only sister. I could have tried harder.

The second thoughts were overrun by third thoughts, the mental traffic jam bruising my ego.

I pulled a hairbrush out of my knapsack in preparation for the last part of my trip. Bad enough I was showing up unannounced. I didn't need to look like a hobo. As I worked the brush through the snarl of damp curls, I once again promised myself I was going to get my hair cut. I pulled long auburn strands of hair out of the brush and let them float away on the faintest of breezes, to be returned back to the land. After doing my part for recycling, the brush went back into my purse, tucked into my backpack.

I brushed the grass off my artfully faded blue jeans. Still clean.

Zipping up my knapsack, I let out one more sigh before I heard the sound of a car coming up over the hill. Maybe a ride.

I twisted to see better, and my heart plummeted all the way down to the stiletto heels of my designer boots as the car topped the hill.

A sheriff's car, bristling with antennas, a no-nonsense light bar across the top.

Did Eric sic the cops on me?

I teetered a bit, wishing I were a praying person. Because if I believed that God cared even one iota about my personal well-being, I'd be reciting the Lord's Prayer, Hail Mary—anything to get His ear right now.

In spite of my sudden spate of nerves, my eyes were drawn to two young girls huddled in the backseat of the cruiser. They didn't look older than seven or eight. What could they have possibly done to warrant the heavy artillery of a police car and two officers?

The passenger door of the car opened, and my attention shifted to the man now approaching me. He wore the obligatory Stetson and tan uniform of state sheriffs. And of course a mass of hardware hanging around his waist, including a pistol.

I swallowed again.

There's no way Eric could know where you are, I reminded myself as I straightened. *They can't arrest you. You did nothing wrong.*

Besides, I thought, glancing again at the two frightened girls in the backseat, *there's no room for you in the car.*

"Good morning," the cop said as his partner got out of the car as well, also wearing the obligatory reflector sunglasses. "Nice day, isn't it?"

Maybe it was the sunglasses. Maybe it was the setting— two men, one woman, empty countryside. I put my guard up quicker than you can say, "Book 'em, Dano."

"Define *nice*." Not a great deflection, and not a good idea, but if I was in trouble, nothing I said would make a difference anyway. If I wasn't, I had just bought myself some time while I further assessed the situation with my razor intellect.

"Would you be willing to answer a few questions?" He had a deep, rough voice that would have reinforced my prickly tendencies, but the beginning of a dimple at the corner of his mouth made me relax. A little.

"If I answer I won't need to enter a witness protection program, will I?"

The dimple deepened a little, and I felt an answering smile. *I think I could like this guy, in spite of the gun and the shades.*

He was about to say something more when his partner

strode over, his uniform and upright bearing conveying "Serve and protect."

"Were you anywhere near a house located five miles down Clarkson Road in the past twenty-four hours?" The other sheriff's voice was quiet, polite, but his tone brooked no more nonsense from me.

"No."

"You know nothing about a party?"

"I'm sorry, I don't." I thought the apology was a nice cooperative touch.

"Have you seen any suspicious activity on this road? Any vehicles? People?"

"Any information you can give us would be helpful," the first officer added.

As my eyes flitted to the little girls with their pajamas and unkempt hair, my mind flashed back to another scene, also featuring two young girls, a hysterical mother, and a social worker who had come to ask a few questions. The social worker had left without Leslie and me, and I learned the first of many varied life skills that day.

"I'm not from around here," I said. "I wouldn't know suspicious from ordinary."

"What's your business here?" the shorter officer asked.

Self-preservation urged me to keep things obscure. "Just visiting."

"Visiting who?"

I wanted to tell him to mind his own business, my usual MO with nosy men, but the badge, the gun, the car, and all the authority invested in him by the state of Montana gave him the right to ask. "My sister. Leslie Froese—sorry—VandeKeere."

The dimple cop frowned. "You don't look like her."

Okay, maybe Leslie, being a mother and all, wasn't the type to be wearing high-heeled boots, a halter top, and a diamond in her nose, but I knew my whole image was way tamed down from what my friends in Seattle were sporting.

"How do you know her?"

"Leslie works in the emergency department of the hospital," he said quietly. "My job takes me there from time to time. I'm Lieutenant Jack DeWindt. This is Deputy Sheriff Diener."

I wasn't up on my Emily Post and wasn't sure if this was the point where we shook hands, so I simply offered a decisive nod. I hoped I wouldn't see either of them again anytime soon. I had come to Harland to lay low at Leslie's while the dust settled back in Seattle. Getting to know cops was not on the list.

"So, you've got nothing for us?" Sheriff Diener asked again.

"Nope." I gave him a quick smile and threw in a "hey, whatever" toss of my hair just to dot the i's and cross the t's.

Sheriff Diener looked convinced and strode back to the car, but Jack lingered for a moment. "I'll see you around," he said quietly, biting back a smile.

I supposed he meant it as a throwaway comment, but something in his eyes hinted at flirtation.

"Not a chance," I muttered through my gritted teeth as I smiled and waved. Eric had soured me on men and relationships for a long, long time.

As they drove away, two pale, forlorn faces stared at me over the backseat, and a shiver crawled up my spine. I wondered what lay in those girls' futures.

Unfortunately, I couldn't spare them more than a moment's sympathy. If I didn't get a ride soon, I would have to switch my footwear again.

I glanced back over my shoulder at the quiet highway, adjusted the straps of my backpack, and headed down the hill toward Harland, Leslie, and her family.

Ten minutes and two vehicles later, a car slowed down.

A young woman slouched behind the wheel. Sparkly barrettes clipped back blond hair, the perky effect negated, however, by her tired smile.

"Do ya need a ride?" she asked through the open passenger window as she leaned one skinny arm across the back of the seat. Her pale green shirt and blue jeans, though worn and faded, gave her a conservative look that inspired confidence.

I pulled open the passenger door.

And stopped when I saw a baby in the backseat.

The girl caught the direction of my look. "Don't worry 'bout Madison. She's finally quiet. Cried all morning, so I thought I'd take her for a ride."

Behind us stretched an empty road devoid of vehicles. Unless I wanted to walk the rest of the way to Harland, this was my ride. I tossed my knapsack in the back of the car, and followed it inside.

"Headed to Harland?" the driver asked as she pulled out onto the road.

"If that's where this road goes."

"This road goes nowhere," she said, steering the car with her elbows as she lit a cigarette. "Every morning, I look out the window . . ."

"And it's still there," I finished the old joke for her.

She waved her cigarette at me. "You want one?"

"No thanks." I wondered if she should be smoking around the baby, but as a rid-*er*, I wasn't about to lecture the rid-*ee*.

"Where you from?" Her question came out on the breath of a tired sigh.

"I'm Terra. I came from out west." *Keep it vague. You don't know her.*

"Amelia," she supplied. The car swerved as she slipped the lighter back into its holder. The baby's head lolled to one side, and I could see the trace of veins in her pale cheeks and in the tiny arms poking out of a stained and faded sundress.

"Do you mind turning the air-conditioning down a bit?" I asked.

Amelia frowned at me. "It's hot as Hades out there."

"Yes, but your baby seems a little cold. Her fingers are blue."

Amelia touched the baby's hand. "Oh, yeah," she said, then reached over and turned the fan down. "This is such crazy weather for May. I thought she was crying because she was hot, so, well . . ." She took another puff of her cigarette. "So, what's in Harland? You know anybody there?"

"Well, I've already met the cops . . ."

"What? When?"

"About twenty minutes ago. They stopped to ask me a few questions."

"Questions about what?"

"A party down the road. They had two little girls with them."

"What?"

"Do you know those girls?"

"No. I don't. It's just . . . I can't believe they would . . ." She let the sentence fade away as she stared straight ahead.

"Can't believe they would what?" Why was she so concerned?

"Never mind." She took another drag off her cigarette,

blowing smoke to the side. "I could sure use a drink right now. You want to come with me?"

And the baby? Did she need a drink, too?

This is none of your business, I reminded myself as I licked my dry lips and lifted my hair off the back of my neck.

The pavement shimmered in front of us, and through the heat waves, I caught a glimpse of the town of Harland coming closer with relentless speed. My heart fluttered.

Leslie's last batch of letters talked about God and faith and how the community had come through for her and Dan when Nicholas was in the hospital. Between the lines lay the unspoken accusation that I hadn't.

What should I have written her? *I'm sorry, but my chaos was more important than your chaos?*

Amelia flicked her cigarette out the window, then looked at me again as if underlining her previous question.

I had time. Leslie didn't know I was coming.

Maybe getting to know a few of Harland's residents wasn't such a bad idea. Give me a chance to scope out the place. What was the worst that could happen?

Chapter Two

I added the numbers on my napkin and factored in some optimism. If I was careful, my cash would last me long enough to visit Leslie and still get to Chicago, too. Emphasis on *careful*. I glanced at the man sitting beside me, blaming thrift for my decision to let him buy me a couple of beers.

Ralph caught my glance and his grin blossomed. "So you ready to party?" He leaned into my personal space, his hand shifting closer to mine.

I was nursing the remnants of my third beer, wishing I'd quit before I'd started, wishing I had the nerve to get up and walk through the smoke-filled room, out the door, and down to my sister's place.

But the longer I sat, the less inclined I felt to drop back into my sister's life. What if Eric *had* followed me? What if I brought disaster down on my sister and her family just by showing up?

Maybe it would be better if I faded out of Leslie's life. Let my little sister forget she ever had a loser sister like me.

I glanced behind me. Amelia was leaving, lugging Madison and her car seat with her. Initially she was going to leave the baby in the car, but I convinced her that taking the baby into the bar was a smarter option.

The jukebox started playing "Bed of Roses," distracting me from Amelia's departure, the music teasing out pictures from the past. Leslie and I taped that song from the radio years ago, playing it until the tape wore out, staring soulfully into the eyes of Jon Bon Jovi as we sang along. I felt the subtle undertow of memories pulling me back. I needed Leslie right now. Needed her badly.

"You seem sad," Ralph was saying. "A drink could chase your blues away."

Or turn me a beguiling shade of green. "No. Thank you." Ralph was quickly losing what little charm he might have had two beers ago.

"Then how about a ride home?"

Home. There was a word guaranteed to make me feel maudlin. All I had with Eric was a fancy condo, a platinum credit card, and too much fear. No home there.

"Just leave me alone," I said.

"C'mon. I bought you two beers . . ."

"And here I thought you were a generous, selfless type." I pushed away the half-full glass of beer that I should have known would have strings attached. I didn't like the smirk on the bartender's face as he took the glass away, nor did I appreciate the wink he gave Ralph.

Ralph slipped his arm around my shoulder. "C'mon. We could have some fun."

Maybe Ralph understood body language better than English, so I pushed at him. "Leave me alone."

His eyes narrowed, and he quickly put his arm back, only this time he squeezed just a little harder. I pushed back. A little harder.

When he tried to kiss me, I elbowed him.

His eyes narrowed and fear slithered through me. "Why, you—" His open hand swung toward me. I ducked, pushed, but as I tried to get away, he caught my arm.

The same arm Eric had grabbed too hard when I told him I wasn't going to stay with him anymore.

And my anger blossomed.

I reached behind me, connected with the solid neck of a beer bottle. When I lifted the beer bottle, it was as if I were watching someone else—simply a spectator trying to warn this wayward hand that if it completed the arc, it would be in deep trouble.

Then the bottle connected with Ralph's head, right over his eye, and I felt one with my arm again. The bottle splintered. Ralph roared and punched my shoulder. Blood poured out of his head as he rained down curses on me and my mother.

I yelled back, still holding the remnant of the bottle.

Ralph grabbed for my arm. I swung and hit him again. Arms grabbed at me from behind. I kicked and stomped, using my heels against shins just like my self-defense instructor taught me.

In spite of my flailing and spinning, I suddenly found my arms pinned behind my back. Ralph held his forehead, blood pouring into his eye, screaming that he was going to press charges.

And when I saw the flashing lights driving up outside, I had this sinking feeling that I hadn't outrun my troubles at all.

Without his sunglasses, Jack DeWindt looked to be on the young side of thirty, until you saw the fan of wrinkles at the corners of his eyes and the faint lines around his mouth. His hazel eyes, fringed with thick, dark lashes, were deep-set, drooping a bit, which gave him a deceptively gentle look. The last time I saw him, he was smiling, but now his mouth had a hard, narrow look of authority.

"You're free to go," he said as the door to my cell slid open. "Your sister came up with the rest of the bail money."

When I was told that using a bail bondsman meant I forfeited my deposit, I went with posting bail myself. Trouble was, I didn't have enough money. Consequently, my first connection with my dear sister was a call from the sheriff's office asking her to literally bail me out.

"And then what?" I asked, stifling a new rush of nerves at the thought of facing my sister. Asking her to get me out of jail after many months and fewer e-mails was more humiliating than having Ralph hit on me and charge me with assault.

I'd tried to claim self-defense, but I was the visiting "lush," and Ralph was the homegrown good ol' boy with friends in low places only too willing to testify on his behalf. So Ralph pressed charges, and though I tried to countercharge, I ended up being fingerprinted, photographed, booked, and now bailed.

"We'll notify you when your court date is set." Jack followed me down the hall.

"Do you have any idea when that will be?" I pushed down a wave of panic. The longer I stayed in one place, the better the odds of Eric finding me.

"Depends on the judge and how booked up she is."

She.

I wondered if Ms. Judge had ever been hit on by a redneck loser. Of course, Ms. Judge probably knew better than to accept drinks from strangers—one of the first few rules my mother tried to impart to Leslie and me.

A final set of doors swung open into freedom . . . and there was Leslie.

She stood behind the plate-glass window separating the receptionist from the public. All I could see of her was a denim jacket, a T-shirt, and her bent head as she signed a paper. Her hair was shorter than I remembered, and streaked. A sudden yearning pulled at me with almost tangible force. My sister.

In spite of my roadside grooming, I knew my hair was a dried-out snarl and my eyes were probably red. My fingers were still black from the fingerprinting ink that simply wouldn't wash off. Add a request for bail money, and I was off to a running start with my dear sister.

I ran my hands down the legs of my pants. Then again . . .

Jack frowned at me. "You okay?"

"I'll be fine."

He lifted one eyebrow as if he didn't believe me, but I didn't have time to be concerned about him anymore.

Leslie looked up as I came closer.

"Hey, Leslie," I said, projecting breezy and carefree. "Good to see you."

"Terra." The word piggybacked a sigh, mom-style.

I'd have to search a long time before I found a sentiment in the card section of the local drugstore to thank her for posting bail. So I decided to keep it simple and real. "Thanks for coming."

"I'm guessing the bar was a detour on your way to see me?" The hurt in her voice twisted through the casual facade I struggled to maintain.

"Of course it was," I said. "Nicholas was just a fuzzy baby bundle the last time I saw him."

"He's walking now."

"I'm sorry, Leslie." What I lacked in originality, I tried to make up for in conviction. "I'm really sorry."

Leslie's smile wobbled. I wanted to grab her and hold on. But I couldn't in this public place and definitely not with Cop Jack watching us.

So I reached over and made do with a quick squeeze of her shoulder. Somewhere in the transition between adolescence and adulthood, she had not only gotten taller—she had also kept her feet planted firmly on the ground.

Leslie turned to Jack. "Can she leave now?"

Jack nodded, standing arrow-straight, hands on hips. "We'll notify you when the court date is set. In the meantime, as a condition of bail, she has to stick around."

How long would it take Eric to track me down? Could he? Had I ever mentioned where Leslie lived? I'd been careful. I had never used his computer to send e-mails to Leslie, had never used the home phone to call . . .

"Will you be coming to the farm to work with your horse?" Leslie asked Jack. I did a double take at the question. Did everyone know everyone else in this town?

"Next time I have some time off."

"We'll see you then."

"Looking forward to it." Jack glanced at me and smiled. His eyes crinkled up, and the tough exterior I'd had the privilege of looking at for the past half hour melted away like frost in the morning sun. He actually looked human.

He actually looked pretty good.

And down that path lies trouble and more trouble.

"So that means we can go?" I asked Leslie. "Like right now?"

Leslie nodded.

"Good." I turned to Jack, staring somewhere over his left shoulder. "I'd like my backpack, please."

"Claim it at the front desk."

Leslie was about to follow me, but Jack beckoned her over with a lift of his finger. "I need to talk to you a minute, Leslie."

She glanced at me as if she wasn't sure she should leave me unsupervised.

"I'll just wait outside then," I said, annoyed at how easily he'd dragged my sister's attention away from me.

The woman at the front desk handed me my backpack with the contents neatly packaged in what I guessed was an evidence bag. *Nice souvenir,* I thought as I dumped the whole bag into my backpack, which I heaved over my shoulder.

The door of the cop shop drifted shut behind me with a pneumatic wheeze. A fly buzzed lazily past my head. A couple of cars sighed past. Across the street an elderly couple shuffled out of the diner, and I heard the thin, reedy voice of the woman complaining about the slow service.

Leslie was still occupied. She and Jack had stepped outside and were frowning, intent on their conversation.

Finally, Leslie nodded a couple of times as if agreeing with what Jack said, and then, thank goodness, we were finally alone.

"You look good," I said quietly, reminding myself that I needed to go slow, make gentle overtures.

The last time I saw her, her face was pale and drawn in spite of the makeup she'd troweled on. Now her short hair framed a naturally tanned face. No makeup. Plump cheeks.

I caught a hint of vulnerability on her face. Her eyes held a brightness that could have been good health or the beginning of tears.

"Terra, why did you . . . Why didn't you . . ." As her hurt-edged words tumbled between us, I caught a note of haunted pain.

We made tentative steps, and then our arms were wound around each other, shutting out the street, the curious pass-ersby, and the rest of the world.

She smelled like fresh air and clean clothes and home. And for the first time since I left the hospital, the knot inside me loosened. Just a bit.

"I missed you," she whispered, squeezing me hard. Then I heard a telltale sniff in my ear. "I missed you so much."

An answering sob trembled deep within me, and for a moment, I wanted to release it. To let her hold me up. But I didn't have a right to her support.

"Hey, what's with the tears?" I drew away with a light laugh, trying to shift the emotional atmosphere back to or-dinary. Back to the Terra she knew and had put up with over the years.

Leslie gave me a shaky smile and swiped at a lone tear track-ing down her cheeks. "Just being sentimental, that's all."

"Can we go?" I said.

"My car is parked around the corner," Leslie said as she dug through her oversized purse.

As we rounded the corner, I spied a familiar little Honda. "You're still driving that old grocery-getter?"

"Don't laugh. It's paid for," Leslie said, sniffing again. "I notice you didn't exactly sail into town in a Jag."

"Actually, it was a Malibu."

Leslie frowned and I held up my thumb.

This netted me another sigh. "I thought you had a car."

"Emphasis on *had*. I sold the car when I moved to Seattle."

Leslie walked over to the car and I waited for her to unlock my door.

"It's not locked," her muffled voice called out. "Harland is not a high crime area. Especially this close to the sheriff's office."

I caught a hint of anger on the last two words. "I'm sorry you had to pick me up here and about that whole bar thing. Some guy was hitting on me. It wasn't my fault."

Leslie fiddled with the ring of keys in her hand. "Is it ever?"

I read disbelief mixed with shame in her expression.

"Were you busy when the sheriff called?"

"I was entertaining Wilma's cousins from Holland. They wanted to stay on the farm. Neither Judy nor Wilma has the room, and Gloria's dealing with her own crisis, so I have them for a few days."

"To sleep?"

"Not many hotels where we live." She clamped her lips down, and I guessed "picking sister up from jail" wasn't going to make a great impression on the relatives.

Apologizing again wouldn't change much, so I ventured into other territory. "How are the kids?"

Leslie shot me a flare of irritation at the abrupt change in topic. Then she sighed and came along. "Anneke is getting even wiser beyond her years. And she's formed an attachment to a red polka-dotted skirt that used to belong to Gloria. Nicholas is growing like crazy. He can say cow, kitty, Sasha, and mama." As Leslie spoke, her expression softened, and I could see that she had changed more than just her hairstyle. I knew she loved her kids, but I had never heard her voice go low and gentle when she talked about them. "Wilma says he's just like Dan was when he was younger."

"And how are things going with you and Wilma Vande-Keere?" Wilma, Leslie's mother-in-law, hadn't approved of Leslie, who didn't go to church like the VandeKeeres did and who had pulled her beloved son Dan out of Wilma's sphere of controlling influence. Wilma didn't approve of me either, so Leslie and I had that in common.

She twisted the key in the ignition. "I can't imagine what she's going to think about my family now."

Each syllable of her last words hit me like a little slap, hurting worse than what Ralph had dished out earlier.

Leslie rested her hands on the steering wheel and pulled in a couple of quick breaths. I hoped her attempt at relaxation proved effective. I clung to self-control with a wavering fist and needed a sister who had it together.

"What were you thinking going into a bar this time of day? It's not even noon!" The words spilled out in a rush of anger.

"I wanted to pay Amelia back. For giving me a ride."

"Did she have her baby with her?"

"Yeah."

"She was at the bar, and here we had an appointment set up for her baby . . ." With a light shake of her head, she flipped further questions away.

Though I was curious about her comment concerning Amelia, I wanted to explain my side of my unfair entanglement with the long arm of the law, but I sensed Leslie was still trying to get her head around the fact that her sister was now a registered felon who had decked a man with a beer bottle. Not the kind of thing you put in the annual Christmas letter. I figured I'd better keep a low profile and wait for the sisterly connection to reappear. Though I didn't come often, up until the past nine months, I'd e-mailed frequently, phoned periodically. We were sisters. I loved her. She loved me. We just needed some time together. And from the way Lieutenant Jack was talking, I was going to be here longer than I had anticipated.

It will be fine. Relax. Don't worry.

I slouched down in my seat, maintaining a low profile.

Leslie said nothing more as she drove through town. The little frown wrinkling her forehead told me we weren't going to get to the laughing and squealing part of our reunion for a few miles yet. I wondered if we'd hit the sharing stories part at all.

So I kept quiet as we went through the third stoplight in town, headed south up over a range of hills, and then broke out into another large valley sheltered by yet more mountains reaching up into an endless sky.

A deep sigh drifted out of Leslie, and I finally saw a smile on her face.

"Isn't this beautiful?" she said, an unfamiliar reverence in her voice.

The view from the hill above Harland was impressive, but this surpassed it by the country miles spread out in front of us. The folded rock of the mountains capped by snow was awe-inspiring, and just behind that I could see the vague outline of even higher mountains standing guard.

The peaks of Yellowstone Park, I guessed, letting the view wash over me.

"You don't see it, do you?" she asked, misinterpreting my silence.

"I see . . . lots of country . . ." Eloquence was not my first language, and the sentence fell as flat as the prairies I had seen in some of my travels. Words were the wrong medium to describe the feeling the sheer scope of the space encompassed by mountains created in me. I became smaller and more insignificant the longer I looked.

Leslie smiled at my feeble response. "When we first moved here, I felt lost. Disoriented. But now, it's home."

The wistful tone on the word *home* hearkened back to another time in our lives. Two girls sitting huddled on a bed under a blanket, making plans for their future while their mother slept in front of the television.

We had each drawn up house plans, envisioned our neighborhoods, and decided how many children we were going to have. Our houses were supposed to be situated in cozy, well-treed suburbs of a nameless city. But, more important, on the same street so we could pop into each other's homes, borrow sugar, and exchange recipes.

Now Leslie lived in the wilds of Montana, and I . . . well, I just lived wild.

It seemed that my dreams had been discarded somewhere along the way, while Leslie's had morphed into the life of a farm wife.

"I understood from your e-mails that you had a hard time

adjusting," I said. "I'm just surprised Harland's become your Mayberry."

"It took me some time to get used to living here," Leslie agreed as her car began the long descent into the valley. "I resented being so far from town, and I resented Dan's family and all the connections he had to this community." She laughed lightly. "With God's help and prayer, I know I've changed."

Unease squirmed through me at her casual mention of God. "So what's with you and this church thing? I didn't think you'd go all kumbayah on me."

The frown made another brief appearance.

"It's not a 'thing,' as you so blandly put it." Underneath Leslie's quiet voice I caught a hint of firm resolve. "I've seen and experienced a lot lately with Nicholas . . ."

The hurt in her voice hit me as hard as her words. I had been a lousy sister and a poor aunt. But I didn't have space in my mind to dwell on that.

"How far do you live from town?" I asked, striking out blindly into the foreign territory that had become conversation with my sister.

"Half an hour. Unless I'm stuck behind some slowpoke driver whose mission in life is to be Keeper of the Speed."

I hadn't heard that term since Leslie and I were young, and I clung to the narrow opening. "Like that lady who used to drive us to school when we lived in that apartment in Pittsburgh? What was her name again?"

"I'm sure her name wasn't Sally Slowpoke, like we christened her." Leslie's smile enlarged the opening.

"I used to be able to finish half my homework on the way to school when she drove," I added.

"I still don't know how Mom conned her into doing that for the six months we lived there."

"Mom had her ways." I had never told her that I was the one conning Sally Slowpoke by promising we would keep Mom's behavior acceptable in return for the ride.

"Have you heard from Mom in the past year?"

I shook my head.

"Me neither."

Our silence made us allies in our disappointment.

"Do you have any idea where she might be?" Leslie asked. "I thought she might want to at least make some kind of connection with her grandchildren."

"I don't know. I was actually hoping we could try to find her."

Leslie tapped her fingers on the steering wheel. "I'm not really interested in trying, Terra."

"Don't you ever wonder if she has any regrets?"

"I would hope so." Leslie shot me a quick, jabbing look. "Why do you ask?"

"I just think she could be pretty lonely."

"That's her choice. And since when have you started sticking up for her?"

I had been critical of our mother in the past. But now? Condemnation didn't come as easily as it used to. My life's choices gave me no ground from which to throw stones.

"I hope she doesn't decide to suddenly show up here as well," Leslie said.

The "as well" tacked onto her complaint piled guilt upon guilt.

Moving right along . . .

"And what about you, Terra? What have you been doing?

Anything come of that guy you told me about in your e-mail? Eric something or other?"

"No. Nothing. Nothing at all. I moved out after—"

"Please don't tell me you were living with him?" Leslie's question was like a shot to the heart.

"Okay. I won't." If you wanted to call what we did *living*.

"Terra—"

I held up a hand, forestalling the lecture that I should have known would be coming. As young girls we'd always laid out the order of our relationships. Boyfriend. Marriage. Sex. Babies. No deviation.

My sister, Miss Leslie, had managed to follow the formula to a T. Then there was me. The only T in my life's formula was the initial of my first name.

"Okay. I don't want to lecture you . . ."

"Thank you."

"But I do worry about you and your lifestyle. Didn't we always say we weren't going to turn out like Mom?"

"I give up. Did we?" I added a forced laugh.

Leslie's poke reassured me that she understood the old joke. "Terra, you know I love you."

Her words dove deep into my heart and dislodged the doubts I'd had about coming here. "I love you, too, Leslie."

"I just want you to be happy."

"I am, now that I'm here."

"I'm happy you're here, too. And now, my dear sister, if you look to the left . . ."

"You'll miss the scenery on the right," I quipped.

"Actually, you'll see the farm."

I obediently looked left, catching a glimpse of a yellow

house and a cluster of barns before the house disappeared behind another grove of trees.

"Home." The word sifted out on a light sigh of contentment.

A finger of envy wriggled in my heart. She seemed settled. Secure.

She didn't need or miss me at all.

Chapter Three

Before turning into the driveway, Leslie unexpectedly slowed the car down, pulled over to the side of the road, stopped, and rested her wrists on the steering wheel.

Sensing she was about to make an announcement, I pushed down a shiver of apprehension. There'd been enough seriousness between us to last a lifetime. I was ready for jokes, a few laughs, and shared memories to cement our relationship.

"Do you remember what happened between you and Wilma at my wedding?"

Oh, yes. Another inebriated moment drawn from the archives. "I remember she was pretty ticked at me," I said, avoiding the obvious.

"Because you had too much to drink and you insulted her." Leslie wasn't above stating the obvious.

"I remember that you were glad I did."

"At the time, Dan and I were in a different place in our life."

"Yeah. Minneapolis."

Leslie caught the corner of her lip between her teeth and gave me a worried look. "I'm serious, Terra. Wilma and I are part of the same family and the same community now. What

she thinks matters a bit more than it used to. And Wilma's at
the house now, and . . . well . . . what with you getting arrested this morning . . ."

"Don't worry, Sis. I'm not about to become a career criminal." I bit back my protestations of innocence, knowing that
I was beating a dead horse. The whole situation still had me
fuming, but right now I was not operating from a position of
strength. Truth to tell, I was getting tired of not operating from
a position of strength. Tired of having my life's choices made
for me by my circumstances.

*It's just for now. Just relax. Breathe. Just get through this little
glitch.*

Leslie laid a hand on my shoulder. "It's just . . . I'm trying
to make a new life here. I want it to work."

"I'll behave." I tried not to resent the fact that she saw me
as a potential liability.

"Thanks. That's all I ask."

And now that she had dealt with her troublesome sister, she
put the car back in gear.

A few minutes later, we pulled up behind a small brown
car and a large white pickup. As we came to a stop, the
screen door slapped open and Anneke came bounding down
the wooden steps of the veranda, Nicholas a few steps behind her.

"Auntie Terra! Auntie Terra!" Her blond hair slapped her
cheeks as she ran.

She remembers me, I thought with satisfaction as I crouched
down to greet my niece.

Anneke threw herself at me, a solid bundle of enthusiastic
acceptance. She had a little more heft to her than the last time
I'd seen her, and she threw me off balance.

A dog barked, the door of the house opened, and another pair of arms grabbed on to me, joining the fray.

I teetered on my stiletto-clad feet, then turned to Nicholas.

His hair, thick as ever, lay like a carpet on his head. Bright blue eyes blinked back at me, then widened as he seemed to realize he didn't know me.

"My mommy! My mommy!" He pushed me away, his head swiveling in panic.

"Gimme a piggyback," Anneke shouted in my ear, her sticky fingers tangling in my hair as the dog's barking rose against the background of Nicholas's crying.

"Sasha, down," Leslie called out, swinging Nicholas easily onto her hip and catching Anneke by one arm. "Anneke, please don't be so loud."

And in seconds, bedlam was banished, and all I could hear was the sound of Nicholas sniffling and the dog breathing down my neck.

How did she get to be this capable mommy? The last time I had come for a visit, Anneke had Dan and Leslie wound around her little pinky.

"But I wanna piggyback," Anneke whined halfheartedly. A single lift of Leslie's eyebrow and Anneke lowered her head, scuffing the ground with the toe of her sneaker.

"Maybe later," I said, ruffling her hair in an effort to appease her.

She slapped my hand away and I heard Leslie's light sigh. "Anneke, you can say you're sorry to Auntie Terra or you can go to your room. Which one do you want?"

Anneke looked up at me as if gauging my effectiveness in the discipline department, then mumbled a quick "Sorry."

"Sorry about that," Leslie said as Anneke slouched back to the house. "She really picks up on people's moods and tends to get wound up when things get tense."

And things get tense when Mommy has to go to Harland to pick up her sister from the sheriff's office.

"She's just young," I said airily, as if I had any clue how a child Anneke's age would behave.

The door opened again, and Wilma VandeKeere stepped out. She had the same high cheekbones Dan had, the same intensely blue eyes. I supposed that the frown puckering her forehead would be similar to Dan's once I saw him again as well.

Her fashionably streaked hair was styled in a bob. Eye shadow dusted her eyelids; earrings glinted from her earlobes. Her tailored shirt was tucked into a pair of khaki pants holding a crease that looked like it could cut.

Wilma looked as scary as the day I'd literally run into her during the rehearsal dinner for Dan and Leslie's wedding.

Nicholas pulled away from Leslie, leaning toward Wilma. "Want Nana!" he called out, his voice filled with surprising joy.

Wilma's features softened as she leaned down to pick up her grandson. He grabbed her around the neck, mussing her hair, but she didn't seem to mind. "You didn't finish your cookie, Nicholas."

Nicholas grabbed her face between his hands. "No cookie."

Wilma's smile transformed her features. "But Mommy made them just for you." She rubbed her nose over his face, brushed a kiss over his cheeks, then turned to me.

"Hello, Terra. It's good to see you again."

If I hadn't seen how her expression softened when she was

with Nicholas, I might have missed the slight stiffening when she turned to me.

"I'm glad to be here." Unoriginal and feeble, but what else could I say under the circumstances?

"Leslie, I was wondering if you had any more cream," Wilma asked. "The pitcher is empty, and I couldn't find another container in the fridge."

Leslie smacked herself on the side of the head. "I was going to pick some up when I ran into town. Sorry, Mom. No."

"Don't worry. It's not a problem." Once again, Wilma's smile held a warmth markedly missing from her little encounter with me. She paused. "Will you be long?"

"Just a few more minutes."

"I'll keep our company entertained. They were hoping to walk over the property in a few minutes." As the door fell shut behind Wilma, I shot Leslie a puzzled glance.

"I thought we had a mom." I dug into my little bag of tricks, trying to find a tone that came closer to teasing than the faint betrayal I felt.

"Wilma is a mom to me," Leslie said, folding her arms over her chest. "She's supportive and helpful. She has her quirks, but she's around. Dependable."

"And our mom isn't."

Leslie gave me a tired look, as if unwilling to go back to this worn, talked-out topic.

Next item.

"Thanks again for picking me up. I didn't know you were so busy."

"And if you had, would you have decided not to get into a fight?"

Apologizing would have been redundant. "I'll pay you back."

The pity on her face bothered me more than her previous request for me to behave myself. "With what?"

I stifled a riffle of panic at the thought that all my available cash now resided in the hands of the sheriff's office of Harland County, Montana.

"Maybe I could help you out on the farm? I could gather eggs, babysit, slop hogs, muck out stalls." I lifted my hands in a gesture of supplication. "I'll do my best *Little House on the Prairie* imitation."

"Except we live in the mountains," Leslie said.

"Little House in the Rockies?"

"For now, you can promise not to get Wilma worked up."

When we were younger, I was the one who made her lunches, who made sure she had clean clothes, who got her out the door and to school on time. My moment of irresponsibility was a glitch in the matrix, not an ongoing problem that needed her firm and somewhat motherly hand.

"I'll lay low and not make eye contact," I promised, stifling a flare of irritation. I knew I was far from perfect, but I was house-trained.

"Just be friendly and ordinary, like I know you can be," she said.

Inside the house, a cacophony of voices in two different languages washed over us, and I knew it would be some time before I had enough quiet time with my sister to make up the ground I had lost this morning and over the past nine months.

An older woman with short, spiky hair, a younger woman with a man beside her, then Wilma and a young girl were perched around the kitchen table. The room held the welcome scent of coffee and cinnamon.

"Femmelies, Siem, Karl, Elsa? I'd like you to meet my sister, Terra." Leslie made appropriate introductions as another teenage girl entered the room. She sauntered over, her eyes wide with anticipation, her hands strung up in the pockets of a pair of gravity-defying low-rise jeans, topped with a bright pink tube top that exposed a generous amount of seventeen-year-old tummy.

Enjoy that smooth, taut skin, I thought, sucking in my own slightly pooching stomach, remembering the twenty minutes my own stomach was as flat.

"Tabitha, this is Terra, my sister," Leslie said. "Terra, this is Tabitha, Gloria's daughter. She's staying with us to help keep our guests' daughter company." As she spoke, Leslie reached over and discreetly pulled Tabitha's hands out of her pockets. "Honey, please pull your jeans up a bit?"

Tabitha sighed but did as she was told. I guessed I wasn't the only wayward person Leslie was setting on the straight and narrow.

"Leslie told me you've lived all over the place," Tabitha said, slipping her hands back into her pants pockets.

"I've been around."

"I've got to serve coffee," Leslie said. "Terra, do you want some?"

I shook my head.

"I thought that was your preferred post-maudlin-mood enhancer?" she asked, letting me catch the faintest twinkle in her eye.

That small moment, that tiny glimpse into our shared past, gave me hope for the rest of my stay here.

"Maybe later. Can I help?" I asked, eager to start my indentured service.

Leslie handed me a carafe. "You can draw on your extensive waitressing experience and refill cups."

"At last, something within my realm of expertise." I took the carafe, but as I walked to the table, Tabitha was hot on my heels.

"Leslie says you went backpacking in Europe," she said. "I'd kill to do that."

"That's hardly an appropriate comment," Wilma said quietly, raising one eyebrow the smallest of millimeters, moving aside so I could fill her cup.

"Sorry, Gramma," Tabitha said, sliding her grandmother a quick smile.

Wilma inclined her head to the empty space beside the young teenage guest, and Tabitha scuttled away. I saw Wilma give me a worried glance, and I sensed her concern over this jailbird leading her granddaughter astray.

"Leslie, this is lovely," Wilma said approvingly at the tray of cookies and brownies Leslie set on the table. "You've been working hard."

Her endorsement pulled a genuine smile out of Leslie, as did the appreciative comments from the guests.

I had to confess, I was impressed as well. The last cookies Leslie served me were some stale Oreos that she had stashed away in the darkened recesses of the pantry of her house in Seattle.

The porch door swung open and a tuneless whistle preceded the person coming in.

"Daddy! Daddy!" I heard from a hallway off the kitchen, and Anneke came barreling in, veering right just as Dan entered the room.

He scooped her up and swung her into the air. "Did ya miss

me, princess?" he asked, lowering her and dropping a kiss on her head.

"So, so much, Daddy," she said, clinging to his hand as if she hadn't seen her father for months.

Dan's hair was blonder than before, his eyes bluer in a tanned face. A spray of wrinkles fanned out from his eyes. His shirt, softened from repeated washings, hung on his broad shoulders like an old friend. He'd lost that intensity I remembered seeing on his face. In spite of the frown now creasing his forehead, his body seemed more at home here in this old farmhouse. More relaxed.

"Hello, Terra," he said, his hand still resting on Anneke's head. "It's been a while. Good to see you again."

Polite words enhanced with a polite upward slide of his lips. Like mother, like son.

"Sorry about dropping in like this." I hoped contrition would cover my misdeeds. "You've got a lovely place here."

"Thanks. We like it." He ruffled Anneke's hair.

If I knew anything about farming, I could have asked him how things were going with the cows or the crops or whatever kept him occupied right now.

As it was, awkwardness and my nine-month absence from his and his family's lives stood between us like an unwelcome guest.

The sound of a chair scraping back broke into the unwieldy silence. "Dan. Hoe gaat het, met je jongen?" The younger male relative hurried over to Dan, then hugged him with great enthusiasm.

"I'm doing just fine, Karl. Good to see you," Dan replied.

Karl said something back in Dutch, and the other visitors all laughed.

I gave Leslie a puzzled look, and she lifted a shoulder in a vague shrug. Obviously, she was out of the language loop as well.

Leslie made more coffee, and I poured and smiled and re-filled the plate with more squares and cookies and in general tried to make myself useful and unobtrusive.

The guests, Karl, Femmelies, Siem, and Elsa, were friendly, but I thought they caught a hint of the underlying tension. They kept looking from me to Leslie, as if trying to put the two of us together in a family album.

I knew we didn't look the same. Having different fathers didn't help. Nor did the feather earrings or the stiletto boots that made a clacking sound every time I walked across the worn linoleum.

I heard a beep from a room off the kitchen. Sounded like a washing machine had finished its cycle. Leslie was about to get up when I held up my hand. "I'll throw the clothes in the dryer," I said, glad for something constructive to do.

"I usually hang them up on the clothesline."

"I'll help you," Tabitha offered, pushing her chair back. She grabbed her coat, then scampered off to the laundry room before Wilma or Leslie could object.

When I got there, she was yanking wet clothes out of the machine and heaving them into a laundry basket.

"The clothesline is outside," she whispered, grabbing the basket.

I followed her through another door leading outside.

She closed the door behind her, peering into the window. "Good, they're talking again," she said, pulling out a plastic bag from her back pocket. It held two squashed-looking cigarettes and she offered one to me. Second time in one day.

"Are you kidding?" I said, hefting the laundry basket onto a stand by the clothesline. "I've more than exceeded my vice quota for the day."

"I've been dying for one for the past hour." She took another puff, the sharp, acrid scent of the smoke wafting past me as she perched herself on the veranda railing.

"Kinda young to be smoking, aren't you?"

"I'm seventeen." Tabitha laughed. "When did you start?"

Thirteen, but I wasn't about to tell her that. A brother of a friend had gotten them for us.

I had quit years ago, but I could still feel the bite of the smoke in my lungs, the faint rush of nicotine in my system, each time I smelled a cigarette burning. And each time, it annoyed me that something so small could create such a longing.

I pulled a shirt out of the tangle of laundry in the basket, untwisting the arms. As I held it up, my plan to help hit its first snag.

"You don't know what you're doing, do ya?" Tabitha asked, swinging her legs.

"Not a clue." My basic method was: Drop clothes into all available washing machines in the Laundromat, pull wet clothes out, stuff into dryer, drag into laundry bag, haul home, make dirty, and start all over again.

The only time I had hung clothes up was when I draped them over the backs of chairs when the dryers at the Laundromat were full or broken down.

Tabitha stuck her cigarette in her mouth, hopped off her perch, and took the shirt from me. "You shake it out like this, grab a couple of clothespins . . ."

The door behind us opened.

Tabitha yanked the cigarette out of her mouth.

"Who is smoking out here?" Wilma asked.

I plucked the cigarette from Tabitha's hands and turned to face her, holding the burning cigarette between my fingers.

"Sorry," I said, giving Wilma my best sheepish smile.

She frowned. One more sin to add to my résumé.

"Tabitha, we're going for a walk. Elsa would like you to come along."

Tabitha sighed. "She barely speaks English, and Terra needs my help."

"I'm sure Terra can manage the laundry just fine."

"I'm the laundry queen," I said with an airy wave of my hand, forgetting about the cigarette burning between my fingers.

Wilma delicately waved the cigarette smoke away, staying behind as Tabitha let the door fall shut behind her. "It's very kind of you to help Leslie," she said once Tabitha was gone. "I'm sorry that she's so busy right now."

I tried to decipher a hidden meaning behind her careful words. The Wilma I remembered had an edge that could cut with the slightest provocation. Of course, I was in quite a provocating mood the last time I saw her. My little sister was getting married and moving out of the apartment we had shared for two years. I was still single, with no matrimonial hopes on the horizon. I was depressed and looking for an outlet.

Wilma, with her pinched mouth and general air of disapproval of my sister and me, had been a worthy adversary.

We almost hit it off, in the literal sense of the expression.

Now Leslie was calling her "Mom," and Wilma was thanking me for helping my own sister. How things changed.

"I'm sorry, too," I said, holding the cigarette down and away from her.

Wilma followed the direction of my hand, her nose wrinkling ever so slightly. "Leslie doesn't like smoking in the house. She still has some concerns about Nicholas. He was quite sick last summer. That was a very hard time for your sister."

"I know."

"Okay, then." Wilma brushed some nonexistent dirt off her pants. "You are welcome to join us, if you wish."

"Thanks, but I should finish hanging this up."

Wilma lifted her hand to open the door, then turned back to me. "I would like to say . . . I don't know how else to tell you . . . but Tabitha is a very young, innocent but impressionable young woman."

Boy, did that impressionable young woman have her gramma fooled, I thought, as Tabitha's cigarette smoldered between my fingers.

"She is easily led," Wilma continued.

I got the gist of where she was headed. "And you think I'm leading her where?"

"I sense you would be a person she might want to emulate," Wilma said carefully. "Tabitha has had her problems in the past. I don't wish to discuss them with you, but you need to know that, well, her parents and I worry about her." Wilma stopped there, and I'd swear I heard the faintest hitch in her voice. "We pray for her. We pray that she will make good choices."

Full-on belligerence from Wilma would have me coming out with all guns blazing, ready to take her on. But this little crack in Wilma's facade caught me off guard.

But what really stuck in my mind was the simple phrase *we pray for her*. I didn't know people who did that anymore. There sure wasn't anyone praying for me.

I was about to tell her that I didn't want Tabitha to emulate me either when Leslie joined us on the porch.

She frowned in puzzlement, then deflected the frown to me as Wilma hurried past her into the house.

"What happened to Mom?" Leslie glanced at the door again before advancing on to me.

"I don't know."

"Oh, c'mon. You come out here to hang up laundry, and first Tabitha comes inside smelling like cigarette smoke, then I meet Mom looking all distraught."

"And you think I did that?" How much power did these people think I had?

"What did you say to her?"

"How about what she said to me? She came out here practically accusing me of leading her granddaughter astray."

"Tabitha *is* easily influenced. Last summer she ended up in the hospital with alcohol poisoning."

"She's older now."

"And not much wiser. And she thinks you're pretty cool."

I mentally skipped over the connection between the two comments. "Wow, first positive stroke I've gotten since I got here, and it had to come from a teenager . . ."

"Terra, please. She's a young girl, and she's made some bad judgments before."

"Before me, you mean."

Leslie shook her head. "No. That's not what I said."

"It's what you meant." I beat back the sharp sting of disappointment. "Ever since you picked me up in Harland, you've been jumping to conclusions about me."

"And where else am I supposed to jump when I find out you've been drinking before the sun is even over the yardarm?"

"It was happy hour somewhere in the world."

Leslie's patronizing look tipped me over the anger barrier.

"C'mon, Sis. As if you've never drunk before, or smoked substances both legal and illegal." The conversation was taking on a life of its own, moving from misunderstanding to anger and frustration. I needed to ramp it down, or words would spill out that we would both regret. Leslie and I had always been close, but like sisters the world over, we knew exactly which weakness to exploit when the gloves were off.

"I've changed. I've found a meaning and purpose to life. You could change, too."

"Really?" I laughed. "You don't know what I've had to deal with . . ."

"And how am I supposed to know if you don't call? Or send letters, or answer e-mails? Or even, I don't know, send smoke signals. *Something.* You drop completely off the face of the earth, then suddenly reappear in Harland and end up in the sheriff's office. I have no clue what's been happening in your life for the past half year or more."

I wondered if my sister, who had discovered purpose and meaning to her life, would understand.

The door opened again and Dan stuck his head out. "You girls coming?"

I turned away. "You go ahead. I want to finish hanging these clothes up."

"We can wait. I'd like to show you around as well."

I shook my head. "I'm tired. I might take a nap while the house is quiet."

"I'll see you later, then." The door clicked and I was alone again.

I pulled a couple of clothespins out of the bag and clipped

the shirt onto the line. In the background, I heard the voices of Leslie and her guests leaving the house, the quiet around me growing as their voices faded away. Tabitha was right. I didn't have a clue what I was doing. But I was a fast learner. In this family, you had to be.

I shifted, pulling the blankets up under my chin, which then exposed my feet. Leslie's leather couch was comfortable enough, but I couldn't settle down.

It had been a busy day.

In the space of an hour, I had been accosted, accused, and arrested. I owed my sister money for the bail she'd posted, and I had none myself.

I wasn't even five days into my five-year plan, and things were going south faster than Canada geese being chased by a snowstorm.

I flipped onto my side, wondering when Jack the Cop was going to call. Wondering what happened to those two little girls he was transporting in his car.

Wondering if he was single.

He was cute enough in a rough way, and he had that air of confident authority that some of the better cops seemed to wear like a second skin. A girl could feel safe around a guy like him.

And you are officially an idiot. Not learning your lessons very well, are you? Remember Eric? No more guys. No more complications. No more being vulnerable.

The care and feeding of relationships required more than I was willing or capable of doing. I couldn't even be a good sister.

Guilt slithered through my gut as I remembered Leslie's look of disappointment in the sheriff's office. Like a mother picking up a stray child.

I flipped again, restless, then sat up.

What was taking cousin Femmelies so long in the bathroom? I knew the Dutch were clean-crazy, but this was taking personal hygiene to a stratospheric level.

I snuck upstairs to Leslie and Dan's bathroom. If I was quiet, they wouldn't even know I was there.

I was about to turn on the tap when I heard Dan's muffled voice. I would have ignored it, but he mentioned my name.

"Why did you have to help her?" The rest of Dan's sentence was lost. He must be lying with his back to the door.

"She'll pay me back."

"With what, if she can't even afford to bail herself out of jail? Putting in the crop tapped us out, Leslie. I need to spray yet, and we need every penny."

"I can work a few extra shifts to cover that, Dan."

"You don't need to cover for the farm. And you don't need to cover for Terra."

"She's my sister."

"You wouldn't know, the way she's behaved."

"What was I supposed to do? Leave her to cool her heels in jail?"

"It might not have hurt her to stay in one place for longer than a week."

Dan's little snippets of conversation bulleted at me, enough truth mixed in with his frustration to hurt.

I knew Dan wasn't crazy about me, so it was a safe bet that Leslie's pulling money out of the household account did not endear me to him. I had to find a way to repay them.

Using my ATM card to pull money from my bank account would be a surefire way for Eric to track me down.

Once I got to Chicago, I could cover my tracks a bit better, but until then a posting from Harland Savings and Loan would give him a good idea of where I was.

What about a job?

I tested the thought. Might be worth a try. Leslie was busy with her visitors, and she didn't really have room for me. I couldn't leave Harland, but I might be able to find a place to live in town.

I crept to the bottom of the stairs and then, finally, the bathroom door opened and Femmelies came out looking all shiny and polished.

"Hello, Terra," she said with a smile. "You use *badkamer?*"

"Yes. I use *badkamer*," I said, then hurried past her, unable to wait much longer.

Neck. Sore.

Awareness seeped into my mind as my body slowly became cognizant of where each part lay. One leg hanging onto the floor. Arm twisted underneath. Blankets askew.

A couch. A living room. Leslie's house.

And then all the events of yesterday brushed away any remnants of sleep with an abrupt hand.

I glanced at the clock, whose ticking had kept me awake half the night. I thought Dan would have been up at first light slopping hogs, gathering eggs, feeding cows, or whatever it was farmers did at the crack of dawn, but so far it seemed as if the entire household still slept.

Within a few minutes, I had the blankets folded and my

clothes packed up again. I slipped my coat on and then my backpack. Time to go.

Remembering Leslie's admonition about communication, I tried to find a pen and some paper, but all I managed to scrounge up was an envelope from a utility company and a worn pencil.

What eloquence could I fit on a 4 X 11–inch piece of paper?

"I'm leaving to make my fortune to pay you back"?

"Sorry about the money. I'm going to make some more"?

"Bye"?

"Where are you going, Auntie Terra?"

I slapped my hand over my mouth, stifling the scream that jumped into my throat.

Anneke stood in the doorway, hugging a tiny body dwarfed by an old ratty sweater covering a faded flannel nightgown. Her hair was a nest of wispy blond, and her cheek still held the sleep imprint of a hand.

"Are you going away?"

I nodded.

"You aren't going to stay?" I saw a glint of moisture at the corner of her eye. Her lips pooched out in a pout that made Angelina Jolie look positively thin-lipped.

I remembered from previous visits that Anneke could turn on the tears and the accompanying drama quicker than a director could holler, "Action."

I dropped my knapsack and ran to her side, hoping I could forestall the coming storm that would probably wake my sister. "It's okay, honey," I said, holding her little body close to me. In spite of the woolly sweater, her shoulders poked through the knit like little knobs of wood, giving her a vulnerability that made my heart clench.

"Anneke, honey, I'm only going to Harland."

"But I want you to stay here," she cried, her voice muffled as her tears dampened my neck.

You're one of the few, I thought, indulging in a moment of self-pity. *Poor Terra Froese. The people you want don't want you, and Eric, who you don't want, does want you.*

"I'm just going to Harland," I whispered again.

Anneke sniffed and pulled back, wiping her nose with the heel of her hand. "Will you come and visit us?"

I smoothed her sleep-snarled hair back from her face. "Of course I will, honey."

"Then you can bring me candy." She gave me a watery smile. "You didn't bring me and Nicholas a present. Karl and Femmelies brought us presents."

The innocent words piled yet another brick on my back. "Maybe next time I come . . ." I was as lousy at this auntie thing as I was at the sister thing.

Anneke wiped her hand over the stomach of her nightie, rumpling the ghostly pattern of a tiny horse.

"Where did you get that?" I asked.

Anneke ran her hand over her nightgown with a proprietary gesture. "My mommy had it."

She had it because one day our mother decided that we needed new pajamas and we were allowed to pick them out ourselves. Leslie's had flowers; mine had horses. Then we went to McDonald's for lunch, and we were allowed to order burgers and milk shakes and fries. I remember our mother laughing out loud that day. I remember that her eyes were clear and her breath fresh and her smile pure and lovely.

Every time Leslie and I wore those pajamas, the memory of

that day was like a beacon in the darker days when our mother was not cheerful or fun or lucid.

I wondered where Mom was and what she was doing. Leslie seemed content with her new life and with Wilma as her "mom." But I wasn't as able to dismiss our mom from my life. Now and again, I would wonder if she was happy, if she had found someone to take care of her. Wonder if she had put herself in as bad a situation as I had.

"I used to wear that nightgown, you know," I whispered, caressing her tiny shoulder with my hand.

"Mommy said you liked it the bestest of all your clothes."

I claimed the memory like a greedy gold digger seeing the flash of gold in a pan. Leslie had shared a piece of our childhood with her children. A connection. "I wanted to wear it to school, but my mommy wouldn't let me."

"Where is your mommy?"

Funny how those innocent words could hold so much. My mommy was as much of a grandma to her as Wilma was, but she didn't see any connection.

"I don't know where she is, sweetheart." I squeezed her shoulder. "Did you know that my mommy is your grandma too?"

Anneke shook her head as she frowned. "I have a gramma. Oma Wilma. Mommy says she's a good gramma." Anneke delivered the information in a matter-of-fact tone that neatly sheared away any bit of family connection I shared with Anneke, Nicholas, and Leslie.

"I'm sure she is," was all I could squeeze out. I heard the floor creaking upstairs. Time to go. I gave Anneke another smile, then brushed her soft cheek with a kiss. "Tell your mommy that Auntie Terra says she's sorry."

Anneke's head bounced up and down as if passing on apologies from a little-known aunt was a perfectly normal event.

"Can I lay on the couch?" she asked. I quickly tucked her in, then before the household came to complete wakefulness, I scooted out of the house. In the distance I heard the faint rumble of a truck, and I jogged down the road, knowing that if I didn't catch it, my chances for a ride would be pretty slim.

Chapter Four

H elp wanted.

We'll see how badly they want help, I thought, adjusting my knapsack as I stared at the sign posted on the window of the Harland Café. Luckily, the first ride I got this morning had brought me most of the way back to Harland. But I'd been on my feet the rest of the day, looking for gainful employment.

I was in an awkward situation. I couldn't use my previous references because one of them was Eric and the other was a friend of his, which created a three-year gap in my résumé that caused more questions I didn't feel like dancing around.

I needed someone who was not just willing but *desperate* to hire me. After hearing too many "No openings" or "Not hiring," all delivered with a suspicious look when I balked at supplying a résumé, I was finally thrown a bone. The young salesclerk at True Value Hardware told me the Harland Café, across from the sheriff's office, was hiring.

I so did *not* want to be a waitress again.

But Dan's voice kept resonating in my mind. To pay Leslie back I needed work, and judging from the sign on the door, the diner needed help.

It was a match made in Harland.

I hitched my knapsack over my shoulder and pushed open the glass door of the restaurant as the tinkling bell announced my entrance.

The diner was one of those authentic frozen-in-time establishments that big cities try unsuccessfully to emulate.

Mismatched chairs were pushed haphazardly around tables that sat too close together, making navigating the restaurant with a full order an exercise in agility.

A few tiles were coming loose in the floor. On the wall beside me hung a bulletin board—every square inch of it papered with notices and items for sale, some hanging by a pin, others tucked into the edges of the wood. From the faded look of some of them, they'd survived a few presidential administrations.

In the past, I had donned my waitressing apron when no other job was available—like now—but most of the places I'd worked easily had more class than this and were much cleaner and quieter.

Willie Nelson was wailing on the radio, and though it was two thirty, traditionally dead-time for restaurants, conversation from a variety of patrons filled the gaps. The smiles and laughter from the people hunched over the tables nursing coffee and digging into flaky homemade pies made me think this could be a good place to work.

I walked to the counter just as a middle-aged waitress scurried past me, her face flushed and her hair slipping out of the ponytail that should have been tightened seventeen hamburgers ago.

Her tired look told me she wished I would go somewhere else to order coffee.

"Table for one?" she asked, reaching for a menu without breaking stride.

"Actually, I've come to talk to someone about the help-wanted sign."

She skidded to a halt. "You're a waitress?" Her whole body wilted in relief. "Do you have experience?"

"I know how to eighty-six an unwelcome customer and how to pump the food out when the restaurant is hopping."

"You need to talk to Lennie." She dropped the menu on the counter and caught me by the arm, dragging me to the back of the restaurant. "He's over there," she said, pushing me toward a door that opened into an office not much larger than a broom closet. "And don't pay attention to his muttering. He's harmless."

A large man, whose wobbling cheeks and protruding stomach made me wonder if he had enjoyed a few too many of the restaurant's fries and pies, hunched over an old oak desk as covered with papers as the bulletin board out front. He stared at the flickering computer screen in front of him. I guessed this was Lennie. He wore a stained apron, and what was left of his gray hair had been combed over to cover a shining bald spot. A pair of worn loafers lay haphazardly on the floor beside the desk.

"Yes, I want to do this! No, I don't want to send an error report." He stabbed at a button on the keyboard. "Just do what I say, you stupid machine."

I cleared my throat and took a step closer.

"Don't even think about closing on me. No. No. No." His large hand slapped the side of the monitor in time to each exclamation.

"Excuse me," I said quietly, knocking lightly on the wood door.

Lennie's head jerked upward and swiveled from side to side, his comb-over listing to starboard.

"Hello," I said again, stepping a little farther into the office.

His bloodshot eyes made him look as if he'd been on an all-nighter. "Whaddya want?" he asked, sniffing deeply and rubbing his eyes.

"I've come about your job opening."

Lennie leaned back in his chair, scratching his stomach. His fingernails were bitten to the quick and stained with tobacco. A thin rime of something I didn't want to know about edged his mouth.

I mentally backpedaled, then hit a wall. My "escape fund" needed to be replenished. I needed to pay back Leslie and find a way to support myself while I was stuck here. This job was my last resort.

"Have you worked as a waitress before?"

I nodded.

"You know anything about computers?"

"A bit."

"I need more than a bit. But I need a waitress more." He blinked, then pushed his chair backward with one stocking foot. With his other, he hooked the wooden chair nearby and pulled it in front of him.

"Come in. Sit down," he said. "Shut the door behind you."

I shut out images from a thousand television shows and movies. This would be where the music got spooky if trouble was afoot . . .

But this wasn't TV. It was my life, and no one knew I was here.

Lennie must have sensed my hesitation. "You can leave the door open if you want. Doesn't matter."

I left it open, sitting on the chair and slipping my backpack onto my lap.

Lennie sniffed again, scrubbing at his face with the palms of his hands before leaning back in his chair. "Tell me about your other jobs."

"I've worked in a couple of hotels, a few lounges, some restaurants. I've done office work for a lawyer and worked as a bank teller."

Lennie nodded and scratched his chin with one finger. "What's your name?"

I told him.

"You live around here?"

"I'm new to town."

"Helen, the other waitress here, might be looking for a roomie. Her friend moved out. Got married." Lennie sniffed and scratched again. "When can you start?"

"As soon as you need me."

"I needed you yesterday."

"So you don't need any references?"

"You ever been in trouble with the law?"

The question sent my heart diving into my stomach. Did my short time in the Harland County Jail across the street count?

And how small was this small town? Would he find out anyway?

"It's okay. If you don't work out, you'll hit the road, curly." Lennie yawned and pushed himself out of the chair. "I gotta get ready for the dinner rush. You got a clean white shirt in there?" He pointed at my knapsack.

I couldn't help but glance at his apron. He caught the direction of my gaze and rubbed his hands over the grease spots that liberally dotted the slightly gray apron. "This doesn't ever leave the back. But you, you need to look your best. So, is it clean?"

"Yes."

"You can change in the ladies' can. Helen will bring you up to speed."

I tried not to let my mouth flop open. I'd worked for some pretty desperate bosses, but I'd never been hired on the spot before.

"Great. Thanks," I said as I got up.

"Welcome to the Harland Café," Lennie said, giving my hand a quick shake. "See how you make out today, and we'll talk wages tomorrow."

I knew it wouldn't be a princely sum, but if today was any indication of how busy it would be, the tips should more than balance out the minimum wage I would probably be getting.

Lennie brushed past me, and I stood there a moment, letting it sink in.

I just got a job.

All I had to do now was prove myself before wind of my recent trouble with the law got out.

Five minutes later I was busing tables that looked as if multiple parties had sat at them back-to-back. I tried to ignore the rumbling of my stomach as I piled one plate with a half-eaten piece of pie on top of another plate full of fries smothered in ketchup and dumped them both into the plastic container.

"Nothing like jumping in with both feet," Helen said as she walked toward me, a coffeepot in one hand and two plates of food balanced precariously in the other. "May as well start you off easy. You can take table eight. The two older men. Cor DeWindt will have coffee, Father Sam will have tea, and pie for both. Tell Father Sam there's no more banana cream, but we've got lemon so Cor will be happy."

I glanced over my shoulder, trying to figure out where table eight was, then saw two older men sitting by the window.

I wiped my hands on an apron that was now as grubby as Lennie's and snagged a half-full pot of coffee.

"Good afternoon," I said as I came near the table. "My name is Terra, and I'm your server."

The heavyset man had thinning hair. A pair of bright yellow suspenders lay against an orange plaid shirt that strained over his generous stomach. When he frowned, his eyebrows obscured his eyes. "Where's Helen?" His rough voice held the hint of an accent I couldn't place.

"I just started here, so for now, I'll be serving you."

"Looks like you have someone new to practice your flirting skills on, Cor," the other man said with a laugh.

Cor. That meant this man, the one with the laughing eyes and dark hair sprinkled with gray, was Father Sam. He wore blue jeans with sandals, and a ratty-looking T-shirt covered by a canvas jacket.

He looked nothing like any priest I'd ever seen.

Of course, the only priests I'd ever seen were the ones on television, so my experience was, you could say, rather narrow.

"Would either of you like coffee?" I asked, wondering how one was supposed to behave around a priest. Considering the fact that I'd messed up so royally with Leslie's family, I figured I'd better walk the line.

Cor pushed his cup toward me. "Where did you come from? I've never seen you around town before."

"Actually, I hitched a ride in," I said as I topped off his coffee.

His eyebrows crawled closer together, two fuzzy caterpillars of disapproval. "That's dangerous, you know. A single girl like you shouldn't be doing that. You are single, aren't you?"

Like I was going to answer that question. I reached over to fill Father Sam's cup, but he laid his hand over his cup. "I'll have some tea instead, please. Earl Grey."

"I'm sorry. I forgot." First slipup. "I was also supposed to tell you that there's no banana cream pie, but there is lemon."

"Hmm. I'm not sure I want tea, then," Father Sam said.

"Oh, c'mon." Cor turned his attention to Father Sam. "You can at least have tea."

"Not without pie."

"Then have lemon pie."

Father Sam seemed to consider, then shook his head.

Cor slapped the table with a large, meaty hand. "Don't be such a hidebound traditionalist. You can't beat lemon pie for freshness."

Father Sam lifted his shoulder in a vague shrug. "You'd like lemon pie. Its tart flavor is very symbolic of your Calvinistic world and life views."

"What? Lemon pie is sweet. Like us Calvinists," Cor said.

"Only because Mathilde redeems the flavor by adding copious amounts of sugar. Which you shouldn't be having."

Theology and pie? These two were a little on the strange side.

Cor harrumphed, then turned to me. "Two pieces of lemon pie. I'll eat his if he doesn't want it."

"And I'll have Earl Grey tea after all," Father Sam said.

"Hey, Terra," Cor called out just as I was about to hurry off to fill the order, "what do you get when you cross an elephant and a kangaroo?"

Oh, brother. One of those kinds of customers.

"I give up."

Cor snickered. "Great big holes all over Australia."

I laughed politely, then rushed off to fill the order. I was aiming for a cross between efficiency and politeness—pleasing the customer and keeping the boss happy.

I almost collided with Helen on the way into the kitchen.

"You're back quick," she said, ringing her order in. "Cor didn't try to pull you in on his biweekly theological discussion with Father Sam?" She pointed to a large glass cooler beside the cash desk. "Pie's in there."

"I did get to hear something about Calvinistic something or other," I said as I slid a magazine-ad-worthy piece of pie onto a plate. The meringue was picture-perfect, lightly browned, artfully swirled. The flaky crust and creamy smooth lemon filling made saliva pool in my mouth. "He told me an elephant joke."

Helen groaned. "He must have gotten a new joke book."

"Is there any chance I can grab a bite to eat?" I asked.

Helen pulled me behind the partition dividing the kitchen from the rest of the restaurant. A little table holding a sugar container, cream cups, ketchup, and napkins was pushed against the wall.

"You can keep your coffee here and any food or snacks you manage to scam when Mathilde isn't looking."

"Who?"

"The cook."

"I thought Lennie was the cook." Light flashed off Lennie's flailing knife as he cut and sliced. His assistant walked a wide circle around him en route to the large walk-in cooler at the back of the kitchen.

Helen rolled her eyes. "He does the morning shift and maybe, when we're stretched, flips burgers at noon, but that's about all the General will let him touch. He thinks he's the best line cook that ever whipped on a hairnet, but every time he works the grill, he drags the side orders. Hasn't mastered the 'everything hot at the same time' concept so vital to quality restaurant fare." Helen glanced at the clock. "If you're lucky, you might be able to grab something before the General comes."

"The General being?"

As the words left my mouth, the back door flew open, and in strode a short, stocky woman.

"Let's get going," she threw out as she tugged off her coat. Her dark brown hair, liberally streaked with gray, was already stuffed into a hairnet. "Lennie, you were supposed to be done with that hours ago," she called out as she stripped off a shabby green coat revealing a full-length apron, striped green-and-yellow stockings, and bright yellow Crocs. "You been fooling with that useless computer again?"

"Behold," Helen whispered as she eased her way out of the kitchen, leaving me to face down Mathilde's beady eyes alone.

"Who's that?" she snapped with a sharp jut of her chin in my direction.

"Terra. I hired her this morning," Lennie replied.

Mathilde's eyes became as small as an iguana's. "You lazy, girl?"

"Not usually." I couldn't come up with anything snappier, but from the set of her jaw and her pursed lips, I guessed I was better off with bland and basic anyway.

"Lennie tell you that if any of your customers skip, it comes out of your pay?"

He didn't. Nor would he meet my surprised gaze. I'd worked for a few other restaurants that did this. It was a pain, and it wasn't fair.

But I wasn't in any place to complain.

"You make sure you try to up-sell whenever you get the chance. No campers except for Father Sam and Cor, and punch your orders in right the first time." Mathilde's eyes swept over me as she delivered that pithy advice before turning her attention to the order screen. "Useless computer is more trouble than it's worth. We're already behind, people," she snapped. "Time is money, and the money belongs to me."

Lennie flapped his hands at me in a *Get going* gesture. He pointed to Mathilde and made a slicing gesture across his throat.

I ran into Helen as I left the kitchen, balancing two pie plates in one hand.

"I thought Lennie owned the place," I whispered as Helen handed me Father Sam's teapot.

"He does, but it's Mathilde's cooking that brings the people in. You want to be best friends with Mathilde. Make her mad, and your tips will be spare change instead of nice, crisp bills. You'll figure her out. If you stay long enough."

Helen's last few words had a faintly ominous tone. Did she mean if I could cut it or if I decided to stick around?

I'd never worked for a cranky boss longer than I had to. But I needed this job. So I would have to put up with whatever Mathilde gave me.

Cor and Father Sam were locked in a heated debate.

"Here's your order," I said when Cor took a breath. "And your tea," I said to Father Sam, carefully setting the teapot in front of him. "Enjoy your pie."

Father Sam sighed and picked up his fork. "If I must, I must," he said quietly.

"Think of it as penance for some obscure sin you don't

even realize you committed," Cor said, winking at me. "And we're out of sugar here, Terra. Can you get me some more?"

"I'm sorry." I was about to get a full container from the table beside them when Father Sam touched me lightly on the arm.

"Terra, my friend Cor shouldn't be having regular sugar. He's diabetic."

"Don't listen to him," Cor said, shoving aside the small ceramic tray full of artificial sweetener packets.

Father Sam looked at me expectantly. I was caught in the middle. On the one side sat Cor, the customer. On the other side, I didn't know if I wanted to fall afoul of a priest. After all, he had connections to realms I respected but didn't know much about.

"I do this out of brotherly love, Cor," Father Sam said, turning back to his friend. "Not just to raise your blood pressure, which, by the way, is probably not good either."

"You're not my mother," Cor grumbled, "or my wife." He glowered up at me, but in the depths of his blue eyes I caught a glimmer of humor. "You look like a smart girl. Do you think I should listen to this man?"

Now he was going to pull me into this? "I was taught that the customer is always right."

Father Sam held up a finger. "Yes. But which customer?"

"Just get me the sugar and no one will get hurt."

"That's my line, Dad."

The gravelly voice behind me sent apprehension dancing down my spine. The timbre and tone were unmistakable and, unfortunately, unforgettable.

I shot a quick glance over my shoulder. And there was my

friend Jack. The cop. He was in plain clothes today, but he still had that cop walk, that air of authority.

Those intense eyes.

"Jack, sit down." Cor slid over to make room. "You want some pie, son? Coffee?"

"Hello, Father Sam," Jack said, his eyes crinkling at the corners. "Father Cor."

"He's such a joker," Cor said, slapping Jack on the back before saying with an expectant tone in his voice, "Jack, have you met Terra? She's new in town."

"I've met her," Jack said. His expression was serious, but I caught the faintest twinkle in his eyes.

Was he laughing at me?

"Nice to see you again, Jack." I pivoted, ready to make my dramatic exit, then stopped mid-spin as the coffeepot I carried reminded me of my job.

I pivoted directly back. "Would you like some . . . ?"

"Could I bother you . . . ?"

Politeness put a stranglehold on our conversation as we stopped, each waiting for the other to speak and then, as if orchestrated by the conversation conductor, started up at precisely the same moment.

"Would you . . . ?"

"If you don't . . ."

Again with the pause, but this time I barreled right on through to the finish line: "—like some coffee?"

"That'd be great," he said, his smile carrying a bit more warmth and, added to that appealing voice, a bit more electric current.

A handsome policeman. Man. Bad, bad combination.

The words clanged in my mind as I poured the coffee,

concentrating to make sure I didn't let any slop over the rim. I was determined to show Jack that I was a capable and efficient woman able to support herself by working as a waitress for whatever Lennie was willing to pay me.

Not an irresponsible lush with a penchant for trouble.

Plus, I could use any tip he might be inclined to drop on the table. Waitresses do not live by wages alone.

"And how was your date last night?" Cor asked, pressing his fork into his pie. "Nice girl?"

"I didn't go," Jack said, his glance flicking over me before returning to his father. "I got a call."

I needed to get moving, not stand here finding out about Jack's love life. I had a good impression to make and limited time in which to make it.

"Do you need anything else?" I asked, ready to leave.

"I'm fine for now, thanks." Jack didn't look up at me, which shouldn't have bothered me because I wasn't supposed to like him.

"Order up." I hurried to the kitchen where Mathilde pushed two plates at me and added a glower just in case I thought she'd gotten soft in the few minutes I was gone.

Helen rushed up just as I took the plates from under the warming lights. "I need Arnie and Elizabeth's special on the fly," she called out. "And where is Anita? Don't tell me she's a no-show again."

"Guess you girls will be running today," Mathilde said. Did I imagine the note of glee in her voice?

"Good luck keeping up with me, no matter how fast you punch orders into that stupid computer. You'll have to call the orders out the old-fashioned way."

I hadn't imagined the glee at all.

"What's with Mathilde and her hate for the computer?" I asked Helen as we exited the kitchen.

Helen laughed. "Mathilde's old-school. She's still ticked at Lennie for putting in the whole POSitouch screen and computer in the kitchen. Whenever it doesn't work, she starts in on him." Helen adjusted her apron. "We'll have to take turns seating people. The regulars find their own place. Just catch the others as they come in."

For the next hour, I managed to stay on top of my orders, seating people, juggling drinks and desserts with full meals, and cleaning up. Anita never showed up.

Father Sam had two more tea refills. Cor had three more coffees and pulled out a cribbage board. Jack joined in, shucking off his coat and rolling up his sleeves.

Father Sam chatted with people who stopped by their table, and indulged in long discourses with Cor and Jack that I caught bits and pieces of as I scurried past with orders and food and bills and more customers. He and Cor looked very much at home in this place, this microcosm of a larger community.

My stomach growled and my head felt like it was lifting off my shoulders. If I didn't get calories in me double quick, I was going to end up falling face-first into one of my customers' plates of mashed potatoes.

Then the door jangled, announcing more customers.

Stifling my annoyance, I glanced around the restaurant. The only table ready for customers was in my area.

A slender young woman backed through the door, carrying a car seat with a baby in it. She was followed by a tall, well-built man with closely cropped hair, a goatee, and a smirk on his face that screamed "cheapskate."

Call me crazy (hey, call me Terra), but after a few years on this job, I could spot a short-tipper at fifty paces with one eye shut.

Then the girl turned around.

Amelia.

"Hello again," I said as I grabbed a couple of menus. "Good to see you."

Amelia's nervous glance flittered from me to the man behind her.

The man sent a frown in my direction. "You know this lady?" he asked Amelia.

Amelia gave me a blank look.

"No, Rod," she said. "Never met her before in my life."

Chapter Five

I knew I had to wipe the stunned look off my face or Rod was going to figure things out.

Though we hadn't shared life histories, Amelia and I had more than a passing acquaintance. After all, thanks to her friends, I ended up in the Harland County lockup across the road.

But in her large brown eyes I caught a glimpse of haunted fear. And as I looked again at Rod hovering over her, his hand on her shoulder, something sinister slid up my spine.

I guessed he didn't know about her little dalliance at the bar the other day. And since that was the only place we'd gone that day, it didn't take an artist to draw the correct conclusion.

"Sorry," I said with an apologetic smile. "I thought you were someone else."

Rod frowned at me.

"Table for two?" I added a bright smile to my chirpy tone, hoping to distract him.

"Yeah."

Fully functional in the vocal department, I thought as I turned and led them to the last empty spot.

Jack, Cor, and Father Sam looked up as I laid the menus on

the table in front of Rod and Amelia. Amelia set the baby seat on the floor beside her, and Rod sat across from her.

"Hey, Rod. Thought you were out of town." Jack half turned in his chair as a genuine smile broke out across his face. It was a good look for him.

"Pawned the trip off on someone else. Thought I'd spend some quality time with Amelia. How's that horse working out for you?"

"Not bad. She needs some ground work yet."

When I came back with coffee, Jack was kneeling down at Amelia's table, gently pulling the blanket away from the little girl's face. "How is Madison doing?"

"Fine." Amelia nudged the car seat closer. "No trouble at all."

"She's just a squirt," Rod said, echoing my own thoughts as he glanced at Amelia. "Uses up all her energy crying."

"I don't know if I'm so hungry," Amelia said, grabbing Rod's arm. "We could go home and I could make something."

"We're here now."

Amelia bit her lip, then wilted. "Sure. It's just . . . I'm a little tired."

"You just need to eat, that's all." Though he spoke the words with a smile, I caught a faint edge in his voice that had my radar tingling. I didn't think I liked this Rod guy. "We'd like to order right away. The baby gets a bit fussy."

"Fine. What will you have?"

Rod glanced over the menu once again and gave me his order.

"I'll have a burger and fries," Amelia said.

"C'mon, Amelia," Rod said. "You always order the same thing. You never even looked at the menu." He opened up the menu and pushed it across the table at her, then looked up at me. "Don't you think she should try something healthier?"

Amelia ran her finger down the various menu items, then gave me a sheepish smile. "I still like burgers and fries the best."

"Good choice," I said. Rod's eyes narrowed a fraction, and I don't think I imagined the flash of hostility that passed over his face.

"Fine," he said a shade too heartily. "A burger and fries it is."

All the while I was dealing with Rod and Amelia, I was aware of Jack watching the three of us. Jack knew I had been with Amelia that fateful morning. But did he comprehend that Amelia was pretending not to know me?

Then the baby started crying, a thin, mewling sound. Like a tired kitten.

"Amelia," I heard Rod say, "what's wrong with her now?"

I should have left the baby alone. Should have walked away. But the pathetic noise drew me toward her.

Kneeling down, I leaned over the baby carrier. Madison's hand flailed out and caught mine. Her delicate fingers, tiny and cool, transparent as fine china, curled around my finger. When her hollow eyes met mine, my head slowly detached from my body and the baby receded into a circle edged by gray.

Large hands caught at my arms. "Whoa, easy there."

I blinked, then breathed deeply as I realized that someone was supporting me, pushing me toward a chair, making me sit down.

"I'm okay," I mumbled, blinking as I tried to pull in air suddenly devoid of oxygen. "Just a bit hungry." On cue, my stomach growled.

"Let me get you something." Jack's gruff voice pushed through the fog surrounding me.

His face finally came into focus as the gray cloud receded. His eyes were like a laser, intent and direct as if he could see deep into my dark, hard soul. I looked away as I stood, figuring out precisely where my feet were in relation to my surroundings.

Helen caught my arm as I lurched past. "What's wrong with you? You're as pale as a ghost. When did you eat last?"

I shrugged.

Helen glanced back at the kitchen, chewing her lip. "If you go to the kitchen now, you'll just run into trouble with Mathilde." She dragged me down the hallway and pushed me into the women's restroom. "Stay here. I'll get you something."

I leaned back against the counter, my world still shifting on its axis. "Can you cover table nine? The three young guys there look like the dine-and-dash type."

"I'll keep an eye on them. Now don't move." She held up her finger as if warning a toddler, then shut the door behind her, leaving me catching my breath in a haze of chemically in-duced orange scent.

A minute later, she edged backward into the bathroom, her eyes flicking about the empty hallway like an agent outrunning the gestapo.

As she turned, the smell of the burger on the plate she set on the counter started a Pavlov-like drool that needed to be checked before it got ugly.

"Eat it quick. Mathilde was asking where you were." Helen waited a beat as I grabbed the burger.

I took a large bite, then had to pause. "This is a great burger," I muttered past the mouthful of food.

"People don't come here for Mathilde's sunny personality. And whatever you do, don't compliment her. She'll think you're trying to suck up to her." Helen leaned back against the counter, her arms crossed over her chest. "I'm thinking you don't have a place to stay either."

"I saw an empty refrigerator box beside the interstate . . ."

"There's a bedroom in the basement of the place I'm renting, if you're interested. It's not big, but it's cozy, and, more important, it's furnished and available."

"Available sounds good," I mumbled, wiping my mouth with a paper towel. "Furnished sounds even better."

"Come home with me tonight after work. You can stay as long as you want. The rent is three hundred dollars a month."

"Sounds good to me."

"I gotta go. Finish up as quick as you can, but leave the plate in here. Let Sunny, the waitress on the next shift, figure out what happened here." Helen gave me a smile and ducked out.

I wolfed down the rest of the burger, washed my hands, rebraided my kinky hair and was about to zip out of the bathroom when Amelia barged in.

"You don't know me." She delivered the obscure statement with an intensity I wasn't about to argue with.

"Okay, stranger." I wasn't going to waste time discussing our relationship or the lack thereof. Mathilde didn't need to find me dawdling.

"I mean it. If Rod finds out I took Madison to the bar, he'll—" She wrapped her arm around her narrow waist. "I don't want him to find out."

I made a locking motion over my mouth and pretended to throw away the key. "I got it." I was about to edge out of the bathroom when she pressed her hands over her face in a gesture redolent of defeat and despair.

I knew that look all too well. "Hey. Are you okay?"

She shook her head, and a shaky sob slipped out between her fingers. "I don't know what to do. I just—"

I couldn't leave her like this, but I couldn't dally either. So I pulled the pad of paper out of my pocket. "I really don't have time to talk now, but I want to. Talk, that is. Give me your number. I'll call you."

The relief on her face as she grabbed the pad of paper was encouraging. I had no idea what I was getting into, but at least I had given her some hope.

"Call me between these hours. Rod is working then."

"He's your husband?"

"Boyfriend."

I glanced at the paper, deciding that I liked Rod even less than when I first saw him. "Okay." I slipped the paper into my apron and gave her an awkward pat on the shoulder. "I'll call. I promise."

She nodded, then swiped at her cheeks. "Thanks."

"Freshen up your makeup, then wait a bit," I told her. I didn't want her boyfriend to figure out we'd been chatting in the ladies' room. I got a vibe from this guy that put me on edge.

Mathilde didn't even look up as I grabbed a plate from under the warming lights, palmed the customer's chit, which told me whose order this was, and read it on my way out.

And almost knocked into Jack, who was just leaving.

"You feeling better?" he asked, stepping back to give me room.

I nodded.

"Good. You looked a little pale."

His concern created an odd storm of feelings deep in me. *Stop now. You fell for Eric's "concern" every time.*

"Are you and Amelia friends?" he asked.

A few moments ago, Amelia had publicly denied knowing me. Jack was friends with Rod. I needed to keep my life simple. Amelia's situation was as complex as a Russian novel, so I went with . . . "No."

Jack acknowledged my pithy reply with a slow nod. He took in a breath as if he wanted to say something more, glanced at me again, and left.

I walked over to table nine to see if they needed anything more before I brought the bill.

The table was empty.

And there went about a fourth of my wages for the day.

Chapter Six

"Ｈow long are your visitors staying?" My feet throbbed and my head ached, but as soon as Helen got me settled into this basement suite, my new home, I phoned my sister. Me. Miss Responsible.

"Another week." I heard a light sigh across the line. "Why did you leave without talking to me?"

Maybe not entirely responsible. "I told Anneke I was going to town to get a job," I said. "And I left a message this morning, as soon as I got to Harland."

"You're lucky you caught me. Mom, Gloria, the relatives, and I are going to Virginia City tomorrow. We're going to stay at a bed-and-breakfast. I had hoped you could babysit. Dan will be busy spraying."

Oh, yeah. Terra Froese, letting her sister down again. "You could have asked me yesterday."

"I would have if I'd known you were going to be gone this morning."

"I didn't know I was going to be gone this morning until—" I caught myself in time. "Anyhow, it was a spur-of-the-moment decision. How long are you going to be gone?"

"A couple of days. Will you be here when I get back?"

"It was a condition of bail, remember?"

I heard a wail in the background. "Anneke . . . No, don't give the toothpaste to Nicholas . . . Hey, Terra, I need to go. I'll call you when I get back."

And thus ended another meaningful conversation with my sister.

I put the phone beside the bed and looked around my new home. *I'm lucky it came furnished,* I thought as I kicked off my shoes. A knapsack, two pairs of shoes, and some clothes don't go far in creating a cozy home decor.

A too-familiar restlessness held me in its clutches. I'd politely turned down an invitation from Helen to go bowling, so I had the house to myself.

I had already availed myself of Helen's computer, which, she told me, was mine to use anytime I needed. However, the only thing in my e-mail in-box was a bunch of spam and a quick note from my friend Amy telling me that she, too, had dropped out of yoga and that she'd write more later.

I needed to talk to a living, breathing person, and my sister was obviously busy.

I reached into my back pocket for a package of gum I had bought on my way home and felt a piece of paper. Amelia's phone number. I remembered her look of fear in the restaurant that afternoon and thought it might be worth a try to call her. If they had caller ID, Helen's number would show up, not mine.

She answered on the third ring. "Hello?" Her voice was breathless. Tentative.

"Hey. It's me—Terra." I burrowed back into the bed pillows, getting comfy, feeling magnanimous. From the little bit I'd seen, the poor girl could use a friend.

"You called. You actually called."

"This is me. Calling you. Present tense."

"Oh. This is so great. Thanks so much. I didn't think you would."

Her enthusiasm was way out of proportion to the simple act of my punching in her number and connecting, but it made me glad I'd made the feeble effort.

"Do you have time to talk?"

"Rod said he was going to be gone for a while, but I never know how long that might be. Madison is finally asleep, so we can talk."

"Okay." And of course, as soon as someone spoke the fateful words *we can talk*, my mind emptied of coherent thought. I could have tried small talk, but that seemed silly, given how I'd got her phone number. So I took the plunge. "So, I'm guessing things aren't too great in your life?"

"What do you mean?"

"You were crying when you gave me your phone number, even though you barely know me."

Silence. Then a slowly indrawn breath. "I just want a friend." Her voice broke. "I don't know anybody in this town, and you seem really nice."

That was the first time I'd been accused of that. But her quietly spoken compliment warmed my heart. And surprised me. "What about the people you met up with at the Pump and Grill?"

Another sigh. "I shouldn't have gone there. I just hope Rod doesn't find out."

"What does Rod do?"

"He owns a furniture store. He keeps really busy and makes good money. He takes good care of me. Takes really good care of me. Buys me stuff all the time—flowers, cute little uni-corns. I like unicorns."

"He and that Jack guy. The cop. Do they know each other?"

"Yeah. They grew up together. They both like horses. Rod wants to get some, but he doesn't have time. Says if you don't get out and hustle, you don't make the money. He works really, really hard . . ." Amelia drew in a breath. She sounded shaky, overly defensive of Rod, and my red flags were waving hard enough to attract every one of Dan's bulls.

"Amelia, are you okay? Is something wrong?"

"Well, yeah . . ." She paused. I waited. "Maybe." Another pause, then a swift indrawn breath. "Oh, no. Rod is back. I gotta go. He wasn't supposed to be back for an hour yet."

"I'd like to talk to you—"

"Meet me at the Harland Hotel bar. Tomorrow night. I'll have the car."

If I was supposed to be turning my life around, going to another bar was pretty much a 180. But I couldn't recommend any other places. "I'll be there."

And then I was holding the phone, listening to a dial tone and wondering about the note of fear in her voice.

"Molson Canadian," I said to the bartender as I slipped onto an empty stool. I didn't see Amelia and wondered if she was going to show.

Work had gone better today. Cor and Father Sam had shown up again, and Jack didn't show up at all.

I'd mastered eating on time and hadn't gotten stung for anyone's bill.

On Helen's advice, I carried the unpaid bill from yesterday

with me wherever I went. Harland wasn't that big. I just might run into my dine-and-dash kids again.

Mathilde had yelled at me four times. In any other situation, I would have bailed. But for now, I had too much riding on the job and sticking around Harland. Leslie, her kids, the money I owed her. I wondered what she was doing right then.

Her life had found a pattern and rhythm I couldn't catch. I thought I had found it with Eric, but that turned out to be one of the bigger missteps in my chaotic life.

And here I was, not even a drop of alcohol in me and already getting maudlin. Any minute, I was going to be pouring out my life's story to the disinterested bartender.

Though smoke hung in the air like a cloud and country music thumped out of the jukebox, the clientele looked more upscale than what I'd seen on my first social outing in Harland. A lot of the customers wore blue jeans, but I also saw a couple of suits, a few dresses.

I gave the bartender a vague smile when he set my drink on a cocktail napkin in front of me.

"This is a nicer place, ain't it?"

She spoke quietly, but I still jumped.

Amelia eased herself onto the bar stool beside me and waggled her fingers at the bartender. "Rye and seven," she called once she got his attention.

"How are you doing?" I asked.

"I'm okay." Though it was warm in the bar, Amelia kept her denim jacket on. Underneath it she wore a sparkly halter top that barely skimmed the beltline of her low-rise blue jeans. She fiddled with her dangly earring, then blew her breath down as if cooling herself off.

"How did you get into town?"

"Rod's gone overnight to Missoula. Some estate sale he was hoping to score some antique furniture from." She gave me a wan smile. "So I'm using the car."

"I'm glad you didn't bring the baby here."

"Yeah. I guess." I caught a note of quiet desperation in her voice and let the issue rest. She didn't need me cross-examining her about her baby. Truth to tell, the girl looked a little spooked.

"So why did you want to meet here?"

Amelia shrugged. "I like being at the bar. I don't know many other places to go. I'm not from around here."

"Where are you from if you're not from around here?" I asked.

"Boise, Idaho. I met a guy there. We dated for a while, and then, well, I got pregnant . . ." She gave me an apologetic smile. "So he talked me into moving here with him. I thought we were going to get married."

"And, big surprise, you didn't."

"No. He left me here high and dry. Not the romance I dreamed about when I was a kid." She swirled the ice around in her drink. "At least I have Madison."

Her pensive smile when she said her daughter's name penetrated my very soul.

I took a big swallow of beer. "Where does Rod come into the picture?"

"I met him one evening at a restaurant. He was good to me. But, well . . ." Amelia tapped her fingers on the bar, distracted by the Dixie Chicks singing in the background. "So, how do you like Harland?"

"In my rearview mirror." But as soon as I said the words,

I realized that wasn't fair. I had scurried to Harland quick enough when I needed a place to lay low for a while. It wasn't the town's fault that the population included guys like Ralph to whom the word *no* was nothing more than a momentary inconvenience.

"I thought you didn't have a car . . ."

"Not anymore." I thought briefly of the little Triumph Eric had bought me, then thought about the Triumph Eric had sold shortly before I left.

"Harland seems like a pretty good place to raise kids. That's what people say."

"My sister, Leslie, thinks so. She was originally only going to stay here for a year, but now it looks like she's here to stay."

"She works in the hospital, doesn't she?"

"Yeah. How do you know?"

"I've had to take Madison to the hospital once in a while. She gets sick a lot. Rod thinks I'm too fussy, thinks I spoil her. But I love her, you know? And they always want to do these tests on her, and it makes her cry."

I thought of the appointment Leslie had alluded to. The one that, I guessed, Amelia was supposed to have kept the day we met.

"And Rod, well, sometimes I think he's not real good with Madison because she's not his baby. I heard this guy on *Oprah*— he said that sometimes the stepfather isn't as connected to the baby because it isn't his."

"That can happen." Or even if it is his . . .

"Rod doesn't fuss with Madison much. But, you know, he's a guy." Amelia half turned to me. "What did you think of Rod?"

Lousy tipper. But I diplomatically kept that to myself. Most girls didn't appreciate disparaging comments about their boyfriend du jour, no matter how sleazy he was. "He strikes me as a definite kind of guy."

"He knows what he wants, that's for sure." Amelia bit her lip.

I waited, sensing that she wanted to say more.

She glanced around, as if checking to see who might be interested in our conversation, then leaned a little closer to me. "I saw Jack talking to you before he left the restaurant. Was that about the bar thing?"

"No. He just wanted to talk."

Amelia ran her fingernail up and down a gouge in the wood of the bar. "I'm sorry about that Ralph guy," she said. "I didn't think he would act like that." She gave me a wan smile. "How much trouble did you get in?"

How much trouble? Let me count the ways.

My sister gets to bail me out of jail, Jack gets to file a report on me, which will probably get put into the archives, and my face will be plastered in post offices all over Montana with a warning to keep any impressionable children away from me. My brother-in-law thinks, because of said moment in sheriff's office, that I'm not to be trusted, and his mother probably would prefer not to think of me at all.

"It was okay." I waved away her concern. "You don't need to worry about Jack," I assured her.

"That's good." She pressed her finger deeper into the gouge, bending her bright pink fingernail. "Because Rod and Jack grew up in this town together. They're old friends. Jack takes Rod's side every time."

I frowned. "Every time what?"

She pressed her lips together, as if regretting this momentary lapse.

"Every time what, Amelia?"

She sighed, then darted a quick, sidelong glance. "Every time Rod hurts me."

I knew she was going to say that. Her nervous air around Rod, her hesitation to talk about him, the little quirks she had—all pointed to a situation I understood.

Yet to hear her speak those words still caught me like a fist to the stomach. Something I, unfortunately, had experienced on a less-metaphorical level. "You don't need to stay with him," I urged, keeping my voice low, trying to keep control as my anger grew like a slow, dangerous storm. "You need to move out."

"He's not always like that," Amelia said with an edge of desperation in her voice. "Sometimes he can be really nice. And he always feels really bad afterward."

If she only knew how clichéd she sounded.

"And he brings you flowers and buys presents, right?" Try as I might, I could not keep the sarcasm out of my voice.

"But it's not always his fault," she said, laying her hand on my arm, willing me to understand this classic relationship. The trouble was, I did understand, and there but for the grace of God, whom I didn't really believe in, went I.

"It's not always yours either," I said, choosing my words with deliberation. Attacking Rod was the wrong move. If she sensed my outrage, she would pull back. She needed to trust me.

Amelia blinked, her brown eyes looking as innocent as her little daughter's. I felt a surge of protectiveness that surprised me.

"Why does he do it, then?"

"Because deep inside, Rod isn't happy with himself. Maybe

he was hit by his own father, and maybe he thinks that's how you're supposed to act when things don't go your way." I was pleased with how reasonable I sounded, considering that all I wanted to do was get a good solid grip on Rod's windpipe and various other parts of his anatomy. "And the real problem comes when he starts getting angry with Madison."

"He hasn't. Not yet."

Her "not yet" gave me more information than she realized.

"Has he been angry with her?"

She pressed her hand to her heart in a gesture of protectiveness, and I knew I had her. "Sometimes. When she cries too much." Her hand clenched in a fist, and her gaze flicked away from me as if she was ashamed to look me in the eye. "What can I do?" she whispered.

"Move out."

Amelia frowned and lowered her hand, then shook her head as I sensed her withdrawing. "I can't do that. I . . . just can't. I . . . I love him."

Frustration bubbled under the surface. I had moved too hard, too fast. I had made her defensive.

"It's good that you love him," I said, forcing a fake calm into my voice. "But sometimes love means doing things that seem hard."

"Where would I go? I can't move out. He would——" Her voice broke. She started crying and I patted her lightly on the shoulder, trying not to make eye contact with any of the curious patrons of the bar.

"It's okay, Amelia. You don't have to. It was just an idea." I hoped I hadn't broken the fragile trust between us.

"You won't tell Rod about this, will you?" She palmed her tears off her cheeks.

And round and round we go. I just hoped that each time we did, I could bring her a little farther away from thinking she had no options.

"Of course not."

She almost sagged in relief. "Good. I can't move out. I got nowhere to go."

"What about your parents?"

"They told me not to come back unless I was married."

Stuck. How ironic that her life was a "before" snapshot of my own situation.

But I left. I made a decision.

I ran away. I didn't confront Eric. Didn't stop him . . .

Amelia sniffed a few more times, then dug into her purse. "Sorry," she whispered. She pulled out a tissue and dabbed at her eyes. "Is my mascara running?"

"You look fine."

"I just wish I could figure out what to do with my life. It's such a mess."

I patted her on the shoulder, unable to offer any sterling words of wisdom, my life being the train wreck it was. I'd scooted out of Seattle with hopes of ducking below Eric's radar while spending time with Leslie. Then, when I figured my past had settled down, I would move on to greener pastures with a blue sky above me and not a care in the world.

At least that was phase one of the life plan I'd scribbled out on a napkin one rainy afternoon at a Starbucks.

"I wish there was something I could do for you," I said, as I glanced around the bar.

Amelia gave me a trembling smile. "You know, that's the nicest thing I've heard since I came here. Thanks."

Her tentative appreciation gave my bruised ego a tender

boost. Leslie should see this. Might make her realize I wasn't such a loser after all.

"Are you meeting someone else here?" Amelia asked.

"No. Just seeing if I know anyone." I thought I might see those boys who had ducked out on paying their bill at the diner. "But I should get going." I resisted the urge to tell her that she should as well. I wasn't her mother.

"Will I see you around?" she asked.

"I'm at the restaurant most days. Stop by next time you have a chance, or call me. I'll give you the number." I dug through my purse, but the only paper I found was an old Visa bill, and I had nothing to write with but a lipstick pencil. "Here's Helen's phone number and address," I said, writing it carefully on the bill. "If you ever need my help or just need to talk, call, okay? Otherwise, I'll be at the diner if I'm not home."

Amelia took it with a grateful smile. "Thanks a bunch. It was nice talking to you."

I laid my hand on her shoulder. "You don't have to stay with him, you know. You do have a choice."

She nodded as she slipped the paper into a zippered compartment of her purse, but I could tell she wasn't convinced. "Yeah. I guess I do," she said. But as I gathered up my purse to leave, she caught my arm and gave me a sheepish grin. "I want to stay awhile yet, but I forgot my wallet . . ."

"Don't worry. I'll get the tab." I signaled the bartender and paid for both our drinks, resisting the urge to slip her a few more bills. I didn't need to encourage her drinking, in spite of her desire to linger. As I slipped off the stool, a bellowing laugh caught my attention. A group of young kids had slipped in while I was having my heart-to-heart with Amelia.

I recognized one of them.

My smile was triumphant as I zipped open my purse and pulled out the unpaid restaurant bill. This was going to be so good. I straightened my jacket, smoothed out my lipstick, and with my smile intact, walked over.

"Hello, youngsters. How are you doing?"

The boy I recognized turned his head with that lazy "I don't care" sneer spoiled teenage boys all over North America seem to have adopted as their signature look.

"I'll have a . . ."

His eyes drifted upward. I held the unpaid bill suspended between us as his sneer stiffened and shifted into fearful recognition.

"Yes. It's me. The voice of your conscience." I waved the bill back and forth, savoring the moment. "You owe me nineteen dollars and seventy-five cents. Plus a fifteen percent tip, which makes twenty-two dollars and seventy-two cents, plus a five-dollar delivery charge, on top of which I could add an idiot charge. But I'm feeling gracious, so your grand total is twenty-seven dollars and seventy-two cents." I slapped the bill on the table. "Which I'll round up, for ease of payment, to twenty-eight dollars."

I love my work.

"But . . . You gotta be kidding . . . You can't do this . . ."

"I can. And I will. Pay up, punk." I held my hand out, knowing full well that when push came to shove, this little twerp wouldn't. Push or shove, that is.

"Hey, wait a minute," his friend said. "This is crazy."

I turned to take him on and found myself looking directly into the wide-open, overdone raccoon eyes of Gloria's daughter, Tabitha.

Chapter Seven

Okay. So I felt a little smug. The VandeKeeres with their family moments and their praying and churchgoing couldn't keep this little minx out of trouble.

But my smug moment was doused when I remembered Leslie's concern and Wilma's comment about praying for her. This girl had all the support and opportunities that Leslie and I never had. And she was royally messing it up.

And why do I care? I've done my good deeds for the night. Listening to Amelia, dispensing advice, paying for her drink.

Okay, so I wasn't Dr. Phil. I wasn't Mother Teresa either, but it bugged me to see this young girl mangle her life.

"What are you doing here?" I asked, shaking my head at the sight. "And how in the world did you get in?"

Tabitha's gaze slipped down as her Gwen Stefani red lips pressed against each other.

"Who are you? Her mother?" one of the young men demanded with that striving-to-be-tough attitude that young men carry until age and experience tell them they're not.

"I'm her aunt." Actually, the sister of her aunt, but I figured it was close enough. I flipped my hand toward Tabitha. "And she's a minor, so unless you want me to report you to the bartender or the sheriff, you might want to back off." I turned back to Tabitha. "Maybe you'd better leave, hon."

Tabitha glanced at the group, then back at me. Though I was alone, she knew I represented a host of adults in her life, so she slowly got up.

The boy that had stiffed me relaxed.

"And you pay up, sonny. You're not off the hook."

He glared up at me, but in spite of his tough attitude, he leaned sideways and pulled his wallet out of his pocket, throwing a handful of bills onto the table.

I sighed, but I decided to leave the teaching of manners to his mother, so I just picked up the money. "Look at this as a growing experience," I said as I slipped the bills into my purse. "Someday you'll thank me for teaching you the value of paying and for the embarrassment of having to do so in front of your friends. Suffering makes you stronger, you know."

I gave the collective group a quick smile, then took Tabitha by the arm and pulled her away from this motley crowd of losers.

As soon as we were out of earshot of her friends, she grabbed my arm. "Why did you do that?" she demanded. "You embarrassed me."

I stopped and caught her by her skinny seventeen-year-old shoulder. "*You* embarrassed you," I corrected her. "This is a stupid place for you to be."

"Then what are you doing here?"

"I was meeting someone, but that doesn't matter because I happen to be of legal drinking age, and you, little scamp, are not."

"What's the big deal?" She blinked, her teeth working at her lips. "Gramma said you were drunk at Leslie's wedding . . ."

Gramma had a long memory and was obviously willing to share, but I wasn't going to get sidetracked.

"I thought I made the underage reference fairly clear."

"But it seemed like so much fun."

"Like that party you were at that sent you to the hospital with alcohol poisoning?"

Tabitha reared back, her eyes wide. "Does everyone know everything about me?"

"Oh, yeah," I said quietly. "But that's not always a bad thing."

Tabitha looked down, wrapping her fingers around each other. "I just get tired of always being . . ."

"Being what?" I prompted, sensing a struggle in her heart.

"Being good. Being sweet and kind." She said the last word like it was a disease. "I play in a worship band; I sing Christian songs. I'm supposed to love the Lord, but sometimes it's so hard. My brothers can get away with all kinds of stuff because they're boys, but I have to be a good little mommy's girl and a good little Christian."

"Believe it or not, you're lucky to have a mom who is involved enough in your life that you can be a mommy's girl," I said quietly, touching her on the shoulder. "And being a good little Christian leaves you with fewer regrets than being a bad pagan. Listen to the voice of experience, honey."

Tabitha bit her lip. "Sometimes this seems like so much fun," she repeated.

"Take another look, Tabitha. A deep, hard look. How many people here are really having fun?"

Tabitha's frustrated sigh answered my question.

"Now, you need to get home. How did you get here?"

"I took my mom's car."

"I do not want to know this," I said, waving my hand at her. "Just head out and clean yourself up and make sure you drive the speed limit."

She nodded, looked back at the noisy crowd in the bar, then with a sigh, left out the back door.

I waited until she was gone, then took another look around. Amelia still sat at the bar, but for now Tabitha was my concern.

The evening air was chilly, and I shivered just outside the door of the bar as I watched Tabitha walk to the car, get in, and drive away.

Different bar, different town. Different, yet familiar. So which way was Helen's place?

As I got my bearings, a rattly diesel truck pulled up to the hotel and two tall young men stepped out.

One of them gave me a slow smile and sauntered over. "Hey, babe. You ready for a good time?"

"Yeah, you know where I can find it?"

The youngster thumped his chest. "Right here, baby. Right here. Let's you and me go back inside, and I'll show you."

I didn't have the time or energy for this. "Sorry, I don't date outside my species."

"What's with you?" he asked, his voice growing belligerent.

"Not you. Now, go inside and make up some new pickup lines."

I turned and started walking away, blinking against the glare of headlights as a car parked down the street. I heard footsteps behind me. The guy was following me.

Did I have "I'm available" written on my forehead? First that loser at the Pump and Grill, and now this character.

I spun around, deciding to take him face-on. "Look, stop

bothering me, or I'm going to call the cops." I pulled out my cell phone, my thumb on the screen, ready to flip it open. He didn't know that my battery was dead. As long as he didn't call my bluff, I'd be okay. And if he did, well, I could always pitch it at him and start running.

"I hope you're not causing trouble again."

That rough voice behind me was way too familiar.

Jack the Cop, and déjà vu all over again.

"No, Sheriff. I'm not." The young man held up his hands and backed away.

I realized with relief that Jack had someone else in his sights, and in spite of my tough talk, I was glad for his solid presence behind me and the authority his uniform and his presence exuded.

"Just talking to the lady, that's all." The guy gave Jack a feeble smile. He motioned to his friend, and they went into the bar together.

I made sure they were gone, then turned to Jack. "You always sneak up behind people and start talking in that gruff voice of yours?"

Jack angled me a curious look. "Sorry."

I relented. "Well, thanks. He was getting to be a nuisance."

"Actually, I thought I'd intervene for his protection." His expression was serious, but I caught the faintest movement of his lips.

I gave in and smiled first. "To serve and protect by keeping the foreheads and insteps of carbon-based life-forms of Harland safe from all newcomers," I joked.

His mouth lifted just a bit.

Tough crowd.

"Are you headed home?" he asked.

"That's the plan." Then, with horror, I realized something else. "I am allowed to go to the bar, right? I'm not breaking the conditions of my bail, am I?"

"Did you start another fight?"

"I didn't start the first one."

"Sorry." He held up his hand as if to stop me from beating on him as well. "So, where are you staying?"

"Helen's."

"She's a good person."

"For now, it's a bed and . . . well . . . a bed." I gave him a casual shrug. Cool and in charge. But I couldn't help wondering why he was suddenly making with the chitchat. I guessed even policemen needed to cut loose from time to time.

The door of the bar opened, emitting a burst of noise and pounding music into the quiet evening. A petite figure stood on the step, looking around as if trying to decide what to do.

Amelia.

She saw me and waved. "Hey, Terra," but when she saw Jack, her hand faltered midair. As she looked from me to Jack, her smile slipped away and her features hardened. Then she turned and left. She probably thought I had arranged to meet Jack here.

"You spent the evening with Amelia?" Jack asked, arching one questioning eyebrow my way.

I deflected the query with a shrug, stuck between the proverbial rock and hard place. "We talked some." And then I caught his next question before he could even ask. "And a friend is taking care of Madison."

"So she comes to the bar." Jack's sigh hit a raw nerve.

"To get away from a guy that . . ." *Gear down, motormouth. Amelia asked you not to tell him.*

"That what?"

"Never mind." I knew the guy code. Man friends are never wrong. Man friends stick together through thick and thin.

Jack gave me a penetrating look, but I wasn't budging. Amelia already thought I had broken her trust—I didn't need to shatter it completely.

A chill feathered down my spine, but I forced myself to hold his intense gaze.

"Amelia's in a bad place right now. I think she needs help."

"She's had offers of help, which she's turned down."

"She or Rod?"

Jack frowned, and I remembered the friendly hello Rod got when he came to the restaurant. Jack probably wouldn't believe me if I told him that I suspected Rod had sabotaged that situation as well.

Time to leave. "Thanks for saving me from the hope-'n'-scope guys. Enjoy your evening."

Jack's expression stayed somber, and as I walked away I had to force myself to keep looking ahead. I could feel his eyes on my back.

Chapter Eight

W hat are you doing spending your evenings in a bar, girl?" Cor DeWindt glowered up at me as I set his coffee in front of him.

"Harland, Montana. Where secrets go to die." I sighed. "I didn't figure Jack for the tattletale type."

"Jack? Did you see Jack last night?" Cor's eyebrows shot up in interest.

Deflect. Deflect. "I went to the bar to meet a friend. So how did you know I was there?"

"My friend was telling me about a pretty young girl with curly hair and freckles who looked like she was laughing at some private joke. I figured it most probably was you." Cor gave the sugar container an extra shake and set it down.

"I thought you weren't supposed to have sugar."

"I thought you were smarter than that. Going to a bar in a strange town."

"Don't change the subject."

"Father Sam isn't here yet—you don't need to do his job." Cor wrinkled his eyebrows at me, but I figured his frown was worse than his bite. "And you, Miss Bar-goer, don't need to lecture me on my habits when it looks like you've got a few bad ones of your own."

"Is Father Sam coming?" I needed to get Cor on another topic. This one was heading to nowhere land.

"He's late this morning. Probably listening to some older woman trying to make her confession, and then he'll give her some job to do, and she'll think it's all over until she sins again."

"At least she has some supervision," Father Sam said, coming up behind me.

"So, Father Sam. Got the flock all sheared and herded up?" Cor asked, giving the half-empty sugar container a surreptitious push back to its original resting place. "Now they're shriven so they can go out and do it all over again."

"It has been a busy morning." Father Sam slipped into his booth and gave me a conciliatory smile. He wore his collar today, and a dark jacket, which gave him a very official air. But official in a comfortable way. He looked like a man a person could trust.

Cor glanced up at me. "You're not Catholic, are you?"

"She has the look of a Protestant, I think," Father Sam said.

I wasn't sure how a Catholic or a Protestant looked, but I wasn't about to become either. God and me—not so much with the talking. He didn't bother me; I didn't bother Him. "Father Sam, would you like tea with your pie? Banana cream is back on the menu."

"That would be lovely. Thank you."

The smile and the extra warmth in his voice touched a forgotten emotion and created a deep, inexplicable yearning for a father I never knew, and for my sister, whom I did know but who was embarrassed by me.

I hurried away, discomfited by my reaction. He was just being polite. And I was speed-reading more into his comment than was meant.

On my way back to the kitchen, I refilled the cups of an older couple buried in their newspapers. The rest of the diner was empty, and Helen had taken advantage of the quiet to duck out to the bank.

The sun shone brightly. The day was off to a promising start. Then I walked into the kitchen and into the whirlwind.

"You're lazy, that's what. Fiddling with that computer when you should be doing books. Reading when you should be prepping." Mathilde's face had turned an alarming shade of purple as she shook her fist at Lennie, her shrill voice piercing the morning quiet. "If it wasn't for me, this place would go down the tubes."

What was Mathilde doing here? The kitchen was supposed to be a no-Mathilde zone for at least another hour.

"Our only customers are Father Sam and Cor and the Dubinskys, and all they do is camp and drink coffee." Lennie rubbed the side of his nose as he spoke, then scratched the side of his head.

"Stop doing that. You look like a moron when you do that," Mathilde screeched.

I was about to make a strategic retreat when Mathilde whirled around and caught me in her crosshairs. "And you!" she shouted, stabbing the air with her pudgy finger, little bits of saliva silvering the air between us as visions of tuberculosis and influenza danced through my head. "Lazy. Sneaking food in the bathroom." She nodded, her eyes narrowing as she glowered at me. "Don't think I don't know about that burger Helen slipped you your first day here."

I should have taken Helen more seriously when she warned me about Mathilde's X-ray vision.

"I'm sorry. I hadn't eaten anything, and I didn't want to eat in front of the customers." I kept my voice even, hoping that reasonableness would do what sucking up wouldn't.

Mathilde's sour look showed no promise of reconciliation.

I swallowed back the retort I so longed to give her as my hands crept instinctively back to the ties of my apron, ready to undo the knot and pull it off. A symbolic gesture that, in the universal language of waitresses, says, "I quit."

And then what? I thought of Leslie—of the money I owed her and of my mostly empty wallet. Of Jack's intent look when he told me I had to stick around.

Whether I liked it or not, for the first time in my life, I was in a situation where I couldn't really afford to quit a job, to walk away. Against my own will, I was stuck. And because I was stuck, I had to find a way to work with this horrible woman.

The idea choked me almost as much as the words I forced through my tight throat. "I'm sorry, Mathilde. It won't happen again."

"You bet it won't." She held my gaze a beat, driving her point home, and I conceded by looking away, giving her the tactical advantage.

I slipped out of the kitchen before she had a chance to ask me where Helen was. The coffee wasn't ready, so I stared at the dark liquid dripping into the pot and wondered what I was doing to myself. When I left Seattle, I promised myself that I was never going to let anyone humiliate me again. I was never going to let anyone have control over my life.

Now, a week after making that promise, it was happening

again. The only way to get through this was to find a way to get into Mathilde's good graces.

The laughter from the television mocked my morose mood. I glanced up at the television set that Mathilde insisted stay on while she was working. A rerun of *Laverne and Shirley,* Mathilde's favorite show, flickered back at me. I pulled a face at their relentless cheerfulness.

And then I had a sudden flash of rare and brilliant insight.

The time was right. The breakfast rush was over, and the lunch rush was still an hour away. The diner was almost deserted except for Father Sam and Cor, who were locked in an intense theological debate while playing their usual game of cribbage.

I punched Cor's and Father Sam's lunch orders into the POSitouch, glanced at Mathilde, who was, as usual, glaring at the computer screen and muttering. Then I took a breath and took a chance.

"Mathilde! A stack of Vermont. Burn one; take one through the garden and pin a rose on it. And frog sticks in the alley."

Mathilde stared at me. The three customers within hearing distance stared at me.

Then, while I stared down Mathilde, wondering if maybe this time I had truly lost my job, I saw the most peculiar sight. Mathilde's face lost its scowl, and—could that be? Was I seeing things? No. There it was.

The glimmerings of a smile.

"You put that into the POSitouch?" she said, catching herself in time, her glare slamming over the glimmer.

"Didn't even have to 9 1 1 it," I replied.

She nodded, acknowledging my comment, pushing a plate

under the warming lights. "Order up, soup jockey." Then she started making Father Sam's pancakes, the stack of Vermont, and Cor's hamburger and fries, the burned one and frog sticks.

Helen was on her break, and as I walked past her to get coffee and hot water for Father Sam and Cor, she looked up from the crossword puzzle she was doing. "What have you started?" she hissed, sticking her pencil behind her ear.

"Get to memorizing, Laverne," I said through the side of my mouth.

The bells above the door jangled, and a peculiar, unwelcome lift rose in my chest as Jack stepped in.

He gave me a little wave as he walked over to his father's table.

I snagged the pot of java and walked over, determined to be a mature adult woman in charge of her life. Or at least taking charge of her life.

"Terra's been giving her orders in that old-fashioned diner talk," Cor said to Jack. He gave me a grin. "What do you call apple pie and ice cream?"

"Eve with a lid, cold cow in the alley."

"You're making that up," Jack said.

"Just the cold cow part. Couldn't find a reference to ice cream," I said, pouring his coffee.

"Well done," Father Sam said. "I think it's fun."

I gave them all a mocking curtsy and as I rose, caught a smile from Jack that didn't bode well for the detachment I was still cultivating.

Then the lunch rush came in earnest. I had a chance to use a few more slang terms, which garnered me an ice-age thawing from Mathilde. Polar ice caps do not melt in a day.

Helen and I picked up the pace, and Mathilde redirected her energy to getting orders out, but the third time I came to Father Sam and Cor's table to give refills, Jack was gone. Cor must have noticed my surprise. "Jack got a call but he left his money, and said to keep the change." Cor handed me a sheaf of bills and added a smirk.

Normally, I'd be thrilled with a tip that high, but knowing it came from Jack created a mixture of embarrassment and discomfort.

I pocketed the money, filled Cor's cup and Father Sam's pot, and ran off to take care of the next tableful of customers.

The rush slowed to a trickle. Kingdoms rose and fell, and still Father Sam and Cor sat, secure in their preeminence over anyone who might want that table.

"I hear confession as a sacrament," Father Sam was saying, leaning back in his chair as I lingered, cleaning up the tables close to them. "Community needs to celebrate God's love in a tangible way, and confession is a part of it. Spoken confession releases sins to the community of believers. As Karl Adams says, 'The absolution granted in confession is more than an expression of hope; it is a consolation.'"

Those words were as much a foreign language to me as the diner slang I had used was to most of the patrons of the diner. But I tucked them away, liking the way Father Sam spoke them. Something small and unformed was resurrected with the words *consolation* and *confession*. I couldn't see my way clear to consolation; my life was too full of mistakes and sins. But maybe Amelia, who had her baby to think of, could use some solace. Some consoling. Some comfort.

"Hey, Terra," Cor asked me as I filled their cups again, "how do you get an elephant into a matchbox?"

"Open it up?" I hazarded.

"Take all the matches out."

I laughed obediently, but as I looked up, my heart fluttered.

Through the large plate-glass window that Cor and Father Sam usually sat beside, I saw Leslie getting out of her car.

Chapter Nine

There she is," I heard Anneke's energetic cry, and then my niece was dodging the chairs in the diner, her arms wide open as she ran toward me. "I missed you, Auntie Terra," Anneke said, catching me by the waist and throwing me off balance. "I missed you so much."

I gave Anneke an awkward pat on the head as patrons in the restaurant gave us both an indulgent smile. I realized that I looked the part of the doting aunt being embraced by a loving niece, but I knew the reality was that Anneke had a forgiving nature mixed with a flair for the dramatic.

"Hey, Leslie," I said to my sister as I gently extricated myself from Anneke's spindly grip. "Good to see you."

Leslie's curt nod told me that in spite of my very responsible phone call before she left for Virginia City, my name was still written in pencil on the birthday calendar, to allow quick removal in case of further familial disappointment. But as she came closer, I caught the heartening glimpse of a faint smile teasing the corner of her mouth.

I pulled myself away from Anneke, grabbed a couple of menus, and led them to an empty table.

"After you hike-hitched, we had a wiener roast," Anneke

said, trotting alongside me, her words spilling out as fast as her lips could move. "And Tabitha fighted with Jennifer, and Auntie Judy burned her tongue on hot chocolate, and I gave her a kiss but didn't give a kiss to Joseph when he got a bloody nose. Auntie Gloria made s'mores, and Uncle Gerrit said they were lec . . . lecable . . . What was that word, Mommy?"

"Delectable. It means tasty," Leslie replied.

"Would you like something to drink?" I asked Leslie as Anneke paused her play-by-play long enough to wiggle onto her chair.

"Sweet tea for me, and Anneke will have a chocolate milk."

"Auntie Terra, Nicholas ate a worm," Anneke informed me, folding her hands primly on the table. "And Mommy said his tapeworm would give it money for the run."

"Thank you for sharing, Anneke," Leslie said as I tried not to laugh out loud. "I'm sure you've given the customers of the Harland Café something else to digest along with their soup and sandwiches."

I hurried away, determined to show myself efficient and caring. Helen came by as I dropped ice into a pitcher. "I'm going to take my break now," I told her. "Then I'm done for the day."

"Sure. I'm guessing that's your sister?" Helen said, poking her thumb over her shoulder.

"Yeah. Leslie VandeKeere."

"Isn't she a nurse?" Helen's question was innocent, but I heard her underlying question: *So why are you just a waitress?*

I knew how our lives compared better than Helen did. "She's the smart one in the family," I said as I pulled Anneke's chocolate milk from the cooler.

Anneke was still chattering, swinging her feet, and making a pyramid out of the plastic cream containers.

She frowned as I set the container in front of her and unwrapped the straw. "This is s'posed to come in a cup."

"I thought you would think it was fun to drink out of the little container," I said, pulling up a chair. I turned to Leslie. "Remember that time Mom gave us some money and you and I went to the corner store and bought chocolate milk for the first time?"

"I thought we got the money from the neighbor," Leslie said.

"No. Mom had some extra cash. I remember seeing her take it out of her jewelry box."

"Wow. She actually had some left over from buying cigarettes and liquor." Leslie's faint sarcasm bothered me.

"She didn't blow *every* extra penny she had," I said, defending our mother.

"Every other extra penny, then." She ducked her head and took a sip of her tea.

Irritation flared through me. It was as if Leslie was determined to see just the negatives of our past. But I had to let that slip. I had my own mistakes to make up for. "So how are the visitors from Holland?"

"They left yesterday." Leslie stirred her iced tea with her straw, the ice clinking against the glass. "Refresh my memory on why you took this job?"

"You know I have to stay until I get this whole stupid assault thing cleared up."

"Is that the only reason?" The hurt in Leslie's voice burrowed deep.

"Of course not. I want to pay you back. And I knew you would fuss if I told you."

Helen came to our table, coffeepot held aloft as she glanced from Leslie to me, still trying to figure out how Leslie got the brains and I got the dim-witted genes. "Can I get you anything else?" she asked.

"I need to pee," Anneke announced.

I pushed my chair back to take her, but Helen laid her hand on my shoulder, stopping me. "You stay and visit. I'll take her."

I smiled my thanks, but as soon as Anneke was out of earshot, Leslie zeroed in on me.

"You don't need to pay me back. I'm your sister. I wanted to help you."

"I think I'll save the financial aid for something more permanent. Like a house. Besides, I know what kind of trouble you've been having with your mother-in-law." I caught a twitch of her lip and felt her infinitesimal shift in attitude, so I pressed on. "My bumping up against her every time we see each other causes you problems. You don't need me complicating matters any more."

"Mom—Wilma—has a tendency to be judgmental," Leslie said with a light sigh, "but she does have her good points."

Mom indeed! "That woman was making you crazy just a year ago." How could she so easily defend Wilma VandeKeere and so quickly find fault with our own mother?

"Things have changed in my life. Wilma and I have come to an understanding. I'm learning to respect her commitment to her family and her faith."

"Faith." As I spoke the word, I tried to fit it in with the sister I thought I knew.

"Yes, faith. I go to church—and not just to satisfy the family like I did at first. I go because it means a lot to me. I find peace there." She hesitated, and I sensed she was uncomfortable telling me this. She should be. My mind flashed back to a scene of the two of us sitting on the balcony of an apartment in a sketchy neighborhood in San Jose. Our legs hung out between the bars of the balcony as we called out rude comments and dropped empty beer cans in front of an older lady on her way to church every Sunday, trying to see how long it would take for her to get angry.

By the time we moved, all we had to do was yell out, "Praise the Lord, sister!" as she stepped into the parking lot and she would shake her fist at us, her Sunday peace shattered before she even got to her car.

"Things have changed for me. I've come to know a God who cares about me and knows everything that happens to me. You should come with me."

"To church?" She had to be kidding.

Leslie gave me a tight smile and nodded.

Not kidding.

"Can you feature me in church? I've been places, done things . . . No."

"Terra. God knows your heart." Leslie stopped, then laughed. "I'm all wrong at this. You should be talking to my friend Kathy."

"How about we just leave the whole religion thing for now. I get enough from Father Sam and Cor over there."

Leslie turned around in time to see Cor waving at her with a benign smile on his face.

Right then, Helen returned with Anneke, saving me from any more uncomfortable discussion about church and God and what He could and couldn't see.

Anneke was full of news about the bathroom and the kitchen and how the icemaker worked.

"Where are you staying?" Leslie asked when Anneke took a breath long enough to blow more bubbles in her chocolate milk.

"At Helen's."

"You can stay at our place, you know." Leslie sounded a little put out, but I let it slide.

"I don't have a car, Leslie, and Helen lives in town. Besides, I think it's a good idea to give us some space."

She gave a tight little nod, which bothered me. I had to confess, I was hoping for a hearty declaration denying my very wise statement.

"So, what are your plans? Or do you have any?"

"I think I'll stick around until I get this court thing done, then head out east. I've never been to Chicago or New York."

Our conversation drifted randomly. The window of opportunity to rehash the past had been shut. We were now moving on to the future. A safer place for me, to be sure.

During one lull in the conversation, Leslie reached across the table and grabbed my hand. "I'm glad you're here, Terra. I missed you." The hitch in her voice caught me as tightly as her fingers caught mine. "I want to find out what's been going on in your life. Any special guy?"

I shook my head. That was a cesspool I'd rather not splash around in.

"There are a few single guys around here . . ." Leslie offered with a hopeful note in her voice.

"I met some, at the bar. No thanks." Even as I gave her those brave words, I thought of Jack and his rescue the other night.

"Expand your horizons, girl. The bar isn't the best place to pick up a guy."

I gave her a wry look. "I keep forgetting: When you met Dan, was it beer you were drinking, or shooters?"

The flush on Leslie's cheeks gave me the first upper-hand moment I'd experienced since I came here.

"Regardless," Leslie said quietly, giving me a warning look. Anneke blissfully slurped down her chocolate milk, unaware of how easily her Auntie Terra had annihilated her mommy's precious argument.

"Regardless of how that happened, you want me to behave differently? Kind of a double standard, don't you think?" I pressed my advantage, but kept my voice down.

"Things have changed in my life. I'm starting to find a purpose beyond being a wife, mother, and nurse. I want the same for you."

Her voice held a faint note of conviction I'd never heard before, and I felt my sister slipping away from me. "Well, my life is pretty much the same as it's always been. You didn't think I needed to change last year. I think I'll stay on course."

"But are you happy?"

Her question shot like an arrow into the hurting places in my life. The places I kept tucked away because rehashing them didn't help and didn't change things. There was no point in looking back.

"Yeah. I'm happy."

But Leslie, who had consoled me when Tom Merrihew took Bethany Aronson to the prom, and who had been with me after I passed my dreaded biology test, knew the Twenty Moods of Terra.

And the skeptical look she shot me proved it.

"Okay, so I'm not ecstatic. But for now I have a job, and—"

"And then what? You'll leave again? Keep moving, keep bending rules until they break? Getting into trouble . . ."

I held up my hand to stop the words that stormed at me, pushing at my defenses. "Innocent until proven guilty, Sis."

Leslie's gentle sigh was like a soft slap.

"You had the same problem here in Harland, as I recall," I said, pulling no punches. "A certain Dr. John?"

"I dealt with it, okay? And nothing happened."

And there we were. Glaring at each other across a wooden table while my niece laid down a burbling sound track with her chocolate milk.

"Anneke, don't make so much noise," Leslie said absently, glancing away from me to her daughter.

"I'm making bubbles," Anneke protested with the peculiar logic of a four-year-old.

"You're making *noisy* bubbles," Leslie corrected as she picked up a napkin and wiped the chocolate-milk mustache off Anneke's face. Then she slipped the cuff of her shirt back and glanced at her watch.

I beat her to the punch and pushed my chair away from the table. "I should get back to work."

Regret tightened her features. "I didn't come here to fight with you or to come across as better than you. I want us to be sisters—to be friends."

"So do I," I said, clutching the back of the chair. "But every time I turn around, I see a different Leslie than the one I used to be able to joke with."

"My life has changed—for the better. And I want the same

for you. The same knowledge that God is in control of your
life. The same comfort."

A chill feathered down my spine. If I didn't know my practical sister better, I would say she had all the makings of a religious fanatic.

Leslie never took on new things without first knowing the
risks and repercussions. She spent the last year of high school
figuring out where she wanted to take her nurse's training,
bookmarking Web sites until our computer crashed. After she
met Dan at the bar, she made a list of reasons for and against
dating him. Then, when he proposed, she kept the wedding
budget on a spreadsheet.

So for her to say that she wanted me to share in this new
religious experience showed me how serious she was about
this God stuff.

"I don't think I want to go there," I said quietly, holding
her steady gaze. "The last thing I need is some all-knowing,
all-seeing God taking charge of my life. Every girl needs a few
secrets." I threw in a quick grin to show her I was borderline
kidding. The thought of some pushy power honing in on my
inmost thoughts did not bring me comfort.

"What secrets?"

I just laughed and waved away her sisterly concern. "The
usual. Passwords to my credit cards. Weight. Bra size."

Leslie stood up and laid her hand on my shoulder. "I care
about you. You know that. You're the only sister I have. I'm
glad you're here . . ."

"And the way you let that sentence trail off, I'm guessing
there's an unvoiced addendum."

"Are you done, Anneke?" Leslie asked, avoiding my comment.

Anneke nodded and ran the back of her hand over her

mouth before Leslie could attack her again with the napkin. "Can I have another little milk box?"

"Maybe next time," Leslie said as she wiped Anneke's sticky fingers. She looked back at me, her eyes piercing. "You don't do things without a reason. You came all the way here for something . . ."

"Sisterly bonding," I protested, uncomfortable with the intensity of her gaze.

". . . and I hope that one day you'll trust me enough to tell me."

She held my gaze a bit longer, as if to underline her dramatic statement.

"The real reason is . . . I missed you . . . and, well, I felt bad . . . about Nicholas."

Her gaze never faltered as I fumbled along.

"I did feel bad about Nicholas," I protested, trying to find the proper tone of indignation. "I should have been here for you. I know that."

Leslie's mouth softened, and I felt like I had gained a partial reprieve. "Thanks, Terra. For that, at least."

I shrugged, gave Anneke a quick stroke on her cheek, and bent over to give her a kiss.

She snaked her arms around my neck and gave me a strangling hug. "I love you so much, Auntie Terra."

Anneke's exuberant outburst started a cozy warmth deep inside. "I love you, too, punkin," I whispered, crouching down to ease the pressure on my esophagus.

Anneke pulled back a little and grabbed my face in her still-sticky hands. "You gonna come and visit me?"

"You could come on Saturday," Leslie suggested. "And stay overnight?"

"Sure. Sounds like fun."

"Let's go, Mommy. Daddy is waiting for us." Anneke ran out of the café ahead of Leslie, and with an apologetic glance, Leslie followed.

As I picked up their glasses, I caught Cor's benign glance. He gave me a thumbs-up, and I guessed that he approved.

Chapter Ten

⸙

"O ne of these days I am going to buy my own car," I muttered as a pickup whizzed past me, ignoring my thumb,
leaving a swirl of dust and paper in its wake. "And when I do,
I'm going to pick up every hitchhiker I see."

I glanced down at my perfectly respectable Eddie Bauer
jean jacket, worn especially for the occasion of seeing my sister. Paired with Diesel blue jeans, I didn't look like a serial
killer. Or a religious fanatic.

I cringed, thinking of Leslie's little chat with me in the
diner the other day. In all my imaginings, I didn't think she
would end up in the clutches of faith and a God whose name I
used only when angry or upset.

If it had been anyone else but Leslie, my calm, by-the-book,
somewhat skeptical sister, I would have brushed the whole
thing off as a phase.

This, however, was something different. Something that
tied in with what Father Sam had talked about. It was unset-
tling and made me think. Something I tried to avoid doing
these days.

I grabbed the strap of my purse, turned around, and carried
on carrying on.

A breeze teased my hair out of its ponytail, giving me, I was sure, that artfully tousled look that models spend hours trying to perfect.

I slipped my hands into the pockets of my jean jacket, enjoying the freedom of the moment. No rain pelted down from the sky. I was walking downhill into Leslie and Dan's valley. Shadows of white, puffy clouds drifted across the valley floor and up the sides of the mountains.

As perfect a day as they come.

I heard the growl of a truck engine and spun around, hope mixing with wariness. Diesel engines meant guys, which could mean either a good ol' boy who was willing to pick up a woman, or a guy who was looking to "pick up a woman."

A fine distinction, but a world of difference.

The vehicle slowed, the tires crunching over the gravel as it came to a halt beside me. The passenger window slid down, and the driver draped one arm over the steering wheel, his face shielded by sunglasses, a half-smile curving his lips. He wore a black shirt, rolled up over his forearms.

Jack DeWindt, channeling Johnny Cash.

"We've got to stop meeting like this," I said, beating him to the punch line as I walked over to the open window.

"I'm guessing you need a ride."

"Are you on official business, or do you policemen take time off between arrests?"

"You going to get in, or do you want to come up with a few more cynical comebacks first?"

I held up my hands, my expression mirrored in the dark lenses covering his eyes. If I didn't know him, I would have walked away from the offer. "I surrender. I don't suppose you're going anywhere near Leslie and Dan's place."

"Right to the doorstep."

"Is this my lucky day or what?" I said with a note of irony as I pulled open the door and climbed into the truck.

"I think you might prefer 'or what,'" Jack said, hitting a button. As the tinted window slid upward, I felt as if the outside world was cut off, underlining his slightly ominous comment.

I slid my purse off my shoulder and set it on the seat beside me, a fragile barrier that was definitely more show than substance.

"Seat belt," Jack commanded as he pulled onto the road.

"If you had asked me politely instead of coming across like a cop, I wouldn't be resenting the fact that I'm doing what you told me to," I said as I slid the buckle into place.

"An obedient narrator," he said, leaning back in his seat, steering with one hand. "I like that in a girl."

"You sound like your dad."

"He likes you. He says you speak your mind. High praise from him."

"Why don't people ever say I'm coy and discreet?"

Jack shook his head, still smiling. "That would be out of character for you."

"And how do you know what my character is?"

"I think I'm a pretty good judge." Jack glanced from the rearview mirror to the road to the dashboard as he delivered this very definitive statement.

Don't ask. You don't need to know.

I should listen to that rational, reasonable voice. I should just smile and nod. But the fact that Jack thought he had me figured out sat wrong with me.

"And . . . what's the conclusion?"

Jack's sunglasses flashed my way. "You're spontaneous. You like to make people laugh but use jokes to keep people at a distance. You try to come across like an open book, but you have secrets that you keep to yourself."

I wanted to hold his gaze as he ran through this list. Hard to do when faced with that barrier of tinted lenses.

"All this after a few chance meetings?" I said, feeling as if he had laid me open and found me wanting. "You're in the wrong business."

"As a policeman I have to make snap decisions all the time. I'm thinking I'm in exactly the right business."

"So you admit that this was a snap analysis?" I said, trying to get my bearings again.

"I'm guessing, from the way you've gotten all prickly, I hit the nail on the head."

"Now he's a carpenter," I said to no one in particular.

"Again she's using jokes to deflect."

I was losing ground fast, and the only graceful thing I could do to save myself some dignity was look out the window.

I should have kept walking when he stopped to offer me a ride. Jack made me uncomfortable on too many levels.

The only sound in the cab of the truck was the ping of gravel on the undercarriage, the tick of Jack's key chain on the steering column, and the faint whistle of the wind from behind my head.

The trouble was, the silence made me even more aware of him.

I heard his fingers tapping out some unknown rhythm on the steering wheel, noticed how the sunlight glinted off the hairs on his arm, off the face of his heavy watch.

His cheeks and chin showed the beginnings of stubble, giving him a slightly unkempt look, so different from the last time I'd seen him. He looked appealing.

This was the second time that word had sprung up in the recesses of my mind in connection with this guy. What was my brain made of? Broccoli? Would I never learn? Men equal problems.

"How long has it been . . . ?"

Jack's sudden question stabbed the air and I jumped.

"Sorry," Jack said.

"It's okay." I took a slow breath. "Try that again."

"I was just wondering when was the last time you saw Leslie. Before this trip," he clarified.

My first inclination was to ask him why he wanted to know. But that would make me sound defensive, which would make him suspicious, which would make me even more defensive.

"I went to see her in Seattle shortly after Nicholas was born."

"Is that where your mother lives?"

I so did not want to go there. The next question would be "Where did you grow up?" followed by the obligatory family history and genealogy, none of which I enjoyed delving into. Dad? Who knew? Home of my youth? Apartments in various cities or small towns—depending on where our mother decided she would stop for a while. Aunts? Uncles? Cousins? Nonexistent as far as either Leslie or I knew.

"I give up," I said, tempering the joke with a smile. "Does she live there?"

Jack gave me an oblique look. "It's perfectly healthy to have a serious conversation from time to time."

"Okay. I'll try." I folded my hands in my lap. "So, Lieutenant DeWindt, how long have you lived in Harland?"

"I've been back for about six years."

"And why did you come back?"

"My dad is still here, plus it's home. I love the area and the community."

"That's nice. Did you always want to be a policeman?"

He shook his head. "I originally wanted to be a rancher, but it costs too much to get started, and neither of my parents came from a ranching background."

"Is your mother still alive?" I figured that was a safe question. Jack's father was very much present, and plain ordinary biology required a mother to be somewhere.

"No. She died when I was sixteen."

"Siblings?"

"A sister in Cleveland and two brothers who decided that San Jose had more to offer than Harland."

"Do you get along?"

"Usually." Jack's mouth curved up in a smile. "See? Painless."

The slight reprimand in his voice should have made me feel guilty about asking him so many questions. But it didn't.

"Well, you know I have a sister, so you didn't need to ask me that. And the rest"—I lifted my hands—"superficial and boring."

"My family history is hardly movie-of-the-week material."

"No. But it is the kind of life that has launched many a television series."

Jack's laugh brought out an answering smile in me. Though the sunglasses still gave him that shielded look, from the side I could see the crinkles fanning his eyes. "I suppose. I know in my line of work I've seen lots of other variations of family."

"Like the family of those little girls you took from their home. Do you think they miss their family?"

Jack's sunglasses flashed toward me. "I'm sure they don't miss being hungry or having dozens of drunk people stumbling around their house."

"Did you ask them where they'd rather be?"

"I could say I was only following the orders given to us by Social Services, but considering those little girls were all alone in a house that looked like Beirut, I'm sure they made the right call. And my first priority is always the safety of the children. Always."

Much as I wanted to keep the discussion going, we were veering a little too close to personal territory for my liking. So I kept my big mouth shut.

After a few miles of silence, he switched the radio on. Classical music filled the cab. Another surprise. "Do you mind?" he asked as his fingers adjusted the volume.

I waved his question off. "I'm just the passenger."

We drove on for a while, the scenery slipping past us, the music adding an elegant sound track to the beauty that changed with each curve we went around, each hill we came over.

The tension holding my shoulders eased away, and I relaxed against the seat. No wonder Leslie stayed. My eyes followed the sweep of the land to the purple-hazed mountains standing guard.

Surprise jolted me when I saw that he was looking my way.

"Beautiful, isn't it?"

I nodded. "It is." Scenery was a very safe topic of conversation. No controversy there.

"I always feel closer to God here."

The way he spoke God's name—so easily and casually—created an indefinable shift in the atmosphere. I wasn't sure where to put this new part of Jack, and it disoriented me for a moment. So much for safe.

"It . . . it is rather awe-inspiring," I conceded. And as if to heighten the moment, the music playing in the background swelled, the violins and brass creating a triumphant counterpoint to what he said, what we saw.

"I think this is what I missed the most when I left," he continued, his voice softening as he stacked his hands on the steering wheel.

"I'm sure Cor will be disappointed to find out that you didn't miss him." I needed to lighten the atmosphere.

"Real men don't admit to missing their dads," Jack said with another smile.

The admission, the smile on top of the previous moment, created a chance to give something in return.

"Jack, when you asked me about my mother . . ."

"It's okay," he said, anticipating my apology.

"No. I'm sorry. It's just that my mother wasn't a textbook case of maternal bonding. I know she had a lot to deal with, and I'm sure she tried. She was around when we were younger, but we were pretty much left to fend for ourselves at a young age."

To his credit, Jack said nothing. Which made me want to say more.

"I mean, I know in your line of work you probably see a lot of bad situations, some probably worse than ours and, well, Mom was around most of the time when we were growing up. It's just that as a rule she didn't work a lot, spent a lot of time at home . . . and somebody please stop me before I start sounding like I should be on *Oprah*."

"You and Leslie have had a fair bit to deal with, then," was all he said.

"I'm sure our mom did the best she could, and even if she didn't, it's done. There are better mothers out there; we just didn't get one, and I'm not going to turn into the kind of person who has 'issues' with her mother or ends up blaming her for the mess her life is." A sliver of panic hooked into my heart at my oblique admission, and I clamped my lips together. Looked away.

Too close. Too close.

"How much farther to Leslie's place?"

"A couple of minutes yet."

My reflection stared back at me from the window, super-imposed over open fields bordered by mountains. The rest of the ride was quiet, and thankfully Jack got the hint that I didn't want to talk.

Chapter Eleven

A few minutes later, just as he'd promised, he drove up to Dan and Leslie's house, parking beside a strange car and leaving the truck running as he got out. I didn't think Leslie was expecting company. She hadn't said anything about guests when I phoned to tell her I was coming.

"Shouldn't you turn the truck off?" I said as he walked behind me to the house.

"I'm heading down to the barnyard," he said, slipping off his sunglasses. Uncovering his eyes gave him a defenseless look.

I realized that I hadn't even asked him why he was going to Leslie's place when I took his offer. I'd just jumped into the truck.

"What do you need to do there?"

"Dan's training a horse for me."

"Oh," was all I could manage as an unwelcome mental image of Jack on the back of a horse slipped into my mind. So very Montana.

I knocked on the door and heard the thumping sound of feet running toward us. Then the door was yanked open, and I looked down into Anneke's delighted face. "Auntie Terra is here!" she shouted over her shoulder as another, younger girl came running up behind her.

Anneke threw herself at me, just as she had at the diner, and I let her hug me hard, glad for the contact, the connection. I hugged her back, stroking her tangled hair. "Hey, little girl, how are you?"

"I missed you so much," Anneke said, breathless with drama. "You're my best friend. Carlene is here, but her brother, Cordell, is with his daddy. They're at an auction. We're helping my mommy."

The younger girl, Carlene I guessed, hung back, watching me with slightly suspicious eyes. I didn't blame her. I was pretty sure she saw me as a usurper.

"Terra, hey. So glad you came." Leslie came out onto the porch, her smile wide. But as she came closer, her eyes flicked from me to Jack.

"Jack gave me a ride," I said quickly.

"But I told you I could easily come and pick you up."

"I was heading out this way anyway," Jack said, forestalling any explanation I might have to offer.

"Dan's in the corral already," Leslie said.

As Jack left, Leslie pursed her mouth in a *Well, well, well* look that I knew all too well, well, well.

I leveled her a warning look, then glanced at Anneke, who was rapidly losing interest in me by the sheer fact that I wasn't paying enough attention to her.

"Jack picked me up because I was hitchhiking," I said, nonchalantly as Anneke took her friend's arm and ran off. "It was sheer coincidence that he happened to be on his way here."

"Well, that's good. That it was a coincidence." Leslie pulled me close.

"And this public service announcement is given to me for what reason?"

Leslie shrugged. "No reason."

I let it lie, but got a shivering suspicion that Leslie was less than thrilled with the whole Jack-and-her-sister scenario. "I told you. Coincidence."

"Sure." She pulled me toward a chair by the kitchen table that was covered with stacks of colored and printed papers, photographs, and assorted other paraphernalia. "Sit down while I make you a cup of coffee."

"What's going on?" I picked up a picture of Nicholas as a baby and smiled. I recognized the cute sailor outfit. I had bought it at Baby Gap.

"Scrapbooking."

"And how does a noun become a verb?"

"Same way looking for something on the Internet becomes Googling?" A woman walked into the kitchen waving a piece of paper as if letting it dry. She flashed me a quick smile. "Good to finally meet you. My name is Kathy. Friend of your sister."

"Terra. Sister of the sister." Leslie had written to me about Kathy, and she sounded like a good friend. I wanted to like her. But though she smiled as she talked, her faint emphasis on the word "finally" pressed down on my guilt, like a finger on a bruise.

"Your printer is awesome," Kathy said to Leslie as she settled herself behind the large table. "These look as good as real photos."

"Kathy and I are both trying to get our baby albums done, so we decided to do it together," Leslie said, setting the cookies to one side as Kathy began whacking the pictures down with determined movements. "Monday didn't work for me, so she came today."

This was not how I'd envisioned spending time with my sister, but then who was I to complain? Dropping in unexpectedly on Leslie's life hardly gave me the right to set out the terms of engagement.

Kathy laid the pictures she had just hacked up under an oval template, pulled out a little blade, and with a few sure movements cut the picture down again. *Why print them out full size if you're just going to make them smaller,* I thought, but I wisely kept the comment to myself and turned to my sister, trying to look ept instead of inept.

"Where's Nicholas?"

"He's with Dan," Leslie said, picking up a couple of pictures and releasing a melancholy sigh. "Look at this little grublet. He was such a cute baby."

I leaned sideways just as Kathy came to look over Leslie's shoulder, pressing her skinny body into what I saw as my personal space. "Oh, look at his hair. It's so thick and dark!" she exclaimed, taking the words right out of my mouth.

I resented her comment. I had seen Nicholas's hair when it was thick and dark. I had held him and snoozled him. Not this woman. This Kathy of the "finally."

Grade four all over again. Alicia Semenuk trying to take Cordy Mueller away from me.

I shouldn't have resented Kathy's presence in the part of Leslie's life I had foolishly hoped still belonged to me. Kathy was Leslie's friend. Leslie and I knew, intimately, how valuable a commodity good friends were.

When we were younger, our very survival in each new school we attended depended on a wise alignment of social groups. We learned to spend the first few days discreetly staking out the territory, watching carefully, then collating the data at home.

In those situations, finding a person who fit the above criteria and who then, on top of that, genuinely liked us and wanted to be with us, was a treasure to be nurtured and guarded.

I didn't begrudge Leslie her friend, but I was jealous of Kathy. And, if I were to be totally honest, of Leslie herself.

I had friends littering the country. But, as with Leslie, I'd experienced a slight cooling trend in relationships in the past months. I didn't have the energy to fan any of them into even a glow, so some of them had burned out.

"What color do you think I should use with these, Terra?"

I looked over her shoulder at a couple of photos of Anneke with her tiny baby brother cradled in her lap, a look of utter bliss wreathing Anneke's face. Nicholas was just a tiny bundle, wrapped in a bright green blanket. In the second picture, a close-up, someone else held Nicholas. All you could see of the person was a hand curved around the blanket.

"Are these the only pictures you have?"

"Yeah. I had another one, but it's out of focus." She handed me a fourth picture. A blurred face was pressed up against Nicholas's.

". . . I just can't figure out who is holding Nicholas, though," Leslie was saying, tapping one finger on the picture as if trying to resurrect the memory.

"That's me," I said. "And that's my hand. I recognize the rings."

Leslie looked puzzled. "I didn't know you'd come and visited."

"Of course I did," I said, letting a slight edge slip into my voice. "I wasn't always irresponsible."

Leslie's expression shifted, her mouth softening as she offered me an apologetic smile. "Of course you weren't."

"In fact, I spent a couple of days with you," I said, building on the fragile foundation I had just established. "I took care of Anneke so you could rest."

"That's right." Her voice shifted upward, putting emphasis on the last word. "You used to take her to the park."

"And we even made a tour of the underground city," I added, further cementing my goodwill moment.

"And you lived in San Francisco at the time?" Kathy said, displaying a surprising knowledge of my comings and goings.

"No. Los Angeles. San Fran came after."

"With all that moving around, I'm surprised you don't have a car," Kathy said, her tone suggesting that I was irresponsible for not doing my part to keep carbon monoxide pumping into the atmosphere.

"Cars require too many decisions," I said, choosing to take her comment at face value and not as a commentary on my lifestyle. "Which insurance policy, how much deductible, what kind of gas, do I speed and run the risk of getting a ticket or tick off fellow commuters by being a keeper of the speed? And at night time there's the whole 'when do I dim my brights' game of chicken to play. And I won't even mention the whole tire issue and what kind of oil to put in. I just can't live with that kind of pressure."

Leslie laughed. On my side again.

Kathy's mouth twitched betraying a mild entertainment. I knew I wasn't going to win her over completely. Her first impression of me was Irresponsible Sister, and she seemed like Loyal Friend. I had a lot of ground to make up.

"So, which color paper to put with them." Leslie's practical comment brought us back to the subject at hand.

"How about the blue . . ."

"There's not enough blue in the picture."

Kathy tapped her jaw with her finger. "You're right. Maybe green?"

They both looked so solemn, I couldn't hold back a chuckle. Or a comment. "My goodness, you two look more serious than Condoleeza Rice negotiating a point in NAFTA."

Kathy's glance bespoke tolerance with an unenlightened mortal, and Leslie looked a tad perturbed.

Oops.

The outside door burst open, and Anneke thundered into the house. "Mommy, I want to go see Daddy." She stood beside Leslie, her hands clasped dramatically in front of her like a supplicant beseeching an audience with the queen.

"I don't want you and Carlene going there by yourselves."

"You come with us, Auntie Terra!" Anneke shouted, grabbing my hand.

Leslie glanced over at me, and I could read between the lines on her forehead. Time to bid a strategic retreat. "I'd like to see Dan's horses anyway," I said, getting to my feet. "You know me. Never really got out of the *My Friend Flicka* stage."

"Can Carlene come?" Anneke shouted.

"We're not across the room, Annie bo Bannie," Kathy said. "And yes. Carlene can go, too."

Kathy's casual reprimand of Anneke and the easy use of an unknown nickname effectively pushed me back to the periphery again.

Anneke was joined by Carlene, and both tugged on my hand with the easy acceptance of young children. "You bring us, Auntie Terra."

Once outside, I had a faint notion of lifting my face to the sun and letting the milieu of country living wash over me in a peaceful wave, but Anneke and Carlene were little girls on a mission, so I let them pull me along and put off appreciating nature for a quieter time. As we came nearer to the corral, I heard the steady thud of horses' hooves and a few brief commands from Dan.

Anneke leaned away from me, but I kept my grip tight on her hand and pulled her back. "If your daddy is working with the horses then you'll have to be quiet and stay by me."

Anneke's features hardened as if to challenge my authority, but I kept my grip firm and maintained eye contact. I knew Dan's opinion of me, and I didn't want to run the risk of his daughter frightening the horses on my watch.

Then her hand clutched mine again and the moment of rebellion slipped away like clouds over the sun. "Of course I will," she said primly.

"Anneke always gets into trouble," Carlene said, as righteous as a nun.

"No, I don't!" Anneke leaned past me, her face full of indignation. "*You* get into trouble."

"You do! You do! You do!"

Anneke was about to protest this intricate argument when I gave both their hands a shake. "If you don't behave, we're going back to the house."

"Are you a mommy, too?"

"She's not a mommy, silly billy," Anneke scoffed. "She's just an auntie."

And from nowhere, twin hands of regret and guilt caught me in a stranglehold.

"You're squeezing too hard," Anneke complained, pulling her hand back.

"I'm sorry," I murmured, easing off on my grip while scrabbling for equilibrium again.

Maybe it was the pictures of Nicholas, maybe it was being around Amelia and her baby that brought out feelings I thought had been dealt with and effectively disposed of.

Obviously not.

Thankfully, I wasn't expected to say anything. I was, after all, "just" an auntie. And I was older than Anneke's and Carlene's mothers. Borderline antique.

By the time we got to the wooden fence on the side of the corral, I had things under control again. Through spaces between the rough planks I saw figures moving. I caught a flash of four white legs, then booted feet.

"She looks a bit Roman-nosed," I heard a gruff voice say.

Jack, I thought, surprised at the little jump in my heart.

"She'll be okay. At least her feet are good."

"That's my daddy." Anneke put her finger to her lips and with exaggerated motions, tiptoed toward the corral.

I heard a faint woof, and then Sasha squirmed under the fence, barking at us, her tail waving a happy greeting.

Anneke pulled her sweaty hand free from mine. I made a quick grab for her shirt, but caught only air.

"Surprise, Daddy!" Anneke shouted as she disappeared around the corner, the dog joining in with a couple of happy barks.

I chased her around the corner in time to see a horse rear and Dan hit the ground with a thud, the reins from the horse's bridle swinging free.

Dan rolled away as Jack jumped down from his perch on the corral fence and caught the reins.

I grabbed Anneke's shirt with one hand and Sasha's collar with the other, and yanked them both toward me.

"Why aren't you at the house with Mom?" Dan demanded. The glare he sent my way did not bode well for any future brother-sister bonding moments.

"Nicholas is here," Anneke whined, deflecting his question.

"Nicholas is sitting quietly by the other gate," Dan said, beating a misshapen felt hat against his leg. "Not yelling and screaming and scaring Jack's horse."

"She wanted to surprise you," I said in Anneke's defense. He didn't need to be angry. Jack had the horse under control and was even now stroking its head, talking in low, almost hypnotic tones.

Dan brushed his hand over his pants, and I saw the smear of dirt on his shoulder and hip. He caught the direction of my gaze, and, to my surprise, a light smile lifted one corner of his mouth. "Sorry. Not my best moment," he said.

"Are you okay?"

Dan rolled his shoulder, as if testing it. "A direct hit on my ego, but otherwise everything is intact." He looked down at Anneke, who was staring at the ground. Sasha sniffed her hand, oblivious to her part in the mini drama.

"Hey, punkin," Dan said, touching her head with one hand. "I'm sorry I got mad at you."

Anneke pushed a clod of dirt with the toe of her shoe, making him wait a second longer for absolution, then she lifted her eyes shyly to him. "That's okay, Daddy."

He gave her a quick hug. "Thank you, Anneke."

He looked back at Jack leading the horse around the

corral. "Whaddya think, Jack? Should we try the round pen again?"

"I can try to get on her again." I couldn't see Jack's eyes past the sunglasses, but I caught a definite smile. "If Terra can keep those kids under control, it's worth a try."

"I'm just the babysitter," I said. As far as snappy comebacks go, this one had all the zip of broken elastic. Jack seemed to have that effect on me.

"Can we watch, Daddy?" Anneke asked, tilting her head to one side in a childish parody of a beguiling flirt.

"You'll have to go to where Nicholas is sitting," Dan warned.

"Come on, Carlene!" Anneke called out. But this time I was wise to her and caught her by the shoulder before she could scamper off.

I knelt down in the dirt, preferring not to think of what my knees might possibly be resting on. Control over my young niece was more important than the state of my new blue jeans. "You have to be quiet, remember? I don't want to get into trouble again."

Nor did I want to see Jack getting pitched onto the ground.

Anneke nodded solemnly, and I gave her shoulder an extra squeeze just to underline my warning.

I held tightly to her and Carlene's hands, and this time not even a murmur of protest was forthcoming from either.

I may not have been a mommy, but I was getting this aunt thing down.

Nicholas was standing on a walkway that ran along the outside of a chute alongside the corral, his hands clutching the rough-hewn wood of the fence in front of him.

As we took our spot alongside him, the beginnings of a squeal gathered in Anneke's throat, but I clamped my hand on her shoulder, and she obediently choked it off.

And the score was two to one for the crabby auntie.

Sasha dropped down into the shade of the fence, her head on her paws, and emitted a sigh, disappointed in our lack of action.

"Horse," Nicholas said, pointing to the horse that Dan and Jack were talking about. Jack held the reins in one hand, the other rested on the horse's neck.

Jack gathered the reins, grabbed them and the saddle horn, and pressed his hands down on the saddle. The horse didn't flinch. Then he put his foot in the stirrup and slowly put some of his weight on the saddle.

Bit by bit, he got the horse accustomed to more of his weight, each time getting off and then leading the horse around the corral before he tried again.

The sun grew warm, and sweat formed on my hairline, bringing out the curl that I'd spent half my life fighting. But the scene in front of us was hypnotically peaceful.

Finally, after a long stretch of slow movements, Jack lay across the saddle, slowly slipped one leg over to the other side, and sat up straight.

The horse twitched her ears and gave her head a little shake, but didn't move.

"I think we're gonna be okay." Jack's voice was a quiet rumble, and Dan gave him a gloved thumbs-up.

Jack gently nudged the horse in the flank, and she took a hesitant step ahead.

"Good girl." Jack leaned forward and gently stroked her neck, then tried it again. And when he achieved the same result, praised her again.

A few more tries and the horse was walking quietly around the corral. "She's doing well," Jack said, throwing Dan a gloating look.

"Don't rejoice too soon." Dan leaned back against the boards, his arms crossed over his chest, his shirt still holding the smudge of dirt from his dismount. "She's unpredictable. Could still get away on you."

"She trusts me." Jack patted the horse gently and kept her moving.

The only sound in the still afternoon air was the muffled thud of the horse's feet as they hit the ground, accented by small puffs of dust. I caught a faint whiff of warm horse as a breeze teased the dead air, feather-light.

Jack looked at home in the saddle. And from the relaxed set of his mouth, at peace. He looked more cowboy than cop.

"You want to try to get her moving a little faster?" Dan asked finally, his voice slipping into the quiet.

"Patience never ruined a horse."

Jack made a few more circuits of the corral, then gently eased himself out of the saddle and hooked his arm under the horse's neck, patting it gently, talking to her in soft, low tones.

That was the first time in my life I'd ever been jealous of a horse.

"I'm thirsty," Carlene whispered.

"Me, too," Anneke chimed in. "Nicholas, are you thirsty, too?" she asked. "Do you want some juice?"

"Stay," was his succinct reply, his eyes intent on Jack and the horse.

Sasha got to her feet, waving her tail expectantly. Maybe this time the humans were going to do something interesting, like chase some cows or, at the very least, go for a walk beyond the boundaries of the yard.

"I'm taking the kids to the house," I told Dan, trying to ignore Jack, who was now watching me. "Nicholas wants to stay."

"Tell Les that we'll be coming in in a bit," he said.

I herded the two girls away from the corral, escorted by Sasha, who ran on ahead, jumping up and down like a rocking horse, her head twisting back to make sure we were still coming.

When she realized we weren't going anywhere near the driveway, she slowed her pace and dropped her head, telegraphing her disappointment with our lack of vitality.

I stroked her warm, dog-smelling fur to make up for our deficiency. "Maybe some other time," I promised her. "I'll come over and we'll go for a long walk." Still petting her, I looked past the farm to the blue mountains beyond, envisioning myself walking over hill and vale, this faithful dog at my side. In my vision, I dangled a straw hat with ribbons that trailed over the grass, a wide peasant skirt flowing in the wind as the dog frolicked beside me. I laughed and turned to the shadowy figure at my side. Not too tall. Brownish hair. Hazel eyes. Long eyelashes. Deep voice, compelling in a rough kind of way . . .

Okay. Enough. I glanced guiltily around the yard for the girls I was supposed to be taking care of. There they were. Heading up the sidewalk to the house, each holding a bouquet of dandelions.

I caught up just as Anneke pulled open the screen door.

"I got you flowers, Mommy," Anneke called out as she toed off her running shoes and kicked them into a corner of the porch.

"Anneke went faster so she could be first," Carlene grumbled, dropping onto the floor and yanking off her shoes. "She always wants to win."

"I bet if you put your shoes away nice and neat, that will make your mommy a lot happier than the flowers will," I said, hoping my feeble words would encourage her.

Carlene looked from me to the shoes as if weighing my authority on the subject. "Mommy says I'm a grub."

Kathy wasn't too far off the mark, I thought, noticing the dirt smudges on Carlene's pants, the orange ring around her mouth, and the tangles in her hair. I gave her a quick smile. "But I bet she loves you anyway."

Carlene nodded, then with a sigh pushed her shoes into a cubbyhole. She grabbed her flowers and slowly got up. "You talk like a mommy."

My heart took a slow, rolling plunge, pulling my smile with it.

But Carlene was already heading into the house, holding her awkward bouquet and leaving me behind to deal with the pain of her innocent comment.

I allowed myself a tiny sting of hurt before I pulled in a breath, conjured up the smile, and joined the party.

Leslie was putting Anneke's flowers in a vase when I came in. "How is Dan making out with the horse?"

"He bucked Dan off."

"What? Is he okay?"

"I know a great orthopedic surgeon who will have those discs fused faster than you can say co-pay."

"Did he swear?" Kathy put in with an expectant grin. Which, in spite of our earlier moment, made me laugh.

"Kathy, please," Leslie protested, glancing at both Anneke

and Carlene, crouched at their feet playing with the paper scraps, as if assessing any potential damage to their delicate psyches.

"Not in front of the girls." I shared Kathy's wink, eager to capitalize on this mini connection.

Leslie's eye-roll expressed her antipathy. "That guy. I thought he would have left bad language behind in Seattle with the mechanic business."

"I had pristine grammar until Nelson decided we needed beef cows to call ourselves proper farmers," Kathy said, positioning a picture on the page. "Of course he ended up getting cows other farmers brought to the auction mart to dump on some unsuspecting slob, a.k.a. us. I felt like putting a Statue of Liberty up in front of our corrals . . . You know, 'Give me your tired, your poor, your huddled masses, yearning to breathe free, the wretched refuse of your teeming shore . . .' "

" 'Send these, the homeless, tempest-tossed, to me . . .' " I finished for her.

Kathy's laughter created another shared moment. "Those homeless and tempest-tossed cows created a tempest in a tossed teapot. Working with them was a time of testing for my faith."

And there it was again. That oblique reference quietly creating a space that I didn't have the tools to bridge. The only faith I spent any time on was not of the supernatural kind. I had faith that the bus would get me where I needed to go. Faith that when I put money into the pop machine, I would actually get a can of pop. Of course that faith was sometimes tested, but not enough to make me avoid pop machines or buses.

Shallow as I was, however, I knew this was not the faith that Kathy was talking about, or that Leslie now shared.

I hadn't bumped up against religion very much in my life, but since arriving in Harland, it had come at me from many and varied angles. If I were a person who actually believed that God did, in fact, care about me personally, I might think He was trying to tell me something.

Kathy glanced pointedly at her watch. "I should get going."

"Speaking of time," I said, "Dan said he and Jack were going to be coming in in a bit. I don't know how long that is, but I suspect you do."

Leslie sighed again, her eyes flicking to the clock. "Guess that means he'll want coffee."

Leslie gathered up the pictures while Kathy sorted and stored.

"Anything I can do?" I offered.

"I want to help!" Anneke called out, jumping up from the floor.

"If you want to help, you have to wash your hands," Leslie said.

"You may as well wash your hands, too," Kathy said to her daughter. "We're going to leave pretty soon."

"You come and help me, Auntie Terra," Anneke commanded.

Though the bathroom was down the hall from the kitchen, I could still hear Leslie and Kathy talking. They had lowered their voices, but I picked up a word here and there.

And then I caught Amelia's name, which sent my radar spinning.

While Carlene and Anneke let the water splash over their hands, I leaned closer to the kitchen, listening intently.

"So what's with Amelia Castleman's baby?" Kathy was asking. "That little tyke looks four months old."

"There's definitely a problem," Leslie murmured. "Malnutrition, developmental delays, but that's only a guess."

"Every time I see that child, she's worse. I can't believe Social Services hasn't taken the little thing away from her."

Here their words were drowned out by Anneke's and Carlene's chatter. I leaned closer.

"Without being able to run tests, I'm guessing she suffers from failure to thrive," I heard Leslie say.

"That baby needs help," Kathy was saying. "It just breaks my heart to see her so helpless and uncared for. I heard through the grapevine that Amelia took her into a bar, leaves the baby in the car when she goes out. That girl definitely has a few lumps in her Play-Doh. I don't know what Rod sees in her."

I clenched my fists, fighting down the urge to barge into the kitchen and defend my friend. Sure, Amelia may not be the swiftest, but all she needed was help and support. Not condemnation and judgment.

The slamming of the screen door announced Dan's, Jack's, and Nicholas's entrance, and Leslie and Kathy changed the subject.

Kathy was all packed up by the time I brought the girls back to their mothers clean and polished. Jack was seated at the table while Dan rummaged through a drawer of the buffet, looking for something. Nicholas was unpacking a puzzle on the floor beside him and Anneke ran to join him. Leslie was grinding beans, releasing the rich scent of freshly ground coffee.

She never ceased to surprise me. Four years ago she would have told Dan, in no uncertain terms, to make his own coffee, and here she was, a June Cleaver for the twenty-first century.

"Hey, peanut. We should get going," Kathy said to Carlene as she slung a large black bag over her shoulder. "Thanks for helping her clean up," she said to me.

All I could give her in return was a noncommittal shrug. I'd thought better of her until I heard her coldly discussing Amelia's situation. I felt a tremble of sorrow that she could so casually discuss taking this baby away from her mother. Children needed to be with their parents. Especially their mothers.

"You're looking very solemn," Leslie teased as I pulled cups out of the cupboard while the coffeemaker gurgled purposefully in the background.

"Life is very serious." I caught a puzzled glance from Jack that pinned and held my own.

Relax. Breathe.

Jack was trained to observe and, I suppose, mistrust. I was becoming too involved. So I gave him a dual-purpose smile. One that would send him off the scent and remind me to relax.

To my surprise, he smiled back, the faint lines fanning out from the corners of his eyes softening his expression. To my even greater surprise, his smile sent a flurry of anticipation scuttling up my throat. Then my stomach fluttered, and while my emotions were flitting about like deranged butterflies I realized what was happening.

In spite of my short but checkered past here in Harland, I could see that Jack was interested. And the trouble was, I was becoming interested as well, reacting to his appeal in the age-old way of women of all ages.

Dangerous, problematic, and simply a bad idea for a slow learner like me.

"Are you going to put those cups out?" Leslie gave me a poke in the ribs that jolted me back into the moment.

"Actually, I figured if I frowned at them long enough, fear would send them scurrying to the table on their own," I joked, scrabbling for control, for humor, anything to deflect unwelcome emotions.

"Leslie, did you find a piece of lined paper on the counter?" Dan shut a drawer and stood up.

"No. Why?"

"It's my prayer."

"Don't tell me you lost it again," Leslie said as Dan yanked open another drawer. Leslie caught my puzzled look. "Dan was asked to pray in church tomorrow, and he wrote out the prayer," Leslie explained.

Dan crouched down by the desk in one corner of the kitchen, yanking open drawers and riffling through papers. "Are you sure you didn't put it away?"

"I wouldn't dare even breathe on it." Leslie poured coffee and rolled her eyes at the same time. "I thought I saw a folded-up piece of paper in the upstairs bathroom."

"Right. Anneke, can you run upstairs for Daddy and get the piece of paper sitting on the bathroom counter? It has lines and writing on it."

"Sure!" Anneke jumped up from the puzzle she and Nicholas were putting together.

"I've been finding the paper this prayer is written on lying on the table, on the back of the toilet tank, tucked in the pocket of his pants." Leslie turned to me. "You'll hear the edited version tomorrow when you come to church with us."

"Come to church?" I released a quick laugh. "You're kidding, right?"

Leslie's features froze into an expression of entreaty, and I knew precisely what she was thinking. I had seen the same look on her face when she wanted me to tell Hayward Atkins, who was in my chemistry class, that she had a crush on him.

Could you please cooperate without making a big fuss over this?

"So . . ." I gave Leslie a bogus smile as visions of sleeping in rapidly slipped away. "Uh . . . what should I wear?" I asked, for lack of a more profound question.

Leslie's face reflected her relief. "I'll help you figure that out tonight."

I thought of the random clothes I had tossed into my knapsack and realized that I would probably be scamming an outfit from her anyway.

Nicholas got up from the puzzle he was now bored with, and as he reached for a cookie, I saw faded scars on his arm.

"What happened to Nicholas's arms?" I asked Leslie.

She frowned, then glanced at her son. "Scars from the meningitis rash he got last year."

Guilt washed over me like a tidal wave as I thought of him lying in a hospital bed last summer while I was incommunicado. Going to church was the least I could do for my sister and her family.

Chapter Twelve

The door to my bedroom cracked open. Light sliced across the darkened floor. "You awake?" I heard Leslie whisper.

Without waiting for an answer, she ran across the floor and vaulted herself onto my bed, her grinning face landing inches from mine.

"Aren't you in the wrong room?" I said, making my voice croaky so she'd think she'd woken me up when, in fact, I'd been lying here wide awake since I said good night an hour ago. Too many thoughts for too little brain space.

"I was finishing up a scrapbook page, and Dan went to bed ages ago." Leslie clicked on the little bedside light, turned, wiggled, and wobbled, settling herself in. "So. Talk to me."

The sight of her face, inches from mine, beckoned beloved memories. After each special event in our lives, she would jump on my bed when Mom was asleep and bark out her curt demand. I always complied. But this time her request chased all lucid thought away.

"I had a good day," was all I could come up with.

"It had an interesting start."

"What do you mean?"

She pulled back a bit, her eyes intent on mine. "What do you think of Jack?"

"I would bet money I'm not his type."

"Really? That's good, then."

"And again I say, what do you mean?"

Leslie rubbed the side of her nose. "Well, it's just that he seemed interested in you . . ."

"Right."

"Oh, c'mon. Don't tell me you didn't notice. You've always had this power over guys. Everywhere you go, guys fall for that long curly hair, that cute nose, and the hint of freckles. You look so sweet and innocent . . ."

"Which we both know I am not."

"I don't mean to put you down."

"Really?" I tried for a smile. "You're doing a pretty good job."

"I did say you had a cute nose."

"Where are you going with this?"

She sighed, then wriggled her own cute nose. "I could see by the way he was looking at you that he likes you. He thinks you're interesting." She held up a warning finger. "Which you are. You're fun, you're pretty, you like to joke . . ." She put her hand on my shoulder and squeezed, as if preparing me for her next onslaught. "I'm so glad you're here, and I enjoy having you around. But I'm not dumb. I know that once this court thing is over and you've paid me back, you're going to get itchy feet and head out again. You'll be gone."

"You should be writing horoscopes."

"That's against my newfound religion."

"There's lots of good money in telling people that Venus is

on the cusp, which means financial success or romance is in their future."

Leslie laughed, then grew serious. "I can't predict the future. Only God can. But I'm pretty sure that your future is down the road once you're done here. And Jack, well, he's been through a tough relationship with a girl who said she was going to settle down in Harland and then left him. He even bought a house."

"Very astute of him. Real estate. Good investment." Leslie's veiled warning made me duck and deflect.

"He's a great guy. I don't want to see him hurt."

"He's not interested in me, Leslie. So your little lecture was a waste of our precious, and as you so perceptively said, *short* time together."

"I didn't mean to hurt you, Terra."

I pressed my hand against my heart. "The truth always hurts, honey. Besides, a churchgoing guy is definitely not my type. And that whole cop thing? Major turnoff."

"You've always had this anti-cop thing. Where did that come from?"

"Childhood hang-up."

"From Mom, then," Leslie said with a dismissive snort.

"I had my own experiences with policemen."

"Like the time that social worker and cop came and you locked the door and pretended to be Mom so they wouldn't think we were alone?"

"And others." I caught her by the hand, willing her to understand. "Mom had it right, Leslie. We were better off as a family. I did what was necessary to keep us together. To keep us a family."

"If you want to call that a family. I still believe if Social

Services had gotten involved in our lives, we would have been in a better place."

My mind flashed back to the little girls I'd seen on my first day in Harland. That could have been Leslie and me in the back of that police car. Somehow I didn't think it mattered how beautiful a house they went to; their first preference would be their own mom and their own home.

"What would you have considered a better place?"

Leslie's soft smile showed me that she hadn't noticed the tinge of anger in my voice.

"I used to imagine that we lived in a house with a yard and a dog . . ."

"Exactly what you have now," I said quietly.

"Yeah." Leslie wriggled again. Hugged me again. "It's nice to have you here in my house, big sister."

I smiled back and gently touched her face. "It's nice to be in your house. I missed you."

"And I missed you."

I knew she meant the comment as a gentle echo of what I said, but her simple words drove a wedge of guilt deep into my heart. I took a long, slow breath and clutched her shoulder, squeezing, as if by doing so I could convey a small portion of my regret. "You need to know that I'm sorry," I whispered, taking the plunge toward the real reason I was here. "I'm really, really sorry I wasn't here for you. With Nicholas."

Leslie held my gaze, then nodded slightly. I was glad she didn't offer me immediate absolution. That would have made my confession seem cheap and meaningless.

"I'm sorry, too," Leslie said finally, her voice a whisper in the quiet that had sprung up between us. "I missed you and wanted you here. I had Dan's family, and they were great, but I needed my own flesh and blood. My own family."

I gave her a wan smile, offering her regret and sorrow space to settle in and be acknowledged.

I caught her clasped hands between mine, covering them. "We don't have a lot of family, do we?"

"I've got more than I used to."

Leslie's quiet comment reminded me of her now-extended family.

"And very, very occasionally that woman we call Mom."

Leslie sighed. "I wonder how a person can abandon her own children."

Now we officially needed to move on.

"Remember how we used to make plans?" I said quietly, letting the past sift through the present. "How we had such a definite idea of what we wanted our lives to look like?"

"I remember cutting pictures out of catalogs and pasting them in our dream books." Thankfully, Leslie was willing to play along.

"You did end up with the dream, didn't you?" I asked. "The house, the kids, the husband."

Leslie's gentle laugh underscored my melancholy. "I saw it as more of a nightmare at first."

"So you said in your e-mails . . ."

"But I know I'm in a good place. I love Dan more than ever. My kids aren't a burden." She laughed, burrowing a little deeper into the pillow. "Well, not all the time. I have help and support in taking care of them. I've discovered faith . . ." She hesitated there, giving me an apologetic smile. "I still feel a little funny talking about God and . . . my relationship with Him. I know you don't feel the same way . . . probably don't even care . . . I should probably be evangelizing you . . ." She let out an embarrassed laugh and stopped there.

I wasn't ready to be on the receiving end of her evangelizing. Church tomorrow would be enough for me.

"But, Terra, I found something when I found faith," she continued, obviously not done with the God stuff. "Something big and deep, with roots in eternity. And I know you're not comfortable with me talking about all that God stuff," she said, resting her hand on my shoulder. "So I'll stop now."

As she spoke, a faint echo of the emptiness I'd tried most of the past ten years to eradicate sounded deep in my soul. The idea that there was something more than this world— something beyond and above it. The yoga classes tried to fill that void, but I grew impatient with the facile answers and mumbo jumbo. Any of the other remedies I'd tried gave me healing with no depth. The self-help books, the motivational tapes, the false intimacy of casual dating, all skimmed over my pain. The life I was working at wasn't functioning.

But God? From what I knew, He required a whole lot more than a quick read, a class one night a week, and a vague promise to practice.

"Hey. Terra. Where are you?"

I tossed her a quick smile, ready to move into another place. "So I'm guessing you threw your dream book away."

"I did." Leslie lifted her head a fraction, her eyes boring into mine, as if burrowing into my brain. "Why did you come?"

"I told you."

"You didn't hitchhike across three states just to ask me about my dream book or hang up clothes with me or work at a diner."

As our gazes locked, a sense of urgency propelled me forward. A desire to spill out all the things I had been holding back.

"Please tell me. I'm your sister."

I licked my lips, then fortified myself with a long, slow intake of oxygen. "I didn't answer your e-mails right away because . . . well . . . I was having troubles of my own."

"What kind of troubles?"

It was a blank question, asked to maintain momentum. I twisted the blanket around my hands.

Leslie pulled the blanket away and wrapped her hands around mine. "What kind of troubles?" she repeated.

I gently stroked her thumb as I struggled to find some secure mental footing.

Don't tell her. Not after all that Christian talk. She won't understand.

It was her next whispered "Please" that tipped my resistance.

I took in a long, slow breath of preparation.

"I was living with this guy." I spoke quietly, gently easing the words out of the pain of my past. "We weren't married. I'd been with him before, but I left him. Well, we got back together again, which was a mistake."

Leslie said nothing.

"It was a mistake because he was abusive."

Leslie's hand flew to her mouth. "Oh, honey."

And then Leslie's arms were around me, holding me tight, anchoring me to our joined pasts.

I pressed my face against hers, letting her sympathy wash over me. For the first time since I'd seen the faintly patronizing looks from the nurses in the hospital, I felt my grief being given consideration.

"I wish I had known. I'm so sorry."

I kept my head down, guilt and shame, like two dark parentheses, bracketing my life.

Leslie stroked my shoulder with her hand, making soft, soothing noises. "I wish you had told me."

"When I got out of the hospital, I found out about Nicholas," I said quietly. "There was no way I was going to put my own problems on your shoulders."

"Hospital?"

"Yeah."

"What happened?"

"I don't want to talk about it." I couldn't tell her. Not yet. Maybe not ever.

"But to have to deal with that all alone . . ." Her voice broke again, and her obvious sorrow nudged more guilt my way. "I wish we could have been there for you."

I wished I could cry. Anything to loosen this horrible knot of pain in my stomach.

"I left him, then moved back once because he begged me to. He said he couldn't live without me. But I found out that what he couldn't live without was someone to kick around. He threatened to kill me if I ever left him. Trouble was, I was afraid he would kill me if I didn't. So I ran away. And came here."

Leslie wrapped her arm around my shoulder, drawing me close. I leaned sideways, drinking in the attention, a balm for my parched loneliness.

I couldn't tell her any more. I just couldn't.

Chapter Thirteen

"Are you sure this outfit is okay?" I hissed, grabbing Leslie's arm.

Leslie pulled her attention away from the lady she was talking to in the church foyer and gave my outfit a cursory glance. "You look fine."

Hardly fine, I thought, tugging on the skirt. Leslie was still a little shorter than me, so instead of hanging demurely at my knees, the skirt I'd borrowed from her stopped a few inches above them. I had topped it off with a camisole of my own and then toned down the streetwalker look with a sedate sweater Leslie had gotten from Gloria as a hand-me-down.

As I looked at the women accompanying their husbands into the church building, all I saw were suits, suitable dresses, or dress pants and blazers. Some of the younger girls were dressed a little more casually, but they were teenagers, and I suspected their choice of clothing was the result of a battle their parents had wisely decided to forgo.

At thirty-two years of age, I couldn't claim that amnesty.

Leslie finished chatting with her friend and turned her attention back to me. When I had asked Leslie if I needed to wear a hat, she laughed, but just to be on the safe side, I tried to tame my hair by pulling it into a ponytail. She reached up to tame a wayward strand that had curled loose.

People milled about, some moving into the church proper beyond two sets of large wooden doors, others chatting and laughing as background music, played by an organist and pianist, created a holy ambience.

An older woman, wearing a tag that read "Greeter," came up to us and, well, greeted me, pressing a bunch of papers into my hands. I presumed I was supposed to use them during the service.

The lady was very friendly. Very nice. A little too much hearty sincerity and unblinking eye contact, though. Maybe she saw me as a potential convert. After all, whatever it was this particular congregation did, it had worked with Leslie. Why not the miscreant older sister?

"Everyone is staring at me." I tugged on my skirt in a futile, last-ditch effort to stretch it to a respectable length.

"They probably are. You're new. I had to deal with exactly the same thing when I started coming here."

My sister. A rock.

"Is Wilma going to be here?"

"I would be surprised if she wasn't." Leslie adjusted Anneke's ponytail, then looked over at me. When her expression softened, I knew she was thinking of last night. "People aren't here to judge you, Terra. They're here to worship."

"Well, you can act all self-confident and know-it-all," I muttered, my eyes darting around, "but don't tell me you weren't afraid when you first came here!"

Leslie laughed me off. "You've never been afraid of anything in your life."

"Prison changes people," I said.

"Prison?" Dan asked, coming up beside us. "What prison?"

"I think she's referring to her little stint in the Harland jail," Leslie said, shaking her head at me and holding out her hand for the papers Dan was holding. Identical to mine. At least we were all on the same page, so to speak.

"Shall we go in?" Dan had just come from the basement after depositing Nicholas in the nursery.

"Auntie Terra!" Anneke exclaimed with all the exuberance a four-year-old could muster. "I want to sit with you." She ran up to me and clutched my hand.

I was about to follow Leslie and Dan into the church when I felt a hand on my arm. "Excuse me. Terra?"

"Gramma Wilma!" Anneke called out.

Her smile for Anneke was warm and friendly, but as she turned to me, it grew tight. Her eyes flicked up and down my outfit.

Don't tug. Don't tug.

"I just want to thank you," she said, though her eyes looked at me like I was the 75 percent reduced rack at the local thrift store.

"Th . . . thank . . . me?" This was a surreal moment, and I couldn't help a quick glance down the aisle, but Leslie was too far away for a discreet cry for help.

I was on my own, and Anneke was no help, jumping up and down beside me, making her hair flop.

"Yes. For what you did with Tabitha."

"Tabitha?" Now I was really confused. The last time Wilma talked to me about her granddaughter, I was officially the stepchild of Carrie with a little Cujo thrown in for artistic expression.

"She told Gloria what happened. At the bar." Wilma's

mouth pressed together, and I gathered that Tabitha ended up with not only her mother down on her, but Gramma Wilma as well. "And, well, I appreciate that you were willing to show, by example, the error of her ways."

Okay. Lesson number one: How to praise and condemn at the same time.

But hey, this was progress, and at least Wilma was, in her own convoluted way, being thankful. She gently laid a hand on Anneke's shoulder, and the little girl immediately stopped her jack-in-the-box imitation.

"I hope she understands what can happen." I edged away from her and glanced down the aisle, trying to see where Leslie had ended up. I could just see her and Dan settling in.

Wilma shook her head and sighed. "You would think she'd have learned the first time."

"Some of us need a few hits before we get it," I said.

I should know.

Wilma gave me a tight smile, then, duty done, turned and left.

As for me, time to catch up to my sister . . .

I scurried down the aisle, clinging to Anneke's hand. People sat askew in the benches, chatting up the people behind them, conversation buzzing all around us, the music still playing. The building sounded like a deranged beehive accompanied by a musical score.

From the corner of my eye I caught a few puzzled glances thrown my way, but I kept my eyes resolutely on the bench where Leslie was sitting.

I passed by some empty spots, wishing I could drop into them. But no, my sister had to pick seats most of the way to the front.

I felt like praying right then and there. Praying I wouldn't fall and praying I would get to Leslie soon.

Finally I slipped in beside my sister, thankful for Anneke, who was clinging to my hand, an underage shepherd single-handedly bringing the stray sheep into the fold.

We sat down, and I concentrated on the sunlight pouring through the stained-glass windows, adding an atmosphere of reverence.

The windows reminded me of a tour my friend Amy and I had made through a couple of cathedrals in Paris. I remembered entering the hushed coolness of the buildings with their mysterious, towering ceilings, the remnants of thousands of prayers trapped in the space, light diffused through the colored glass of the windows.

While we toured the church, making jokes about the statues, chuckling at the pieces of paper tucked into the crevices of the building, a young girl came in from the outside and walked confidently up the aisle. She didn't look much older than seventeen. One would expect a teenager to be too busy thinking about boys and makeup and parties to go to church in the middle of the week, but here she was. She stopped halfway up the aisle, knelt, crossed herself, and bowed her head.

Then she went into one of the booths along the wall. A confession booth, I found out after. Amy and I lingered long enough to see her come out again, light some candles, and kneel to pray. She stayed the entire hour we were walking around. Amy made a joke about her, but I couldn't join in.

I was jealous of the young girl's familiarity with the routines that seemed both archaic and comforting at the same time. She knew her way around faith and church. To her that wasn't just a building; it was a sanctuary, and, from the beatific look on her face when she left, a refuge.

We were in that church to satisfy our curiosity and to soak up some culture.

The girl had come out of conviction.

I wondered if I would feel the same thing here as well. Glancing around, I found myself looking directly into an all too familiar pair of hazel eyes.

A faint smile curved Jack's lips as he nodded in my direction. I didn't want to think about Leslie's little warning last night. Jack wasn't interested in me, and, I reminded myself, I wasn't interested in him. Never mind the mesmerizing voice that made him sound all tough and I-mean-business, offset by his droopy eyes and thick eyelashes.

Not interested at all.

Then Cor dropped into the pew beside him, caught the angle of his son's gaze, and looked toward me as a huge smile almost cracked his face in half.

"Terra. It's great to see you here." In case anyone missed the happiness in his booming voice, he underscored the greeting with a wave of his large, meaty hand, as if he were saying howdy to a friend across the street in town.

I returned the smile and opted not to return the wave. I could see a few puzzled frowns, a smattering of grins—people obviously knew Cor—and a few faces that I recognized as customers at the diner.

"Father Sam and I missed you on Saturday," he called out, unconcerned with the jab Jack gave him.

I, however, was caught between continuing the conversation by yelling back at him—he was a bit deaf—thereby drawing way too much attention to my infidel self, and ignoring him and possibly hurting his feelings.

Jack dug into his father's ribs with his elbow and finally got his attention.

Cor turned on him, frowning his frustration. "What do you want?"

Jack leaned closer to his father, and all I heard was the quiet rumble of his voice. Cor's frown slid away. I had no clue what Jack might have told his father, but for now I was thankful for the reprieve.

The auditorium filled, and slowly the buzz of conversation died down. Then the minister stood at the front of the church, his arms raised up over the audience.

I noticed that Leslie had bowed her head, so I did the same.

For the next few minutes I took my cues from Dan and Leslie, looking up at the song-lyrics screen when they did, opening a book from the pew when they did. Standing up, sitting down, reading responsively.

No wonder our mother never went to church if it took this much choreography, I thought as we all sat down after singing yet another song. Keeping track of her favorite television shows was enough of a stretch for her. Never mind the liturgy of a church service.

Leslie pulled a Bible out of the pew as the minister announced a passage he was going to read. Psalm 139.

Anneke pulled out the Bible and laid it on my lap. "You have to find it. I don't know how."

And she thought I did?

I flipped open the book at random. *Leviticus,* I read at the top of the page. Wrong. Deuter . . . something or other. Still wrong. Where in the world was Psalms? I started flipping faster. How was anyone who knew nothing about the Bible supposed to figure out which book was where?

Leslie came to my rescue, leaning sideways and whispering the page number.

I found it just as the minister started reading. With Anneke hunched over the book beside me, I followed along. And the minister's words started a flutter of nerves deep within my abdomen.

" 'Where can I go from your Spirit? Where can I flee from your presence?' " Did this mean God could see me always and everywhere? A chilling thought. Was He watching me now?

Anneke poked me and pointed back to the Bible. Her disapproving frown scared me almost as much as the passage did. She looked exactly like Wilma.

" 'For you created my inmost being; you knit me together in my mother's womb. I praise you because I am fearfully and wonderfully made . . .' " My breath tangled in my throat. " 'My frame was not hidden from you when I was made in the secret place. When I was woven together in the depths of the earth, your eyes saw my unformed body. All the days ordained for me were written in your book before one of them came to be . . .' " The letters blurred and danced over the page. " 'Search me, O God, and know my heart; test me and know my anxious thoughts. See if there is any offensive way in me, and lead me in the way everlasting.' "

The words slammed back and forth in my mind.

"Where can I flee from your presence? . . . My frame was not hidden from you . . . All the days ordained for me were written in your book."

I put the Bible back in the holder in front of me, my hands shaking, and sat back, running my damp palms over my filmy skirt. I could do this. Didn't I return a five-weeks-overdue library book without flinching? Hadn't I often lined up in the "10 Items or Less" express lane at the grocery store with eleven—sometimes twelve—items?

Slowly the deep breathing took effect. By the time the minister closed the Bible and started the sermon, my pulse had slowed down. My mind flitted over the events of the past week, trying to distract myself while the minister spoke.

I thought of Amelia and her baby, Madison. Wondered if Madison was doing better. Wondered what was wrong with the baby. I hadn't seen Amelia since our visit in the Harland Hotel bar. I would call her when I got home. See if she needed any help.

I wondered if God, who apparently could see everything, was watching Amelia trying to deal with her problems.

". . . We need to realize, of course, that from the moment of conception, we are God's . . ."

A chill formed around my heart. I tried to expand my lungs, suck in what precious oxygen was left, and glanced quickly around. No one else seemed to be having the same problem.

"We need to know that He knows everything about us," the minister was saying.

I didn't find that concept comforting.

"But at the same time, knowing that God, from the beginning and before our own beginning, was and is with us is a comfort. We cannot make it on our own, no matter how hard we try. We need God. And in Jesus, God gives us the answers to our unspoken questions. Jesus is the answer—a simple but complete concept. Jesus, in His death, reconciled us with the God who knows and sees all. Jesus became the expression of the love God shows us in this psalm."

Each word the minister spoke caused a shift of the shaky foundations I had tried to build my life on. But did I dare replace that with what this minister was suggesting? A God who was everywhere, who knew everything?

I felt warm. Lightheaded. I leaned over and gave Leslie a poke. "I'll be back," I whispered. I didn't want her coming out after me—a Froese entourage heading out of church.

As I got up, eyes followed me, heads swiveling as I tottered toward the exit. I stumbled through the doorway, and then, thankfully, I was outside. The air was cool on my heated cheeks, fresh and plentiful. Slowly equilibrium returned, and I leaned back against the wooden siding.

What was I doing here? I didn't belong in church with these people. With my sister and her little family.

From deep within, a flicker of regret breathed to life. I closed my eyes and willed it away. Nine months of hard work and strength of will had lifted me above my emotions. Had given me control of the regret, the guilt, the shame. I couldn't let a preacher's meanderings or a few words from a Bible I'd never read take that away.

I pressed my hands against my cheeks, pushing the past back down.

"Is something wrong?"

I clamped my hand over my mouth and spun around, my poor overworked heart doing an Olympics-worthy leap.

Jack stood in front of me, flipping his cell phone shut, his eyes intent on me.

"What are you doing here?" I pressed my hand against my chest, trying to hold my runaway heart in.

Jack held up his cell phone as if that explained everything. "I'm on call, and, well, I just got a call."

"You scared the living daylights out of me," I said, taking on the role of the challenger to the questions I could see forming behind his eyes.

"You do look a little pale."

"The curse of my complexion." My breathless voice gave him too much to work with so I turned away, hoping my flip reply would put him off the scent. As I folded my arms across my chest, I saw him in my peripheral vision. He wasn't leaving.

"Shouldn't you be doing something about that call?" I asked, keeping my eyes on the mountains, my hands clutching my elbows. "Heading out to defend the innocent. Keeping Harland safe for carbon-based life forms?"

"I just needed to answer a question."

"They keep you on call to answer questions? Sounds like the sheriff's office doesn't have enough to do."

Jack didn't reply to my taunt, which made it sound like exactly what it was: the childish response of a defensive woman. A last-ditch effort to get rid of him. I was barely hanging on to my equilibrium. I wanted him gone.

To my horror, tears pricked my eyelids.

I clutched myself harder, ducking my chin, not caring anymore what my actions looked like, concerned only with getting through these next few moments with a spectator.

But if anything, his presence intensified my emotions, made them harder to keep in check.

Then, to my amazement and, yes, horror, I felt his hand on my shoulder. Large, gentle, and warm.

Connection. Contact.

Consolation.

The word gently teased out of my subconscious reminded

me of what Father Sam had talked about. How could I find healing in church when I was continually reminded of how far I fell short of what Leslie's God required?

I shouldn't have come, I thought as my tenuous control unraveled. I mentally grabbed the ends, frantically trying to bring it all together again, but they slipped through my grasp, slowly pulled away by the faint sob that rippled through my chest.

Not here. Not in front of Jack. Please, God, not now.

And why was I calling out to God? He hadn't heard me then. He wouldn't hear me now.

"What's wrong?" Jack's voice grew quiet, comforting, almost drawing me out.

I concentrated fiercely on the grass at my feet. Green with a bit of brown. Twisted leaves, intertwined, reaching down into the dirt . . .

I was almost centered again when Jack's rough finger touched my chin and gently lifted it up, forcing me to look at him. Though he didn't have to force too much. My head willingly lifted itself. My eyes willingly drifted to his.

He knew nothing about me, nothing about my history. But still he looked at me as if I was important. I hadn't been looked at like that in a long time. And the compassion in his gaze was almost my undoing.

I pulled away as my history, the reality of my life, and Leslie's lecture stiffened my resolve.

"What's wrong, Terra?" he asked again, pressing gently against the walls I had hastily thrown up.

"Nothing . . ." I stumbled a moment, trying to find my normal voice, knowing that someone didn't charge out during church because of "nothing." "It got a little stuffy in there."

That was dead-on the truth. Just depended on which truth one wanted to grab on to. "I'm just not one for church, I guess."

He tipped his head to one side, studying me like he would a child. "I just thought I'd check." He waited a beat, as if he knew I was hiding something. But I kept my lips tight. Finally, he retreated a step, turned, and left, taking his skepticism with him.

I waited as the door of the church opened and slowly sighed closed behind him, then allowed relief to wash through me. I had fooled him.

Oh, right, mocked my intuitive counterpart. *He knew you were hiding something; he just knew he couldn't get it out of you.*

Didn't matter. He was gone for now, and I had time to figure out what my next step was. I could wait for Dan and Leslie and put up with their questions. Or I could start walking.

Running away again, are we?

Just like Leslie said you would?

Just like Mom?

Chapter Fourteen

A re you sure you're okay?" Leslie asked me for the fourth time, her eyes doing that little-sister thing as she pulled out of the church parking lot. Dan had elected to stay behind for coffee, and Nicholas, big surprise, decided to stay with him. Anneke was going to a friend's for lunch. Once again, Leslie and I were alone.

"Just feeling woozy. I'm sorry."

No sooner had the last notes of the last song died away inside the church, than the outside door flew open and I heard Leslie calling my name.

When I told her I wanted her to drive me back to Helen's, her disappointment made me thankful I didn't go with my first inclination to leave without telling her.

"I'm sad you missed Dan's prayer. It was really good."

"I'm sure it was. Maybe you could give me a copy?"

"The way he had that thing marked up and rewritten—only he could have deciphered it."

"Maybe next time."

Leslie shot me a quick sideways glance. "What was Jack doing outside?"

The undertone of her question hit me wrong, and I reacted the way I shouldn't. "Trying to seduce me."

"Terra!"

"He came out to answer a phone call, okay?"

"I'm sorry."

"And I get the whole 'he's not suitable for you' thing, okay? You don't need to hammer it home with a sledge."

"Again, I'm sorry. I am." Leslie was quiet a minute. "So, are you going to come back to the farm again soon?"

"Do you want me to?"

"Of course I want you to. I want to have my sister around. I want to see you settle down." The last comment held an unspoken note of longing that hooked into my heart.

I had hoped to rebuild my connection with Leslie while I was here, but it seemed that at every turn I was reminded how far our lives had shifted from any hope of convergence.

Besides, if getting closer to my sister meant getting involved with a God who, it seemed, knew everything about me, I wasn't sure I wanted to be here any longer than I had to. This morning in church was not something I wanted to repeat.

And yet . . .

The psalm the minister had read echoed in my mind. *"If I settle on the far side of the sea, even there your hand will guide me, your right hand will hold me fast."*

The words held both fear and comfort for me.

I pressed my fingers against the low-level headache pushing against my forehead with all the insistence of a siding salesman.

"You're not okay," Leslie said, pulling the car into the parking lot of Albertson's grocery store. She turned sideways, brushing my hands aside as she rested her palm against my forehead, her fingers at my wrist.

"My sister. Always with her finger on the pulse," I joked, trying to regain control of the situation.

"I'm sorry. Was the service hard for you?"

"A lot of things were hard for me," I said quietly as another insistent thought pushed against me. *Why not tell her everything?* The quiet question hovered in the gloomy recesses of my mind, tugging on the old memories, trying to draw them to the surface.

"My frame was not hidden from you . . . All the days ordained for me were written in your book."

A married couple walked past the car. In the silence that settled between Leslie and me, I could hear their muffled argument. It sounded halfhearted, as if they weren't completely committed to it but pride required that they carry it on.

I wondered about our mother and her relationship with our respective fathers, both of them men we knew nothing about. I had long suspected that our mother would have had a hard time picking either of them out of a police lineup. But that didn't change the connection between Leslie and me. Nor did it change my feelings about my mother.

According to all the birth-order books, as the oldest girl, I was supposed to be the responsible one. And prior to Leslie's getting married, I had been.

I got both of us to school on time, made sure Leslie wore the right clothes, and when there was money in the house, I bought the proper food. I was the one who made sure she did her homework. And when someone picked on her, they had to answer to me.

I turned my head slightly, studying Leslie as if seeing her for the first time. The only features we had in common were our long eyelashes and a vague similarity in the shapes of our noses and chins.

"For you created my inmost being; you knit me together in my mother's womb . . . See if there is any offensive way in me."

"Does it bother you that I lived with Eric? That I wasn't married?"

Emotions tumbled across her features. "For your sake, yes. For me? I'm not going to judge you." She slid me a sympathetic glance. "No one is perfect—especially not me."

"I should have left him long ago. I don't deserve your sympathy."

"I wish I'd known—I wish I could have helped you . . ."

"You were living the dream, Leslie. I was living the nightmare. You didn't need me messing up your life."

"You wouldn't have messed up my life. You're my sister."

In the once-dark center of my life, a faint glow began, brought to life by her approbation. "You know I love you," I said quietly. Leslie grabbed me in a tight hug that fanned the faint ember to flames. We sat that way for a while, until I noticed a couple of young boys watching us, laughing. The reality of the outside world intruded, and I pulled away.

"You should get going," I murmured. "I'm sure Dan won't appreciate waiting so long. You didn't tell him about last night, did you?"

Leslie shook her head. "Of course not. But I'd like to tell him, if I may?"

"Please. Don't." I couldn't stomach the idea of Dan, or anyone else for that matter, knowing what I had told Leslie.

"I think he needs to know. It will help him accept what happened . . . last summer."

I laid my hand on her arm and shook my head. "Dan comes

from a different place. I'm sure the whole loose, abused woman thing wouldn't work with him."

Leslie and I had grown up in a different circle of expectations and morals. We were raised by a single, unwed mother. We had absorbed this fact of our lives as easily as we accepted the color of our mother's eyes—clear brown, or bloodshot. Realities we accepted with a *whatever* shrug.

In spite of his own mother's divorce, Dan might not be accepting of our background or how it affected my life. I knew that his Christian upbringing might not stretch far enough to take in the reality of my life.

"But he needs to know."

"Let me be the judge of that—"

"Dan cares for you."

"I know he's not crazy about me. He never was. He puts up with me because I'm your sister, and your children's aunt. And I've messed up royally in that department, too, haven't I?"

Her silence underlined my comment.

"You should get going," I said again, letting her off the hook. The last thing I wanted was for her to feel like she had to ping-pong between me and her husband, trying to defend one against the other.

"Are you sure you're going to be okay?" Leslie asked.

I caught her hand and gave it a reassuring squeeze. "I'll be okay. This didn't happen yesterday."

"I'm going to call you every night. And stop in at the diner when I can."

"That sounds ominous." But it didn't really. It sounded comforting.

Leslie started the car again, and a few quiet minutes later we were parked in front of Helen's place.

"I'm glad you came and stayed with us," Leslie said as she slipped the car into park. She left the engine running this time, though. "Next time, just give me a call. I can come into town, or pick you up after work, if it works out. Don't hitchhike again."

"I got a ride from a very reputable person last time."

"But there are a lot of disreputable people around here," she said. "I don't like the idea one bit."

I leaned over and gave her a quick sisterly kiss on the cheek, her concern touching a hidden chord. "Okay," I conceded. "Until I get my own transportation, I'll call you or get a ride from someone. Maybe I'll buy a car," I said with a bright smile, deflecting her anxiety.

"That would be great. You haven't had one for a while," Leslie said, brightening.

"Like I said to Kathy—too many decisions." I pushed open the door, half turned, and gave Leslie a quick smile. "Thanks, Sis. For listening."

Just as I was about to close the door, she leaned forward, stopping it with one hand. "I'll be praying for you, Terra."

That was unexpected. I gave her a feeble smile. "Thanks. I think."

She held my gaze. "I mean it. There is power in prayer. I know it from personal experience."

I wanted to make a joke, to push away the intensity she was projecting, but as my throat closed up, I felt the brush of something ethereal. As if Jesus had laid a hand on my shoulder.

Chapter Fifteen

"Cow paste on whiskey, down with a cowboy, Adam and Eve on a raft, blowout patches, zeppelin in the alley," I called out as I punched in the order.

A smile teased the corners of Mathilde's mouth as she nodded an acknowledgment of my order. That almost-smile still felt like a major triumph.

"What did you think of the church service last Sunday?" Cor DeWindt asked me as soon as he got settled into his usual booth, his booming voice drawing its normal attention. I poured him his coffee, and while I waited for the other order to come up, continued with my side work.

This time of day the café was quiet, so I figured it would be more pleasant to fill sugar containers by his table than to drag them all back to the workstation. But if I had known he was going to come at me with both barrels blazing, I might have opted for working behind the scenes.

"It was . . . okay." I watched carefully as the white stream of crystals slid into the jar. Then as I screwed the lid on, wondered if I was creating a temptation for Cor.

Cor leaned in, narrowing his eyes and flicking his finger downward—a signal for me to come closer. I set down the sugar container, brushed my hands, and leaned over.

"Why did you walk out?" he asked, lowering his voice.

What a surprise. Cor, being discreet.

"I wasn't feeling well," I whispered back. And that was all I was going to tell him. Monday was my day off, so today was the first chance he'd had to quiz me.

"Jack said something like that," Cor whispered again. He sat back with the expectant look of a proud father. "I heard you met Jack at the VandeKeeres' place."

This was going to get awkward. "He gave me a ride. When I was *hitchhiking*." I stressed the last word, hoping to distract him.

A frown beetled his brows. "I thought I told you not to do that anymore."

Bingo.

"Well, Cor, this may come as a shock to you, but I am all grown up and"—I grabbed the sugar container off his table—"you're not my father." I frowned at the five grains of sugar in the bottom, then at him. "And where did all this sugar go?"

He ignored my question. "Well, your father's not around."

"Truthfully, Cor, my father probably doesn't even know I exist." I filled the container, gave the lid an extra twist, and set it as far away from him as I could without making it look obvious.

Cor frowned at the placement of the sugar dispenser, then at me. Busted.

But he got the hint as, with a sigh, he ripped open a couple of packets of artificial sweetener and dumped them into his coffee. He took a sip, pulled a face, then sat back, his arms folded over his bright yellow suspenders and purple shirt. A Crayola storm if ever I saw one.

"A father should be with his children. Should be interested. That's wrong."

"That's my life."

"Order up!" I heard Mathilde say, glad for the distraction. I didn't want to talk about a father I never knew and, I had to confess, sometimes wished would come rolling into my life full of remorse. Money wouldn't hurt either.

I brought the order to the three men sitting close to the kitchen, honored the now-standard request to translate my diner-speak, then returned to Cor's table to collect the sugar container.

"So your father has never contacted you?"

Can you say *persistent*? "Never," I said, adding a smile to show I didn't care that much.

Cor's glower took over his forehead. "What was your mother like?"

I wiped the last sugar container down and set it on the tray to dry. "I guess free spirit would about cover her description."

Cor's direct gaze bored into me. "You ever hear from your mother?"

"Not for the past six months or so."

"And you don't know where she lives?"

"She doesn't know where I am, so it goes both ways."

"And you probably couldn't go see her even if you did."

"Why not?"

He held out his thumb. "No car. But I have a car you might be interested in. I've got my truck, so I don't need two vehicles."

"I'm not really in the market for a car right now. I have debts to pay." And money to save up. I was getting closer to my goal, but I still hadn't heard about a court date.

"I'll give it to you cheap," Cor said, continuing his campaign to prevent me from thumbing rides on the roads of Harland County. "Don't even have to get a loan. I'll finance it. You should come have a look." He slapped his hand on the table. "Could you come tonight? And stay for supper. That would be nice." The faintly wistful tone of his voice snagged my attention.

I knew he spent so much time at the diner because he was lonely, and going to his place to look at a car wouldn't kill me. Looking didn't mean buying.

"I could come for supper. But let me bring something."

"Why don't you bring dessert?"

"Dessert I can do."

"You don't have to go to a lot of trouble. The co-op has a special on black forest cake. You could just pick one up."

Or not. I was thinking fruit platter. A healthy alternative and possibly a chance to teach him some better eating habits. "What time should I come?"

Cor pulled one corner of his mouth down as he thought. "How about seven o'clock? That would give you time to change, and I could come pick you up—"

"It's gorgeous weather. I'll walk."

He frowned and waggled a finger at me just as the jangle of the doorbell announced another customer. "You won't hitchhike?"

"Hard to do in town." I glanced over my shoulder and smiled at Father Sam.

He patted me gently on the shoulder then slipped into

the booth across from Cor. "And how was your weekend, Terra?"

"She went to church," Cor said. "*My* church." He put heavy emphasis on the "my."

"It's not a competition, Cor." Father Sam looked hurt. "Though I'm sorry to hear that the homilies of our resident priest, Father Jorgenson, don't match up to the thunder-and-lightning sermons of Pastor Hofstede."

"He preaches the Word of the Lord," Cor said. "That's what we need to hear in this day and age. Pure preaching of the Word."

"But does he preach comfort?" Father Sam asked.

"Of course he does." Cor looked at me for verification. "Does Pastor Hofstede preach comfort? What do you think, Terra?"

Did I look like a theologian? "I think it's time I brought Father Sam his tea," I said, taking the coward's way out.

Conveniently, a new group of people came in just then, and a few minutes later the restaurant was buzzing again. I filled orders and refilled cups and tried out some of my own versions of slang to describe food I couldn't find on any of the Web sites I had checked out. And all the while, Mathilde grew more and more mellow. At least as mellow as someone with a permanent scowl pressed into her forehead could get.

"So we'll see you tonight?" Cor asked when I brought the bill. He leaned sideways to pull the wallet out of his back pocket, his expression hopeful.

"I'll be there. With dessert." Which I could probably buy with the tip I knew he would leave me.

The look of anticipation on his face almost gave me second thoughts about my plan to bring healthy food.

Then I noticed the half-empty sugar container.

And Father Sam didn't take sugar in his tea.

So, which pineapple to buy?

I held up two likely prospects, examining them closely, hefting them in my hands as the gentle strains of Muzak threatened to zombify me.

You have absolutely no idea what you're doing. Just pick one.

I didn't want to get home, cut open the pineapple, find a brown spot, and wish I'd bought the other one. I wanted to get the sweetest, tastiest pineapple I could so that Cor would eat it and declare himself done with sugary desserts. I wanted him to be converted to healthy eating habits, and to stay healthy after discovering just how good fresh pineapple could taste.

That was a lot of responsibility to put on a single piece of fruit.

A woman rolled her clattery cart up the produce aisle, reached past me, and with a decisive swipe, pulled a pineapple out of the bin. She dropped it into her cart and carried on, the rattle and squeak of her wheels following her.

How did she know?

I made a snap pineapple decision, then turned around in time to see a familiar sight ahead of me. I hurried to catch Amelia as she turned down the cookie aisle.

"Hey there, Amelia."

She spun around, the look of fear on her face slipping into relief when she saw me. She had Madison in a car seat tucked in the cart, a few groceries stashed around her. The little girl was sleeping, her head angled to one side, a little pink bow slipping out of the tuft of hair it had, at one time, been anchored to. Her mouth was pursed in a glistening pout, her stubby eyelashes a whisper of color on her cheeks.

The frayed blanket that had covered her had slipped down, and I gently pulled it up and very carefully, trying not to disturb her, tucked it back around her. She was so tiny and frail—I was afraid that even this small movement would disturb her.

Her cheeks were flushed and as I leaned closer, I could hear that her breathing was labored. And I caught a whiff of dirty diaper.

I thought of Leslie and Kathy's conversation.

"How is she doing?" I asked, brushing my finger lightly over her warm cheek.

"I dunno. Okay, I guess."

"She seems warm. Did you take her temperature?"

Amelia sighed and fiddled with her earring. "Well . . . I don't have a temperature thing."

"Thermometer. Come with me."

I led her to the pharmaceutical aisle. "Here," I said, handing her a blister package. "Thermometer. Directions are written on the back. Make sure you clean it with rubbing alcohol, not hot water." While I talked to her, I glanced over the contents of her grocery cart. Wieners, skim milk, Kool-Aid packages, some baby cereal, and macaroni-and-cheese packages. I had already interfered; I figured I may as well take it one step further. "That milk. Is it for you?"

"No. For Madison."

"You don't give a baby skim milk, Amelia."

Amelia chewed her lip as she fiddled with the thermometer. "My mom always gave me that milk."

Was this part of the reason Madison wasn't growing properly? "You don't give skim milk to a baby." I took her to the next aisle, handed her a can of infant formula. "This is what you feed a baby."

"It costs more, though."

"But it's better for her. And, Amelia, there's a changing table in the bathroom. You might want to use it to change her."

"Oh, yeah. I forgot."

I wondered how she could have forgotten something that made its presence known in no uncertain terms. For a moment, I understood Leslie and Kathy's concerns.

"And if you are really worried, take her to the hospital."

"But if I go again . . ." She stopped, her hand reaching up to her earring.

I moved a little closer, touching Madison's cheek again. Her very helplessness clutched at my heart. "If you go again, what?" I said quietly, sensing Amelia's fear.

"Your sister—Leslie?" Amelia wrapped one arm across her stomach, her other hand flipping her earring back and forth, back and forth, her nervous movements creating a jangling sound. "She said . . . she said something about taking Madison away."

My heart turned to ice in my chest. "Did she say exactly that?"

Amelia's face grew confused. "Not exactly."

I tried to keep my voice calm and even. I could see I was making Amelia even more nervous. "What *exactly* did she say, Amelia?"

"Well . . . she said it looked like Madison needed some

help, and then she said something about tests. I don't want them to take her away for tests. What if they don't give her back to me? She's okay, you know. She just needs love, and I love her lots."

"If you love her lots, you'll take her for those tests, Amelia." I hesitated, then figured after giving her advice on nutrition and child care, I could go all the way. "There is something wrong with Madison. She's too small for her age. She doesn't look healthy. You need to find out what's the matter with her so you can make her better."

"I'm scared." Amelia wrapped both arms around her waist, as if protecting herself. "I saw your sister and Rod talking together the other time I went to the hospital. They were whispering. I know they were talking about Madison and me."

"They won't take her away, Amelia. I'll help you keep your baby."

"You promise?" Her desperation leached into her voice.

"I promise."

She nodded. "Okay. I'll go change her. Except I don't have another diaper."

I led her one aisle over to the baby needs, picked up a package of diapers, and pulled one out. "I'll pay for this while you're changing her. Meet me at the cashier's when you're done, and I'll give you the rest."

"Okay. Thanks." Amelia took the diaper from me.

"And don't forget to wash her up after you take off the old diaper. You want her bottom completely clean."

"Right. Clean her bottom." Amelia stuffed the diaper into the pocket of her coat.

I watched her go, wishing I had my cell phone. I wanted

to call Leslie. To ask her what she and Rod had spoken about. I wanted to give Leslie the benefit of the doubt, but at the same time, when I thought of the conversation I overheard between her and Kathy I got angry. I gathered my groceries into a bag.

"You have to pay," the cashier called out just as I was about to leave.

"Sorry, I wasn't thinking." Which was a lie, I thought as I swiped my card, jabbing at the numbers with my forefinger. I was thinking too much.

I forced myself to calm down while I waited for Amelia. She didn't need to get any more stressed than she already was.

Ten minutes later, I realized that somehow she had snuck past me. No-show.

Now I was out six bucks and I had a package of disposable diapers. Just what every single woman needs on hand.

As soon as I got home, I called Leslie. But she didn't answer and she wasn't at work, and I wasn't about to start working my way through the Harland phone book to track her down just to satisfy my anger.

I had to calm myself to make up the fruit platter for that night anyway. Anger and knives are a recipe for bloody fingers and a quick trip to the ER.

Twenty minutes later, I had the fruit arranged on a plate and covered with Saran Wrap and I was on my way again. The walk calmed me down, and as I walked, my mind spun through the variables of Amelia's life. Rod, who didn't seem supportive, talking to Leslie, who didn't object when her friend Kathy said Madison should be taken away.

And why do you care? You're not going to be here forever. Don't get involved.

But I couldn't just walk away. Amelia's situation was eerily close to my own.

As my feet pounded out my steady waitress rhythm on the sidewalk, my mind flitted back to something the minister had said on Sunday. *Atonement.*

Maybe I needed to atone for my bad decisions, I thought. Maybe atonement—helping Amelia—would help erase the stupid mistakes I had made, straighten the wrong turns my life had taken.

Maybe helping Amelia would take away this nagging feeling that my life was heading in the wrong direction. Maybe I could have a moment of purpose before I moved on.

Who are you kidding? You can't help anyone. You've got a court case coming up—or have you forgotten the reason you've stuck around as long as you have?

I tried to brush the errant thought away. I had lots of reasons to stay awhile. Leslie. Nicholas. Anneke. I needed to connect with all of them.

Leslie comes with a whole load of other stuff you aren't ready to take on. Church. Family. Expectations. Everything comes at a price. Staying with Leslie could cost you more than you're willing to pay.

Leslie was my family. She was all I had.

And what is she going to think once you get hauled through the court system?

I stopped, closed my eyes, and willed the thought away. Ever since I'd been fingerprinted, I had tried to ignore the ignominy of the situation. My focus had been paying Leslie back. I hadn't given much thought beyond that.

I'd need a lawyer, probably. And how was I supposed to pay for that? Legal aid?

Stop. Stop. You're going to have supper with Cor. Think about that. Only that.

I straightened my shoulders and stepped around the corner.

Jack's silver pickup was parked on Cor's street.

Chapter Sixteen

I stopped so fast the pineapple I had spent so much time working on almost slid off the plate.

I was not ready to see Jack right now.

I still got a faint shiver when I remembered the intensity of his gaze on Sunday, the warmth of his hand on my shoulder.

An aluminum screen door slapped open, and Cor stood on the concrete step of his little stucco house. "Hey, Terra. There you are." He waved as if he hadn't seen me in days instead of mere hours. "Come on in."

I saluted him with the fruit tray, my fate for the next hour sealed.

Maybe Jack had just stopped by to check Cor's hot water tank, maybe put salt in the water conditioner, I consoled myself as I trudged up the cracked sidewalk, edged by overgrown grass. Maybe he was leaving soon.

"Guess who's staying to have dinner with us?" Cor boomed in my ear as he pulled me close in a hug. "Jack!"

Maybe I was delusional.

"My, isn't that nice." A tad insincere, but I could be excused for not jumping up and down with paroxysms of jubilation. Jack was too quickly becoming . . . interesting.

After I finished my good deeds, I had every intention of leaving Harland and leaving intact. Jack was a complication, and even though I didn't quite believe Leslie's assertion that he was interested in me, I had no intention of becoming a complication in his life either.

"Come in, come in. Supper is almost ready." As Cor ushered me into the house, he looked down at the plate I'd brought and his smile faltered. "What did you bring me?"

"Some lovely pineapple, some delicious melon, scrumptious orange pieces, juicy grapes, and fruit dip."

"Well. That sounds—"

"Nutritious," I supplied, then took an exaggerated sniff. "And it smells wonderful in here." I caught the distinctive scent of onions, garlic, and something else I couldn't define.

"Come on in. We're just about ready to eat." He took the plate from me and led the way, wheezing as he walked, which made me doubly glad I had brought the fruit.

He led me through a cramped and cluttered living room—papers lay stacked in a precarious pile against a chair; paperback and hard-covered books blanketed the coffee table. A tattered afghan hung over one arm of a cracked leather chair.

A man's domain.

And then we were in the kitchen. And there was Jack, standing by the stove.

He wore blue jeans again and a loose cotton shirt. The country music wailing out of the radio competed with the sizzle from whatever Jack was frying. He glanced up at me as Cor and I entered the small kitchen. Gave me a neutral smile, which made me relax. A little.

"Hi. Welcome to Chez DeWindt. Would you like something to drink?" He gestured toward a table decked with a brown-

and-gold-plaid tablecloth and three place settings made up of mismatched dinnerware.

Two pitchers, one holding water and the other orange juice, sat on the table, condensation slipping down their exteriors onto the tablecloth.

I shook my head. My little jaunt here had made me more hungry than thirsty. That, and the fact we'd been so busy at the diner all day, I hadn't had a chance to grab more than a random bite from a hamburger Lennie had set aside for me.

"It smells good in here," I said.

"As soon as the Iron Chef is done, we can eat," Cor announced, giving me an encouraging smile as he pulled open the refrigerator door and put the fruit platter inside. "Hey, Terra. How do you know you've had an elephant in your fridge?"

"I don't know."

"You can see his footprints in the butter." Cor laughed, slapping his knee.

"Can I do anything?" I asked, hoping he wouldn't come up with another joke.

"No. You sit down and let us serve you." Cor pulled out a chair at the far end of the table and motioned for me to come sit down.

From that vantage point I could see the entire kitchen. The counter was strewn with vegetable peels and seeds and plastic bags. Among the detritus of vegetables were nestled two cutting boards, knives resting across them as if waiting for the next onslaught.

"Jack's a very good cook, you know," Cor said, plunking a cup of water in front of me.

Very subtle.

"Jack lives on his own place, of course. But sometimes he comes here and cooks for me." Cor beamed at his son, obviously his pride and joy.

I gave Cor a careful smile as I balanced my interest between . . . well . . . interest and . . . not interest.

The look Jack directed at me started out as *What can I do?* then changed as our eyes met. His expression started a familiar prickle at the nape of my neck.

Too late I caught Cor's gaze flicking from Jack to me and back again.

"Jack's been fixing his place up himself, you know. He's real handy with a hammer . . ."

"You can put the rice on the table," Jack said, tipping his chin toward the pot on the back burner of the stove, stopping Cor mid-admiration.

Cor scurried over to the stove, grabbed the pot, and dropped it directly on the table with a muffled *thunk*. Lines of brown streaked the sides of the pot.

"You could put it in a bowl, Dad," Jack muttered. "Or at least put a hot pad under it."

"Nah. The table can handle it, and a bowl would just give us one more thing to wash up." Cor rubbed his hands. "What else?"

"Spoons?"

"Right." Cor yanked open a drawer and rattled through it, pulling out a misshapen spoon with a triumphant grin. "I got one."

"We'll need two, Dad."

"Gotcha."

"Is the salad ready?"

"Not yet."

For the next few minutes, I watched Jack order an increasingly flustered Cor around.

Cor ran his fingers through his hair, washed his hands, adjusted his suspenders, picked up a knife, cut up some more salad—all the while his eyes flicking from me to Jack and back again.

I offered to help a couple of times, but each time Cor waved off my suggestion with his knife, which frightened me more than the erratic chopping did. Cor didn't relax until the food was on the table and we were sitting down. He glanced at Jack again, smiled, then looked at me. "We usually pray before our meals," he said.

"Of course."

I waited until Jack bowed his head, then followed suit.

"Our heavenly Father," Cor prayed, his voice taking on a deep, reverential tone, "we come before Your throne of grace to thank You for the blessings You have given us out of Your bountiful hand. We ask You to look upon us, Your children, in Your love and bless us in our work."

In spite of the formal tone and the religious language, his words created a space that sounded well visited, a path well trod. I could imagine that this God he was talking to could well be the same God that Father Sam spoke of when he talked of consolation. A connection, as thin and insubstantial as a spider's web, anchored them together as Cor's prayer showed me his relationship with God.

Intrigued, I followed along as his voice ebbed and flowed. I was surprised to hear the love and connection to God in his voice, his tone. A love that seemed at once utterly foreign and utterly desirable as he referred to God as Father.

I thought of Cor's comment about my oblivious father, and for the second time that day, my emotions trembled.

I squeezed my eyes shut, trying to pull myself out of the insidious snare Cor wove with his voice and his conviction as he named each of his kids and prayed for them in turn. Even Jack, who was sitting right beside him.

"And, Lord, we pray for Terra . . ."

My heart jumped. *Me?* He was bringing my name before this God he was speaking so intimately with?

No. Not a good idea. I preferred to stay out of God's line of sight, thank you.

"Be with her in her work, and give us a good time together this evening."

Well, that sounded innocuous enough. "Help her feel Your presence in her life. Give her comfort and encouragement . . ."

I bit my trembling lip against the swell of yearning that his innocent words brought up.

Chapter Seventeen

Give me your plate and I'll scoop you up," Cor said, holding his hand out.

"She can help herself." Jack placed the pot of rice beside me.

"Look how skinny she is. She needs good food," Cor protested.

Jack let his eyes drift upward in a "Help me" moment, then lifted the lid off the pot. "Here you go. Help yourself to some china."

"What?"

"Oh, c'mon. I thought that was diner slang for rice."

"You've been doing your homework," I said, trying to regain some of my shaken equilibrium.

"I like to keep up."

"Not hard to do with me when I'm on foot most everywhere I go."

"You check out my car after," Cor said as he spooned a mound of soft, fluffy rice onto my plate. "It's a good car. A Shadow."

"Of its former self." Jack passed the stir-fry spoon. "That thing has been around the world. Twice."

"Don't exaggerate." Cor grabbed the spoon and dropped a huge pile of steaming vegetables and chicken on top of the rice. "It only has a hundred and eighty-seven thousand miles on the odometer."

"My bad. Seven and a half times. It's ready for the junk heap."

"What do you mean? I drove that car until I got my truck."

"You've had your truck for four years, Dad."

"Only two." Cor filled a small bowl with salad, poured a liberal amount of dressing on it, and pushed it my way.

"You bought it when Harland put that right-of-way through to the interstate. That was four years ago."

I ate, and they argued. But their argument held no rancor. It was as if they both felt obligated to spar and parry. I got a sense that beneath the surface bickering lay a relationship that had depth and roots. A relationship not easily shaken.

I didn't mind not having to participate, content in my role as spectator. The food was good, spicy with a hint of ginger. The house was cozy—as worn and lived in as an old sweater. It had that early sixties look with its turquoise Arborite countertops and blue-and-brown-striped wallpaper. A few of the pale green tiles on the backsplash were missing. The varnish around the curved brass handles of the kitchen cupboards had been worn away by countless hands opening their doors. This house had history, I thought, taking in the scuffed line and pencil marks by the door, marking off the heights of the various DeWindt progeny.

I wondered how often Cor's other kids came home. I wondered if they knew that Cor prayed for them. Every day, I was sure.

Did they just assume that would happen, or did they really appreciate it? Did Jack?

"I'm sure Dan could fix it up for you if there are problems. Right, Terra?"

With a start I pulled myself away from my contemplations and back into the conversation.

"Does the car have problems?"

"I don't know. I haven't run it for"—he raised his eyebrows toward Jack—"four years, according to my know-it-all son. But if you bought it, you wouldn't have to hitchhike everywhere. It would be much, much safer for you, girl."

He sounded so excited about the prospect, I hated to rein in his enthusiasm. "That would be pretty cool, but I can't afford to buy a car and then spend money on repairs."

"I would sell it cheap."

I looked from Cor's almost pleading expression to Jack, who was watching me with curiosity. Probably trying to figure out why a thirty-and-change-year-old woman couldn't afford a vehicle. Of course, the fact that he'd caught me hitchhiking twice might have clued him in to the fact that I wasn't exactly listed in *Forbes*.

"You wouldn't have to pay me right away," Cor continued, emphasizing the point with his fork.

"I had hoped to save the money first," I said, patting my mouth with the paper napkin Jack gave me. "I don't like being in debt."

"You have to go into debt for the big things," Cor protested. "Right, Jack?"

Jack shrugged.

"Jack just bought a house outside of town. He's fixing it up himself, bit by bit." Cor's teasing manner showed Terra what he thought of that idea. "I keep telling him to borrow the money and finish the job."

"It's biblical," Jack said. "When Luke talks about someone wanting to build a tower, he writes, 'Will he not first sit down and estimate the cost?' I'm making sure I can finish what I start."

"The longer you wait, the more everything goes up. Interest rates will be higher; lumber is going up."

"I've got the kitchen done."

"You're too cautious." Cor turned to me. "Tell my son he has to take a chance once in a while. Stick his neck out."

Like I, with my very patchy résumé, was in any position to give Jack DeWindt life skills advice.

"Sticking my neck out has never done me much good." His quiet comment momentarily flicked aside the curtain to his past. I thought of the girl Leslie had told me about. Of course it made me curious.

But of course I wasn't going to ask.

When we finished dinner, Jack cleared the table, insisting that I stay where I was, which I did. Gladly. Having two men wait on me hand and foot was a novel experience.

Cor brought out my fruit plate. From the casual way he put it on the table, I once again sensed his disappointment that I hadn't stopped at the co-op and picked up the heavily-hinted-at black forest cake.

"This is a great idea, Terra," Jack said, filling up a plate with fruit after I'd helped myself. "Tastes good, doesn't it, Dad?"

Cor gave me a polite smile and took a couple of pieces. But a few minutes later, he had a few more.

"So, do you think you want that car, Terra?" Cor polished off the last piece of pineapple, then returned like a terrier to his previous topic. "I can give you a good deal. In fact, I can give it to you, period."

"I don't want you to do that." From the look of his house, I guessed he lived on a fixed income and could use all the money he could get.

"It's in good shape." While he kept at me, Jack got up and took out a large black book from one of the kitchen drawers behind him, setting it in front of Cor along with a pair of glasses. I caught the glint of the words *Holy Bible*.

This time, however, I was prepared for whatever would come out of that book. When Cor began reading, I sat back, folded my arms, and let my mind slip away. I wandered to Leslie's place, imagining her and the kids working in their yard. *I should call her and see about coming on Friday.* Visit her in the wide-open spaces of the farm, bounded and protected by the surrounding mountains. My mind slipped with ease to the daydream I'd had the last time I was at her place. Me, wandering like Julie Andrews, minus a guitar and all those kids.

But with Jack.

A slow chill drifted through my chest as my eyes were unwillingly drawn to him. Why this inexplicable attraction? He hadn't encouraged or nurtured these fluttery feelings that, of late, came over me whenever I thought of him.

. . . How he could make me smile.

. . . His hand on my shoulder after church.

. . . The concern in his voice when he checked on me.

I mentally shook away the memories. I wasn't going to settle here, and Jack and I each had our own histories to deal with.

Jack sat with his arms crossed, his eyes staring sightlessly at

the empty fruit platter as he listened to his father. Then Cor's
words caught my attention.

"'And if he finds it, I tell you the truth, he is happier about
that one sheep than about the ninety-nine that did not wander
off. In the same way your Father in heaven is not willing that
any of these little ones should be lost.'"

Cor pulled the silk ribbon bookmark between the pages
and slowly closed the Bible, as if afraid to disturb the words
within. Then he looked across the table at me, his watery
blue eyes intent on mine. Did he think I needed rescuing?
Like that single sheep that wandered off? Did he think I was
worth rescuing?

I was glad when he said nothing, just turned to Jack and
asked him to pray.

Jack's prayer was short and took a different tack from
Cor's. Thanks for the food and company. Prayers for the safety
of family and friends.

". . . and be with those of us here who are lost and
hurting . . ."

I doubted that either Cor or Jack were the "us here" who
were lost, so I guessed he was praying for me. The thought was
like a shot to my chest. What did I matter to him?

When he said, "Amen," I kept my eyes on my hands, now
folded tightly in my lap.

A moment of silence followed Jack's prayer, as if it needed
time to settle. Which it did. I didn't know where to store this
new information.

Why did he pray for me?

And what was going to happen to me now?

But in spite of my questions, the idea that he would lift me
up to God, a God I spent minimal time even acknowledging,

took root and developed, creating feelings I had neither the
time nor the patience to examine.

"Well, I have to walk to the mailbox and get the mail,"
Cor announced, pushing himself away from the table. "I didn't
have time earlier today. So you two will have to do the dishes."
Then he blithely walked out the back door without a backward
glance.

"As if that wasn't obvious," Jack said, taking the plates from
the table. "Sorry about that. Dad has his moments . . ."

"That's okay. I planned to do the dishes," I said, purposely
misreading his apology. "I just don't think it's fair that you have
to help."

"Dad cooked the rice, set the table, and made the salad. In
his mind, that makes him exempt."

But more important to Cor I was sure, it made me and Jack
alone. In spite of my nonchalant attitude, Jack's prayer inter-
laced itself through the memory of that moment in the church
parking lot, weaving a low-level tension around us.

We worked in silence, which, if Cor were around, would
have been a grave disappointment to him. After all the work
he had done to bring about this moment, I was sure he would
not have been pleased that Jack and I only murmured the
occasional "Excuse me" when our elbows happened to brush
together.

I wiped the last pot and set it beside the stack of mismatched
but clean dishes. "Anything else?"

Jack took the damp dishtowel from me and hung it over the
handle of the oven door. "By the way, the fruit was a great idea,"
he said, buttoning the cuffs of his sleeves.

"I know Cor eats way too many sweets."

Jack grabbed the back of his neck in a gesture of frustration. "Dad thinks that if he ignores his diabetes, it will magically disappear."

"Is he on pills or insulin?" I handed Jack a pile of plates.

"He was on pills, but they're losing their effectiveness. He thinks once he goes on insulin, he's halfway to dying." He pushed the plates into a cupboard and closed the door.

"That would mean injections, wouldn't it?" See Terra show off the little bit of knowledge she gleaned by Googling *diabetes* on the Internet.

"I think he's scared of the whole needle idea," Jack said as he took the glasses I handed him and pushed them into another already full cupboard.

"I can sympathize." I shuddered. "I hate needles."

"You're nothing like Leslie, then." Jack chuckled.

"That I'm not."

"You don't need to be. Like Leslie."

I shouldn't have been surprised that Jack caught my derisive tone. What did surprise me was how his simple comment created a warmth that no man had kindled in me in a long time.

I didn't know where to put these emotions. Jack was exactly the wrong person for me. Besides the whole police gig, he was churchgoing. Solid. Dependable. Probably planning to live in Harland forever.

And I couldn't?

You need to keep moving. Stay in one place long enough, and you start having expectations of people. They'll always let you down. Always.

I thought of Eric. Thought of the dreams I had when we first started dating. Dreams that I had slowly but surely compromised the longer we stayed together. First it was intimacy before marriage. Then it was moving in before marriage.

Then pregnancy.

During my time with Eric, what dreams I hadn't discarded or compromised had been broken or twisted beyond recognition.

I wished Cor would come back.

"Listen, about that car . . ."

"I can't buy it." I was about to tell him that I couldn't afford much of anything right now, but I held back. I looked like enough of a loser for now.

"Dad would give it to you. He really worries about you hitchhiking." Jack folded his arms across his chest and leaned back against the kitchen counter, tapping his fingers against his arms. "He'd feel better if you took it off his hands."

"But he could use the money. I mean, he doesn't seem to have a lot."

Jack just laughed. "Trust me, he's got boatloads stashed away."

I looked around the kitchen with its worn floor, the old-fashioned table with the cracked vinyl chairs.

Jack caught the direction of my puzzled gaze. "Dad could give Ebenezer Scrooge tips on how to pinch pennies."

"But he tips really well."

Jack just nodded, his crooked smile once again doing those silly things to my stomach. "Dad likes you."

"Why?" I couldn't recall anything I had done that would have endeared me to him. I didn't treat him special.

"For one thing, he thinks you're cute."

"What?"

Jack grinned and spread his hands in a *What can I do?* gesture. "He's perfectly harmless, if that's what you're worried about."

"No. No. Of course not. I mean, I don't . . . 'cause he's . . ." I stumbled over my words, taken aback.

"He feels protective toward you. He told me that he sees deep hurt inside you." As Jack spoke, his smile faded and his gaze became intense. The kitchen grew smaller, and Jack seemed closer.

I remembered our conversation in his truck. Each time we met, something shifted between us. I recognized the signs.

And it scared me.

"That hurt he sees is probably the indigestion I get from the burgers I have to wolf down so Mathilde doesn't think I'm slacking off." I tossed off the comment with a smile, trying to break the atmosphere.

Jack's expression didn't shift. His eyes stayed on me, but I managed to hold his gaze, even though inside my chest, my heart wobbled and spun. Then his hand came to rest on my shoulder, his fingers curling around it. I wasn't going to lean toward him. Wasn't going to let him pull me close. Wasn't going to let his lips lower to mine.

But I did. And he did.

And next thing I knew, I was being held close against a hard, warm chest, strong arms holding me tight.

"What's happening, Terra?" he whispered, his fingers tangling in my hair as his hand cradled my head against him.

"I thought you'd done this before," I whispered back.

"I have."

"So why don't you know?"

He drew back, his fingers still woven in my hair. "I just don't know about you."

"You arrested me . . ." I was scrambling here, trying to find the strength to pull away from him. To do the right thing. I was supposed to be a liberated, free-living woman. In spite of Eric, or maybe because of him, being supported by Jack's strong arms created a haven I was loath to leave.

"All I got from that was your date of birth and the fact that you had no previous convictions." He shook his head. "I don't want to talk about that."

"What does that leave?"

He finger-combed my hair back from my face, his eyes following the movement of his hand. "You. Leaving once things are settled here."

The reality of my situation finally gave me the willpower to pull away. I thought of what Leslie had said about Jack's previous girlfriend and knew that this moment of weakness wasn't fair to Jack.

"I'm sorry" was all I could say.

"Of course you are."

He was about to say something more when the door flung open, announcing Cor's return. I was off the hook.

Chapter Eighteen

So what do you think?" Cor patted the hood of the Dodge Shadow, and a few more flakes of white paint peeled off. He brushed them aside with a casual gesture. "That's just surface stuff. They had problems with their paint that year. Don't let the looks fool you. It runs real good."

I walked around the vehicle once more. The little white car had definitely seen better days. Better years. In places, the paint had peeled so badly I could see gray primer underneath it.

Cor unlocked the driver's door and held it open. "Sit in it. See how you fit."

I hesitated, remembering the little spiel I'd heard from a used-car salesman—insert favorite used-car salesman joke here. He told me that as soon as a customer touched the car, he started calculating his commission.

As I settled into the seat, the chemical scent of orange air freshener drifting past me, a force beyond my own took control of my feet and will. Seconds later, I was holding the steering wheel in my hand, the plastic seat cover warm under my legs, as my eyes flicked over the dashboard, taking inventory.

At least I refrained from making *vroom-vroom* noises.

An incongruous orange-colored pine tree swung from the rearview mirror. Stereo with old-time cassette deck. Automatic transmission.

From what I could see of the seats past the dusty plastic, they were in immaculate condition. The floor mats were new.

Lots of room in the back.

"Do you want to take her for a spin?" Cor dangled the car keys in front of me, tempting me.

"I don't know." My hands still clutched the steering wheel, kneading it as if to test its reality.

Cor reached past me and stabbed the key in the ignition. "There. Take it out."

It had been months since I had driven my own car.

Cor slammed the door shut, and the orange smell intensified. Nerves fluttered in my stomach as I reached for the key. What could it hurt? It was just a test-drive. No commitment.

And this is how sad my life had been of late. That the thought of driving an old beater car got me all fluttery.

Of course, my emotions were a little shaky yet after the encounter with Jack. Thank goodness, he left shortly after Cor returned. Which of course made Cor curious. So to forestall his inevitable cross-examination, I asked him to show me the car.

And here we were.

Cor flapped his hands at me in a shooing motion.

He wasn't going to quit until I went. So I started it up, pulled the gearshift into reverse, and backed out of the driveway before my sensible side took over.

I turned onto the road, and from there it was a few minutes to the outskirts of town, and from there . . .

Oh, the freedom! The unbeatable bliss of choices. The idea that I could turn down that road. Or that road. Or that one.

Or get to the interstate and just head out on the open road.

Keep going. Who's gonna know? Eric hasn't found you yet. No one's gonna go after you over some lame trumped-up assault charge. You can dump the car.

And what about Leslie? Anneke? Nicholas? Amelia?

Relationships and expectations that were put on you. You didn't take them on.

But I did. I didn't need to go running to Leslie. I could have gone in any direction, but I came here. To my sister. For the first time since Leslie had left for college, we were in the same place.

And I had that stupid pending court case. I should have asked Jack about it, but in my flustered state, I'd forgotten.

I twisted against the restrictions of expectations, but they held me fast. So I turned the car around and drove slowly back to Cor's place. As soon as I parked the car, he was through the gate and standing beside the door.

"And? What did you think? Runs pretty good, doesn't she?" he said as I handed him the keys.

"It does." I waited a beat, then took a plunge. "How much do you want for it?"

Cor pursed his lips, thinking. "Well. Jack said it's not worth much. How about three hundred dollars?"

"No. That's way too low."

Cor put his hand on my shoulder and gave it a light shake.

"I really want to get rid of it, and the longer it sits in my drive-way, the less valuable it becomes. You'd be doing me a favor, honey."

I thought of the freedom the car would give me. Thought of what I could do with it. The possibilities. If three hundred was all Cor was asking, I could stay a little longer after I paid Leslie back and maybe save up enough to get a decent start in Chicago.

Unless, of course, Ralph's assault charge sticks.

I couldn't go there. If that happened, I was here for who knew how long trying to pay for a lawyer, dealing with a court case, throwing money in seventeen different directions.

Think positive. Think positive.

"Two hundred," Cor said, misreading my hesitation.

"Stop already."

"Buy it already."

"Okay. Okay. It's a deal. But at three hundred."

"No. Two hundred, and you pay me when you have enough money together." Cor squeezed his hand tighter on my shoulder and then unexpectedly pulled me close to his barrel chest in a quick hug. He patted me on the back before drawing away, looking sheepish at his sudden outburst.

"I'm glad you're buying the car," he said. "I don't like the idea of you walking home from work late at night." Cor put both his heavy hands on my shoulders, his intent gaze holding mine.

"Harland. The high-crime center of Montana," I said, trying to brush off his concern.

"But I do worry about you. In more ways than one. I was

glad to see you in church, but that's only a start, girl. God is looking for you, and I'm going to be praying that you'll hear His voice, hear Him calling you."

"I'm not so sure I like the idea of more voices in my head. What if I don't want to answer? Or the line is busy?"

Cor gave my shoulders a little shake. "Joke all you want. It doesn't change the fact that God loves you like a father. You don't know exactly what a father's love is. Or even a mother's. But God put His only Son's life on the line for you. Terra Froese. You need to know that." He pulled me close in another awkward hug, patting me heavily on the back.

"Oh, Terra, Terra," he said with a sigh, holding me tight. "What are we going to do with you?"

I closed my eyes, feeling the rough texture of his shirt, the strap of his suspenders pressing into my cheek. *If I had to make up a father, this is what he would feel like,* I thought, my arms barely reaching around him as I returned his hug.

In that fleeting moment, I felt like a daughter. A beloved daughter.

As far as God's loving me, though . . .

Snatches of verses slid through my mind, memories of the church service, of what Father Sam had said.

Forgiveness. Atonement.

I pulled away and gave Cor a quick smile. "You're not going to quit your campaign to bring me into the fold, are you?" I said, though I wasn't feeling as breezy as my voice made me out to be. "Even though I'm a stubborn, hitchhiking mongrel?"

"Well, Jesus said He would go after some dumb sheep who didn't know enough to find his way back when all the others managed to. What makes you think you're any different?"

His blue eyes held mine with an intensity that made me realize where Jack got the gift.

"Nothing can separate you from His love," Cor said, adding another salvo to the ongoing crusade. "Remember the Bible passage the minister read on Sunday? 'Where can I go from your Spirit? Where can I flee from your presence? If I go up to the heavens, you are there; if I make my bed in the depths, you are there . . .'"

"That's all well and good, but you're forgetting the second part—the part that talks about slaying the wicked and blood-thirsty men. Not so much comfort in that piece."

Cor frowned at me, as if I had spoken some heresy. "But it ends on a good note. The psalmist talks about God searching his heart, and about asking God to lead him. That can be a great comfort." Cor patted me on the shoulder. "God knows your heart. He knows your struggle. He's calling you to come to Him, and He's waiting."

I didn't want his simple words to influence me, but I couldn't let them go. Nor could I process them completely. All my life I'd held a basic concept about God. I didn't bother Him; He didn't bother me. But since I'd come to Harland, I had bumped up against God and Jesus again and again.

"I've done too many things wrong. I'm sure God doesn't really want to go looking for me."

"Well, you know sin is like a big hole between you and God, but when you confess those sins, they become the bridge."

"Then I'd have a pretty big bridge." I tried for a quick smile. "But in the meantime I guess we have some paperwork to do," I said, bringing the conversation out of the heavenly realm and back down to earth.

Cor gave me an odd look as if he understood what I was doing and was resigned to it, but he wasn't happy with me.

He led the way to the house and I followed.

Little mongrel, lost lamb.

"I wasn't sure what would come up, but look at these." Leslie knelt down by a patch of bright yellow and purple irises. "Try putting these colors together in an outfit, and you'd be banned from polite society."

"Even impolite society," I said, brushing the petals of one of the irises with a finger. "I can't believe you did this," I added, completely impressed with my little sister.

"I just put the bulbs in the ground. Sort of like that one Bible passage about us planting the seeds but God watering and giving growth."

I had no clue what Bible passage she was talking about. Since I had come to Harland, I had been inundated with Bible facts, so I figured I should have some clue. However, I also knew the Bible was a fairly hefty and confusing tome and had a lot more words than any other books I'd been exposed to, so my ignorance could be excused.

"Well, He did a good job with that growing part," I said. "They're lovely."

"I planted lilies as well, but they won't be flowering for a couple of weeks yet." Leslie pushed herself to her feet and looked around her yard, a woman content with her world. "Next year I'm going to try to start some of my own bedding plants. Judy said she would help me set up a small greenhouse. I'm looking forward to trying some squash and peppers. Maybe cantaloupe or muskmelon."

"And maybe you can buy yourself a little bonnet and apron and have a little booth at the farmer's market to sell all your stuff."

Leslie shot me a frown. "Don't tease."

"I wasn't."

Leslie's frown deepened.

"Well, maybe a little." I laughed. "C'mon, Leslie. The last time I visited you in Seattle, your houseplants were begging me to put them out of their misery, and now you're making plans for vegetable and fruit self-sufficiency."

"I enjoy it, and it still surprises me that I enjoy it."

"Surprises me, too." I shivered as a breeze whisked the warmth of the sun away. I grabbed Leslie by the arm and pulled her toward the house. "How about you serve me some of your iced tea made from tea leaves that you grew and dried yourself?"

A few minutes later, we were sitting on her deck, our feet up on lawn chairs. Nicholas and Anneke were with Dan on the tractor, so my sister and I were alone.

"I have something for your kids," I said, reaching into my backpack. I had been a little disappointed to find out that Nicholas and Anneke were gone when I arrived. This time I had done my auntly duty and come bearing gifts. A Polly Pocket for Anneke and a tiny plastic farm set for Nicholas. I had even wrapped them up.

"That's so sweet," Leslie said, taking the packages. "You can give them their presents when they come home. You are staying for supper, aren't you?"

"I plan to." I dug into the knapsack again, pulled out an envelope, and, with a flourish, handed it to her. "And this is for you."

Leslie took the envelope with a light frown, which turned into a pleased smile when she pulled out the thank-you card. "Well, thanks for the thanks . . ." She stopped when a bill fluttered out. She bent over to pick it up. "What's this?"

"It's what I owe you." By saving every penny of my tip money and begging Lennie to give me an advance on my wages, I had managed to scrounge together the exact amount of what Leslie had lent me.

"I said you didn't have to pay me back," Leslie said, holding the money between her finger and thumb as if it were contaminated.

"But I want to. I have to." Every time I pocketed another tip, Dan's words had tiptoed around my subconscious. "Now we're even, right?" I toasted her with my iced tea.

"I would have gladly given you the money. We're not that broke."

That wasn't the impression I got from Dan. "Doesn't matter. I owed you, and I pay my debts."

"I'll take it, but I'm not happy about this." Leslie tucked the money back into the card and set it beside the presents I had brought. "Are you sure you're not shorting yourself?"

"What's to short? I have a cheap place to live for now, and once this stupid court thing is out of the way, I'll be able to save up some more."

"Do you have a lawyer yet?"

"Lawyers cost money. I'm going to defend myself," I said with a flippant grin.

"Defending yourself was what got you into this mess in the first place."

"At least you admit it was self-defense."

"Jack told me."

I almost choked on the ice cube I was sucking on. "Jack admits I was telling the truth? Why did he arrest me, then?"

"He said Ralph had corroboration and you didn't. He had no choice. Besides, Ralph was the one bleeding, not you."

"So I really don't need a lawyer after all . . ."

"You cut Ralph's forehead open, though after what you told me about Eric, I understand that scenario better, too." Leslie focused her attention on the ice cubes in her drink. "I wish you had told me earlier about Eric."

"I probably should have, but I thought things were getting better between us. I thought I just had to learn to go through some of the ups and downs of a relationship." I shrugged. "Trouble was, the downs were often on the floor. Our relationship was such a classic scenario, I'm surprised Social Services didn't use my story on a pamphlet as a 'loser' warning."

Leslie swirled her ice cubes around her glass. "Are you afraid? That he'll try to find you?"

Her voice was casual, but underneath I caught a faint note of concern for her own family. "He won't find me. He doesn't have a clue where you live. I've never told him, and I never called you or wrote to you from our home phone or our home computer." I gave her a smile that I hoped was comforting. I wished she would drop the subject. I'd started moving to a better place in my life in the past few days. I was starting to make some plans. Dwelling on the past brought doubts and headaches. Today was bright and full of promise, and once I was free to go, I could move on to a fresh new stage of my life.

"Ever since I became a Christian, I've been praying for you," Leslie said quietly.

Her words pulled me up short. Another person praying for me. Should I feel flattered or afraid? "What exactly were you praying, pray tell?" I tried to laugh, but it fell flat.

"I prayed that you would come here. I think your coming here is a sign of those prayers being answered. A sign that you need to be here."

"Honey, the only signs in my life are the ones that say 'Now Leaving Harland' and 'Welcome to Chicago.' There are no other signs." She spooked me out with her talk of signs. Like some kind of magic got me here. There was nothing magical about Eric who was the catalyst for my trip.

"But you're here. And I've been praying that you would experience what I have."

"This faith thing?" I tried for mockery, but my heart wasn't in it and the tone fell closer to question than derision.

"Yeah. This faith thing." Leslie's gaze locked onto mine.

"You know, you want me to go to church, but I'm getting enough sermons hanging around Harland," I said, throwing up one last feeble defense.

"Who else has talked to you?"

"I got a mini agricultural lesson on lambs and Jesus looking for a lost sheep from Cor."

"He got that one right. I think you are lost, big sister."

"What do you mean? I have a plan. I'm going to Chicago . . ."

"And then?"

"Find a job that pays me more than a buck over minimum wage and tips."

"And then?"

I squirmed, wishing she would stop. "I don't know. Join a rock band."

Leslie's exasperated head shake dismissed my silly comment. "You've been running for the past few years. Running against the wind."

"Don't knock it. I like that song."

"You should. It's been your life's theme for too long now. One of these days you're going to get tired of this restless, windblown wandering. You'll be old and tired, and you won't have a place that's your own, and you'll realize that one really is the loneliest number."

"Leslie's greatest hits." I was really scrambling now. Scrambling for a foothold on the place I used to stand. But I was losing ground. Fast.

It wasn't fair, I thought, curling my shoulders as I cupped my hands on my elbows. I had come here feeling vulnerable, and now Leslie was hitting me again and again and I didn't have the strength to fight back.

"I've been hoping and praying you would come here. Hoping and praying I would be given a chance to talk to you about what's happened to me. And here you are."

I felt a surge of protective anger. "I'm here because you're my sister and because I needed to lay low."

"There are a lot of other places you could have gone to avoid Eric. But you came here. To the only family you have." Leslie put her cup on the table, leaned forward, and gently dislodged one of my hands, holding it between hers. "I think you came here because in your subconscious you thought you might find healing here."

"I came . . . I came because . . ." I stopped. I looked down at her hand holding mine because it was easier than looking into her eyes.

"I've found a meaning to my life here," Leslie pressed on,

obviously sensing my wavering. "I've seen you watching me, as if you're wondering yourself what is going on. I know that God loves me, and He has given me purpose in my life. I want you to find that purpose, that meaning."

I wanted to shut out what she was saying. Yet, as she spoke, in spite of my resistance, her words quieted the angry voices and created a silence and stillness I had never felt before. "You know this still seems a little weird to me, don't you?"

Leslie smiled. "I know. You need time. I did too." She got up, went into the house, and returned with a small book. I knew what it was before she even placed it on the table beside me. "I want you to have this for now. It's small enough to fit in your backpack. If you have a chance, read it."

I held the book, tracing the gold letters on the cover, then slipped it into my purse before I gave in to an impulse and opened it up. Though my resistance to all this faith stuff was shrinking, it was still a scary proposition.

This faith thing means losing control. Don't fall for it.

As if I have so much control over my life now.

"Does this come with Cliff's Notes?"

"No. But if you're really stuck, I'm sure Father Sam or Cor could help you out." She waited a beat. "Or you could come to church again."

"I could." I nodded, declining to accept the offer. Church hadn't turned out all that well the last time. I wasn't eager to repeat the humiliation. "So tell me about Anneke," I said as I zipped up my purse. "What's her latest new thing?"

Leslie brightened, distracted by any mention of her daughter. "The other day we went for a walk and she said she hoped there weren't any 'hopgrassers' around this year. It was so cute, I had to write it down." She told me about Nicholas's new words. Dan's latest plans.

The tension in my neck loosened and my shoulders dropped as the calming influence of the commonplace settled my churning thoughts.

Finally, the muffled ring of the phone summoned her. The door fell shut behind her and I settled back in my chair, letting my eyes follow the contours of the land as silence wrapped itself around me.

This is nice, I thought, momentarily thankful for the hiatus my little adventure in the bar had created. Had I not been forced, how long would I have stayed here? A week? Maybe ten days?

I was getting comfortable here. I was connecting with my sister, something that hadn't happened in a long time. Nicholas and Anneke didn't stare at me with that puzzled look, as if to say, "Who are you?"

You don't belong here . . .

I pushed the cynical voice aside. She was getting shrill and boring. I leaned back in the chair and sighed lightly. Aside from all the faith stuff, I enjoyed being with my sister again.

The screen door creaked open, and Leslie stood in front of me, holding out the receiver. "It's for you," she said with a puzzled lift of her eyebrow.

My heart gave one long, slow thump of fear. Had Eric found me?

"Hello?" I said, swallowing down my fear.

"How are you doing?" Jack's deep voice turned the thump into a flutter.

"Fine," I said cautiously. "How did you find me here?"

"Lennie said you had the day off, and there was no answer

at Helen's, so I assumed you were at your sister's place. I've got good news. Ralph agreed to drop the charges."

"So that means?"

"You're free to go. I can't release your bail money for a couple of days, but you'll get that back eventually as well."

"Really?" I sat back in my chair, suddenly boneless.

I would have my money back. I could start making plans again.

I could leave.

Leslie hovered over me, her eyebrows lifted in a tell-me-as-soon-as-you-hang-up look.

Did I really want to go? Start all over in a new city, a new place?

"I was also wondering what you're doing this Friday night."

This pulled me back from my mental meanderings. "Working. Why?"

"Yeah, but you get off at seven o'clock. Would you like to go to a movie, maybe coffee afterward?"

"With you?"

"I usually like to arrange my own dates, yes." Jack had lowered his voice, creating a gentle intimacy that, in spite of the warmth of the day, sent a faint shiver dancing down my arms.

And I didn't know what to say.

"If that's a problem . . ."

"No. No problem." Complication, yes. Problem, no.

Leslie's hovering was making me nervous. I knew what she thought of Jack and me, and while part of me didn't care, another part of me wanted her to approve. I liked Jack. I was attracted to him. Why not go out on a date? What could happen?

"Yeah. I think I will," I said. I gave Leslie a *Don't worry* smile. "So I'll see you Friday, then."

I said good-bye, disconnected, and laid the handset down on the table beside me.

"And? What did he want?" Leslie pulled her chair closer, as if proximity would pull the information from me quicker.

I leaned back in my chair and wrapped my hands around the back of my head as I digested this latest piece of information. Should I tell her? She'd find out sooner or later anyway . . .

"I have a date." My eyes flitted over her, then past to the mountains edging the valley.

"Jack phoned to ask you out on a date?"

I nodded.

"And you're going to go?" Leslie's frown did not bode well for any encouragement about my date. I didn't want her disapproval ruining the quiver of pleasure that curled in my midsection at the thought of going out with Jack.

"Oh, yeah, and I won't be needing a lawyer after all. Ralph is dropping the charges."

"So you're free to go."

"Yes."

"And will you?"

I held her steady gaze as conflicting emotions pulled me back and forth. *Stay. Go.*

"Well, I have a date for Friday night, so I'll be around at least until then."

Leslie gave me a feeble smile, but I could see that she was less than impressed with my current life's plan. "You make sure you don't hurt him."

"It's just a date."

"When you're a single guy over thirty and living in a small town, there's no such thing as 'just a date.' Please don't lead him on."

Leslie's concern for Jack's well-being would have been touching if I wasn't the one she was warning.

"I won't lead him anywhere, Sis. Don't worry."

Chapter Nineteen

I'm going on record as saying I'm sure I've been more bored at some point in my life, but I must've expunged that memory from my mind," Jack said, putting the key in the ignition of his truck.

"I'll bet the credits would have been interesting," I said, tucking my hands in the pockets of my jacket as I leaned back against the seat, "if you'd let us stick around to see them."

"And let that movie suck even a few more minutes out of my life?" Jack started the truck, then glanced at me. "I know you said you didn't want to do coffee, but I can't take you home yet. I'm sure you need some time to recuperate from that traumatic experience."

I was surprised he persisted. With Leslie's faint warning echoing in my subconscious, I had told him that I needed to go directly home after the movie. I hadn't counted on enjoying his company as much as I did. He knew exactly how to mock bad movies, bad acting, and sentimental music.

A movie critic after my own heart.

And even better—he didn't think he had to get his money's

worth by sticking around, when it was obvious to both of us the only thing that would redeem the movie was the projector breaking down.

So he tugged on my hand and said that he was ducking out and if I valued the time that was still allotted me in my life, I would follow him.

I laughed, was hushed by an anorexic-looking woman with dreadlocks, and, giggling, followed him up the darkened aisle and outside.

Which brought me to this place. Not ready to end the evening, and unwilling to go home to an empty basement suite with Helen watching pay-per-view upstairs.

"Sure. I can do coffee."

"Great." He started up the truck and pulled out onto the quiet street. The first place we went to was closed.

His truck's dashboard clock glowed 10:10. "I think we're too late for any establishment that doesn't serve alcohol." Jack frowned, tapping his fingers on the steering wheel. "I forgot how late it was." He sighed, then gave me a quick smile. "How about we just go for a drive? I can give you a resident's tour of Harland."

"Sure." That sounded harmless enough.

He took me past his old high school, shining his headlights on the football field. "Where I didn't play the game that didn't win the state pennant," he said, sighing.

"That's funny. I would have pictured you as a football star."

Jack shook his head. "Spent too much of my high school years reading. By the time I pulled my nose out of my books, prom was breathing down my neck, and all I could think of was how to work up the nerve to ask someone." He reversed out of the school yard and continued the tour, turning down another road I was unfamiliar with.

"Did you go?"

"Yeah. Kathy's sister, Phyllis, took pity on me."

I laughed. "I doubt she accepted out of pity."

The lights of the dashboard cast a greenish glow on Jack's face. In the half-light, his eyes shone with a familiar glint. Interest. Expectations. Our banter was slowly shifting to flirtation. "I'll take it as a compliment," he said.

"Glad I could be of service to your self-esteem."

Jack pointed out a church building with a towering spire. "That's the Catholic church. Father Sam's old parish. He lives in that little house beside the priest's residence."

A light shone out from one of the upper rooms. I wondered if Father Sam was praying. And whom he was praying for.

"How did he and your father meet?" I asked, curious about the relationship.

"Father Sam had visited my mother when she was in the hospital. My dad connected with him there. In fact, Father Sam was with my mother when she died."

"What did she die from?"

"Non-Hodgkin's lymphoma."

This was one of those occasions when I wished I was better with words. Wished I could say the right thing. "Sorry to hear that" just didn't pay the bill.

Yet I felt a curious kinship with him. Even though my mother was, to my knowledge, still alive, I'd lost her, too. "How old was she?"

"Forty-three." Jack shook his head. "Funny how that goes. Her death wasn't unexpected. We had lots of preparation. But still, when it came . . ." He gave a short laugh. The kind people give when they don't really know what else to say or do. "It's been over seventeen years, but I still miss her." He looked at me. "Do you miss your mom?"

"The last I heard from her was an e-mail she sent about six months ago from Yellowknife. That's in the Northwest Territories. Canada."

"So, not around the corner, then?"

"Not even in the neighborhood." I had told him what I needed to on our little trip to Leslie's place. More than that was just whining.

Jack turned into a paved parking lot, and I was spared more rehashing of the family history.

Large trees shadowed the empty park, edged by a waist-high hedge. During the day the trees would have offered welcoming shade. Now that night had slipped over the sky, they created an intimate atmosphere.

A fountain gurgled from a small man-made lake in the middle of the park, the spray diffusing illumination from a spotlight.

"Do you want to sit here a minute?" he asked.

I hesitated. Sitting in the park with Jack, after dark. The equation was adding up to more than I might be ready for. But neither was I ready for the evening to end. So I nodded, got out of the truck, and walked to an empty bench.

Jack was right behind me. He sat down, then leaned forward, man-style, his elbows resting on his knees, his hands clasped between them.

"I never knew about this park," I said, leaning back against the rough wood of the bench, content, for now, to make simple conversation.

"I used to come here with my friends after school and play

baseball in that far diamond." Jack pointed to an open space between the trees. I saw a backstop and some old bleachers in the reflected light from the fountain. "Used to play Little League."

"What position did you play?"

"Shortstop, which, for me at that age, was sort of like rubbing my nose in it." He gave me an apologetic glance. "I was vertically challenged for many of my formative years."

"You're not too short now."

"Thankfully, the formative years come to an end."

I hugged my knees to my chest. Jack sat back and stretched out his long legs in front of him, crossing his booted feet at the ankles. He folded his arms, the picture of a man content with his world.

"So, what do you want to talk about now?"

"We could discuss the difficulty of finding a radio station that plays your favorite songs," Jack said quietly.

"That's where an iPod comes in."

"Only if you care to figure out how to use it."

"It's not as complicated as building a house." I felt myself relax. Ordinary conversation was my forte.

"And how would you know?"

"Between Google and Wikipedia, I know a bit about joists and headers."

Jack chuckled. "Don't trust everything you read on the Internet."

"You mean I can't get four million dollars if I give that nice Nigerian woman the number of my bank account?"

"Nor will Bill Gates donate money every time you forward an e-mail."

"Rats. I sent it to my entire address book twenty-eight times."

Jack laughed, and a curious but comfortable silence enveloped us. He surprised me. The comfort level I felt around him surprised me even more.

With Eric, I'd always felt like I was trying to prove myself. Trying to show I was worthy. With Jack, I knew I wasn't. He had seen me at my worst. I had nowhere to go in his estimation but up.

What surprised me the most was that in spite of what he had seen, he still wanted to spend time with me.

I heard the faint coo of a dove, followed by the trilling of a nighthawk. The night was coming alive, and I felt myself relax even more in this man's presence. This was a curious phenomenon for me. Relaxing around a guy.

I could get used to this.

"What did you think—" He held up his hand. "Sorry. That was going to be a dumb question."

"And that's a loaded statement. Now that you've admitted it, you have to ask it."

"No. I don't."

"You have to tell me because I'm going to keep nattering at you until you ask, and let me warn you—I'm a nattering nabob. A tsunami of talking. Leslie and I had a talking-without-stopping contest once. I wiped the floor with her. I can do the same with you. Of course there's no floor here, just dirt—and that could get messy. But I'm sure I can rise to the challenge . . . "

He pressed a finger to my lips. "I concede."

I raised my eyebrows at him, my unspoken question.

"I was just going to ask you what you thought of the church service. But we both know how that turned out."

I ducked my head, suddenly interested in my cuticles. I

needed a manicure in the worst way. I couldn't remember the last manicure I'd had.

"Like I said, dumb question."

I sighed, folded my arms on my knees, and leaned forward, staring into the gathering dusk. "No. It's not a dumb question. I felt kind of challenged. Kind of unworthy, I guess."

"None of us are, you know. Worthy."

"Not even you?"

"Especially not me. The Bible tells us that no one is righteous, not one. I can't begin to presume that I'm exempt."

"Leslie gave me a Bible." I opened my purse and pulled it out to show him. "She also gave me a little sermon about purpose and meaning."

"Have you had a chance to read this yet?" Jack took it from me and flipped it open.

I shrugged. "It's small enough to pack around. I thought if I had some free time, I might read it. I kind of ran out of steam at Exodus—all that talk about the tabernacle and cubits and ephods and stuff."

"So you haven't had a chance to find a life verse yet?"

"A life verse being?"

"A passage of Scripture that speaks to you. That guides you in making a decision for Christ."

"For Christ and against whom?"

Jack shot me a puzzled look.

"If I make a decision for someone, doesn't that automatically mean I'm against someone else? Like in hockey or football?"

"No. Sorry. Christian lingo. I'm not very good at this."

"That's exactly what Leslie said," I replied. I watched as he leafed through the Bible, watched his expression soften into a smile as he read. "Why don't you read me your life verse?"

"I was teasing you," Jack said, his eyes flitting over the tiny type. "When I went to Bible camp, we were always encouraged to find our life verse. I was a bit of a rebel and used some obscure verse from Deuteronomy. Something about . . . the western border was the Jordan in the Arabah, from Kinnereth to the Sea of the Arabah . . . The joke backfired on me."

"How so?"

"They made me write out every verse I could find that dealt with geography. Kept me busy every night for the rest of camp." Jack laughed. "God tamed my rebellious streak through that, and as a result I did find one of my favorites." He shot me a quick glance. "You want me to read it?"

I'd been on many dates and gone to many places, but I didn't remember ever having a man read the Bible to me before. Of course, Jack wasn't the kind of guy I usually dated, so the lack of precedent was understandable. "Go crazy."

" 'For I am convinced that neither death nor life, neither angels nor demons, neither the present nor the future, nor any powers, neither height nor depth, nor anything else in all creation, will be able to separate us from the love of God that is in Christ Jesus.' " Jack's deep, rough voice lent an air of gritty reality to the words, and I found myself jealous of the certainty of his faith. Jealous of the conviction that rang in his voice as he read. "I get a lot of comfort from that."

There was that word again. *Comfort.*

I thought of the stillness that seeped into my soul when Leslie talked about God. Here in this park, with Jack reading a passage that spoke of power and strength, I yearned to experience the same thing again. My mind cast back to the empty moments after coming home from the hospital. The inexplicable yearning for comfort, for a reason. For some kind of meaning to an existence that had slowly spiraled out of control.

You'll get it back. You just need to get your feet under you.

And when would that happen?

"Anyway, that verse really speaks to me," Jack was saying. He handed the Bible back to me.

I took it, ran my fingers over the embossing on the cover, and slipped it back into my purse. "I guess this is why I don't feel like I need to go to church," I said. "Your dad told me I was like a lost sheep, and Leslie said that she has found purpose in her life." I tried to force a light laugh, tried to find the old Terra. "I've had a lot of religion since I came here."

"Then I'll back off." He folded his arms over his chest again, looking out over the park. "So, now that you're a free woman, what are your plans?"

"I'm not sure. I'll wait until I get my money back and then probably head out."

"I'm sure Leslie is going to miss you. She's pretty happy having you around."

If Eric caught up to me, Leslie might not be so happy to have me around. I had no idea what he would do to me or anyone connected to me if he ever found out where I was. And I had no intention of finding out.

"She'll be okay. She has Dan and the kids."

"Amelia might miss you. You two seem like friends."

"I've spent time with her. Listened to her story."

"Does she listen to you?"

"What do you mean?"

"Would she take advice from you?"

"Why do you want to know about Amelia?"

Jack sighed, ran his hands through his hair again, then leaned forward. "I was hoping you could convince her to think about foster care. Or at least a custody agreement."

A chill crept into my chest. "Was that the reason for this date?"

"No." Jack turned to me. "Not at all. Nor was the reason some opportunity to reform you or turn you into a Christian."

"So why are you asking me these things?"

"Because you're here, no one else is around to hear us talk, and I'm concerned about Madison—and I know you are, too. Amelia is not cooperating with the hospital or the doctors. I wanted you to know that I have a friend in Social Services, and she's been making noises about removing Madison from Amelia's care."

Chapter Twenty

A chill spread from my chest to my arms and legs, followed by the heat of anger. "You aren't serious."

"I am. And so is Rod."

I wrapped my arms tighter around my knees. Hugging myself against a sudden chill. I didn't want to think that Jack was on the wrong side of this struggle. Didn't want to acknowledge that the first date I'd had in years that made me feel comfortable around a man had an ulterior motive because of my connection to Amelia.

"Rod doesn't want Amelia to have Madison," I said, my voice holding a sharp edge. "I wouldn't trust that snake farther than I can spit."

Jack's sigh showed as much denial as his body language did. "Amelia was supposed to take her baby to the clinic for tests to find out why Madison isn't growing, but she's never shown up. She won't listen to the nurses or doctors at the hospital. Rod is worried about Madison, too."

I shouldn't have been surprised that he would take his friend's part. None of my friends or Eric's friends had believed he had a wicked backhand either.

I leaned back on the bench, staring out at the trees. An evening breeze had sprung up, dancing through the leaves, creating a sibilant hiss. Though I couldn't see them now, I knew that beyond the trees were the mountains. Solid, firm. Surrounding this valley. They'd stood in their place long before we puny humans got here, and they would stay long after.

And within this bowl of beauty swirled sadness and sorrow. Broken lives and deception.

"Rod's not as worried about the baby as he is worried about losing control over Amelia," I said quietly. "Madison is a way to keep control over Amelia. She's scared of him."

Jack gave a disbelieving chuckle. "Rod? What's to be afraid of?"

"You'd be surprised," I said quietly, rubbing my arm. I glanced down at my hand and stopped the nervous gesture, twisting my arm away to hide the scar.

Jack massaged the back of his neck and sighed. "Regardless of what you think of Rod, something needs to be done for that baby," Jack said, ignoring my little interjection. "If you could talk to her, we might not have to do anything drastic. She could stay completely involved in Madison's life. In fact, her involvement would be integrated into any program Social Services recommends."

"And if Amelia doesn't cooperate?"

"Social Services will have to go with something stronger than a custody agreement."

"And you'll play right into Rod's hands."

Jack's eyes narrowed. "How do you figure that?"

"Don't you understand? He wants Madison out of Amelia's life. Madison is competition for her attention . . ."

"Are you accusing Rod of neglecting Madison?"

"I'm accusing Rod of making it very difficult for Amelia to

take proper care of a baby who isn't growing properly, who seems to need special care. Why doesn't he help her more?"

"Rod doesn't know how to take care of her, and Amelia won't let him."

I could see we were on opposite sides of this problem. I didn't want to be on the opposite side of Jack. I wanted us to agree. I wanted him to see what was going on.

"I know Amelia needs help, but she doesn't need her baby taken away from her. Mothers should be with their babies. She hasn't always made bad choices. She chose to have that child. She could have swept that child from her life . . . Could have . . ." I stopped there.

Too close. Too close.

I clamped my lips together, holding back any more confessions that might spill out.

"You're not just talking about Amelia anymore, are you?" His quiet question slipped past defenses that had begun crumbling from the first conversation I'd had with this man. Under normal circumstances, I would have gone into high-defense mode and scrammed.

But for now, I was stuck here, Jack's deep voice creating an intimacy I had never felt before.

I felt Jack's hand rest on my neck, his fingers tangling in my hair. "Why don't you tell me?"

"I know what it's like to be in a relationship where you have no power," I said, pleased that I sounded fairly together. "Where people doubt you and are quick to believe the man who abuses you."

My mind slipped back, resurrecting the anger I needed to keep my distance from Jack. To keep my mind off his hand resting on my neck. A small comfort I wanted to give in to, but didn't dare. "Amelia is not a loser; she's just lost. She needs guidance. Why don't you let Madison stay with Amelia and put them both in a place where they can be taken care of?"

"I don't know if Amelia would agree to that."

"She certainly won't agree to your taking her baby away."

"You act like you don't care about other people, but you really care about this girl." His hand still lay warm on my neck. "And I want you, no—I need you—to know that I care about her, too. I'm not deliberately trying to hurt her. I do have a heart, you know."

A shiver trickled down my spine as his fingers lightly caressed my skin. I knew he had a heart. I also knew he was pursuing me. And oh, how I wanted to lean into his touch. To be held by a good man.

"I care because Amelia is me. Her life is mine." My voice faltered.

"What do you mean? How is her life like yours?"

I tried to stop the words, but they poured out of me like a river breaking through a dam that had slowly been cracked by steady pressure. "I was pregnant. I was going to have a baby. Amelia managed to keep hers."

Jack's fingers stilled. "What happened to your baby?"

My emotions teetered, but I clamped down. Regained control. "I had a miscarriage. I lost the baby." I kept my voice even. It was just a fact. Just a fetus.

"Oh, Terra. I'm so sorry." The sympathy in his voice was almost my undoing, but I soldiered on.

"I didn't deserve her."

"What are you saying?"

What *was* I saying? I waved his question away.

"What do you mean you didn't deserve her?" he pressed.

As if it had its own will, my hand crept up and caught his hand as it rested on my shoulder, craving the stability he represented.

His fingers tangled in mine, rough and large, squeezing as his concern washed over me like a subtle undertow and my grip on my emotions loosened.

A sob heaved through my chest. Before it ebbed and I could stop it, another followed. And another.

And without knowing how it happened, I felt myself pressed against his chest.

His hand gripped my shoulder, his other arm held me at my waist, anchoring me to him while an unnamed sadness coursed through me. And then from nowhere came hot tears slipping out like a stream, dampening his shirt.

The sorrow washed over my feeble resistance, laying bare the pain and sorrow I had kept hidden all this time. The tears I couldn't shed in the hospital or in the weeks following, the tears I couldn't release even around my sister, now became a deluge.

He just held me, saying nothing, stroking my hair, holding me against him.

A quiet refuge.

I allowed myself a few more moments in this calm place, letting his strength hold me up. How long had it been since the feel of a man's arms around me created a shelter? I couldn't remember.

But slowly reality intruded into the little haven he had created for me.

The buttons from the pocket of his shirt dug into my cheek, and my arm tingled from being pressed between us, so I drew back.

I dug in my pocket for a worn tissue. Then his hand cupped my chin. He took the tissue from me and gently wiped away my tears.

The moment trembled between us, and even though I knew I was flirting with trouble, I looked up into his eyes. In their hazel depths I saw gentleness and caring.

I was on the verge of nurturing this moment and letting it take a new shape in my life, even as a joke bubbled up that would break the fragile spell Jack's tenderness wove around me.

But as Jack brushed my damp hair back from my face, I felt his kindness and concern in the light touch of his hands, the way his eyes drifted over my face, waiting for me to open up.

Jack didn't deserve to have his benevolence treated with disdain just so I could keep a hedge around my emotions.

His hand lingered on my cheek, the calluses on his palms snagging on a few strands of hair that still clung to my face.

I gave in to an impulse and covered his hand with mine. As my hand tightened on his, something in his eyes shifted. And then he came nearer, his face became a blur, and his lips were on mine.

I wasn't going to do this. I wasn't going to let this happen.

But my unstable emotions didn't let me hold my ground, and, Lord forgive me, I leaned closer. Let my free hand slip around his neck and hold him there.

My hungry, lonely soul drank in the slightly salty taste of his lips, the connection created by our mouths.

And when his arms pulled me close again, the abrupt shift from the tenderness of his previous embrace to the longing I now felt both in him and in myself gave me the strength to pull away.

"I'm sorry," Jack murmured, but he didn't immediately lower his arms. Didn't immediately let me go. "That wasn't fair."

I had to close my eyes so I couldn't see his face. I knew one look at his eyes, and I would be undone.

I wasn't the woman for Jack DeWindt. My heart might not clue into the fact, but my head knew it for a certainty.

I had been in dark, hard places. He deserved someone with a whole lot less baggage, and I didn't need to get involved with another man. What had I done? I had told myself again and again, with every footfall as I left Seattle. *No. More. Men.*

This vulnerability was precisely the thing I needed to avoid. I couldn't take a chance on letting anyone get ahold of a piece of my heart. Eric's snide erosion of my self-worth made moving on an easy decision.

Jack? Different man. Different story.

Much, much harder.

I pressed my fisted hands against my stomach, and thankfully Jack read my mute request. But when he withdrew, the lonely part of me wanted to snatch back what he had silently offered and what I had refused. He confused me, and I didn't like the feeling.

"So now what?"

I had no answer. I had told him something I hadn't even told my sister. Becoming connected to Jack hadn't been part of my Harland scenario. Leaving was not a matter of speculation; it was simply a matter of time. I had to keep moving.

"I'd like to go home now."

"I'll drive you."

I shook my head. At the moment I felt vulnerable and needy.

Putting that mix into the confines of a pickup truck, in the evening, with Jack, would be asking for trouble. "I'll walk."

"It's dark out."

I chanced a glance at him. "So now I'm getting an astronomy report?"

The barb served its purpose. Jack's face tightened and he pushed himself to his feet. "I don't want anything to happen to you."

Warning. Don't read more into his comment than he meant.

The way he pulled the sides of his mouth in made him look all tough and "I mean business."

"I'm a big girl in a small town. I'll be fine."

Jack's eyes narrowed as he held my gaze a heartbeat more, but I stood my ground.

He got up. He started to leave, but stopped in front of me, his hands on his hips in his cop stance. "I know what happens in this town after dark. You're not walking."

I wanted to protest again but didn't have the energy or strength. So I simply nodded and followed him to his truck.

As we drove, I kept my eyes ahead, trying not to relive his kiss. Trying not to remember how good it felt to be in his arms. How I felt safe. Protected.

Trying not to remember what I'd spilled out while he was holding me.

We pulled onto my street and Jack stopped in front of the house. I was about to thank him for the ride, but he was already getting out of the truck.

This guy is killing me with kindness, I thought as I waited for him to open my door.

"Thanks for the ride," I said, slipping out of the truck.

"I'll walk you to the door."

"You know, I'm one of the criminal elements you're trying to keep me safe from in this town."

"You're not a criminal," he growled, an unexpected edge to his voice. "Ralph is an idiot, but I didn't have any choice. Not when he had four of his buddies backing him."

The streetlight shone in my face, cast his in shadows. All I saw was the glimmer of his eyes. Then his head blotted out the light and his lips touched mine so lightly I might have imagined it.

"That's in case you thought the other one was simply for pity," he said, brushing his knuckles over my cheek.

I couldn't breathe. I needed to breathe, or I was going to fall over.

"Thanks," I said, my voice a feeble whisper.

Brilliant. You can't breathe and you can't think. A handsome, appealing, caring guy kisses you, and all you can come up with is, "Thanks."

"You're welcome." And I caught a glimmer in his eyes and a flash of white from his smile. "I'd like to see you again."

"I'm always at the diner. Stop on by." I gave him a casual wave. Somehow I had to get this evening on a footing I was more comfortable with, but just as I was about to step away, he caught my hand.

"You know what I mean." He twisted his fingers around mine.

Don't do it. Don't fall for it. You just broke down in his arms; you're all mixed up.

"I think I do," I said, tightening my hand in his.

Leslie warned you against him. Are you going to go against your own sister's advice?

And since when did my alter ego care about Leslie?

"I'd like to try again," he was saying. "Could we do dinner sometime?"

Don't get tangled up with the Christian cop before you go.

For once the cynical voice in my head held a tinge of truth and wisdom. Getting involved with Jack was the wrong thing for me to do.

"We'll see," I said vaguely.

"Let me know." He lifted my hand and brushed a kiss across my knuckles. "But just in case you get all panicky, there are no expectations. I just like being with you."

Oh, c'mon. Is this guy for real?

His eyes held mine and stillness pervaded my being. As if a quiet strength that was the essence of Jack was slowly seeping into me.

No expectations.

I had stayed with Eric because of his confidence. His self-possession made me hope that by being with him, I might absorb some of that confidence. But it had gone the other way. Eric had absorbed me; had slowly sucked away what self-confidence I had.

With Jack, I felt as if I was receiving, not giving.

I didn't know where to put this in my guy experiences. This was a novelty and, I was afraid, an illusion.

Panic clustered around my heart. Panic and a touch of fear that had nothing to do with Jack's strength or his confidence and everything to do with what I had just told him. Everything to do with the way he was looking at me now. The way his thumb was slowly caressing my hand.

No expectations.

He leaned closer and waited, the moment stretching out

between us, rife with waiting, and I knew what he was doing. He wanted me to make the next move.

I closed my eyes, wavering between my past and the hesitant promise that trembled in the moment between us.

Don't do this. You're heading down a dark, dangerous path.

I wanted the voice to be quiet, but I let the panic take over and pulled away.

I had to go.

I had to get out of here before this guy got a stronger hold on my heart.

I pushed past him. I would go pack up. Head down the road. I had a little bit of money left over after paying Leslie back. I could ask Lennie for my wages tomorrow. Then leave. I might not get as far as Chicago, but maybe I could find something in eastern Montana, or the Dakotas. I found a job here. It shouldn't be too hard someplace else.

"So I heard you and Jack were at the park Friday night," Cor said as I poured him another cup of coffee.

I wasn't going to blush. Wasn't going to let that memory intrude on the cold light of today.

Cor and Father Sam hadn't shown up on Saturday. Nor, thankfully, had Jack. I appreciated the reprieve and the opportunity to gather my wits. To get lost in work. To make my plans. Yesterday I took on the Sunday shift to give Helen a break and, of course, to earn what extra money I could. I had no intention of going to church.

When Leslie called to ask how my date went, I kept things vague, remembering how less than pleased she was with the idea of my going out with Jack.

"He's a good boy, my Jack," Cor was saying, adding his own sting to my self-flagellating thoughts. "What time do you get off work? I can drop off your car," Cor said, pulling a face at the foam from the fake sugar that bubbled up as he stirred his coffee.

"I can pick it up."

"No. I don't mind." He looked up at me as if daring me to say anything different. "I can use the exercise." He waited a beat, giving his tea another stir. "I went to the doctor yesterday. He told me I needed to get more exercise. And he started me on insulin."

I wanted to tell him that was great, but could I rightly celebrate the fact that he would be jabbing himself two or three times a day from now on? "This is your first step toward taking control of your health," I said in my best imitation of a television doctor.

Cor glowered at me. "I thought it might get you, Jack, and Father Sam off my back."

"We nag because we care."

Cor leaned back in his chair and folded his arms over his ample chest, a smile flickering over his rough features. "You do?"

I looked at his face, the ever-present suspenders over the wrinkled shirt, and felt a flood of warmth for this dear man. "Yes," I said quietly, touching him lightly on his shoulder. "I do."

"Well . . . good." He cleared his throat and nodded, then bent over his coffee and gave it another stir. "So, what time are you off?"

"I can pick up the car . . ."

"What time are you off?"

I relented. "Seven. I'll be home at seven thirty."

"I'll bring it then."

"Good."

"Hey, Terra. Why did the elephant cross the road?"

"To get to the other side?"

"Nope. It was the chicken's day off." He slapped the table, laughing at the sad joke. "So I'll see you later?"

"I'm looking forward to it." And, to my surprise, I was.

"Order up, Terra," Mathilde snapped as I came into the back.

She had been in a snit all morning because the fryer wasn't working properly and the repairman had to order parts from Cleveland. She'd been so cranky I was tempted to hitchhike down to Ohio myself to pick up the missing part.

I wondered what she was going to be like after I left. Helen, Sunny, and Anita—the other waitresses—would bear the brunt of her ire. Remorse watered down the relief of not having to deal with her anymore. I wondered if they would find someone to replace me right away.

Don't start. You need space. You need to breathe.

I also needed to talk to Lennie about collecting my wages and tell him I'd be quitting. I knew how crazy things got here, and I knew I would leave them short-staffed. Lennie hadn't made up the new schedule for next week yet. I had to tell him before he did.

Maybe I could leave tomorrow . . .

My heart sank as I looked at the calendar. Next week was Anneke's birthday party. I had even bought her the cutest present—a pair of plastic high heels, a tiara, and a magic wand.

Don't go there either. You've never been one to spend a lot of time with the kidlets. Drop the present off before you go.

If I went. Maybe I could stay a little while. Get some more money together.

The longer you stay, the harder it will be to leave.

My thoughts battled one another as I walked to my customer's table.

Nothing's changed. You were always going to leave. Stick with the plan.

But as Jack's face swam into my mind, I realized everything had changed. For the first time in my life, I felt like I had met someone I could spend more than a few days with. Someone with depth and character.

Don't go.

Don't stay.

Maybe what I needed was some kind of sign. The kind Leslie talked about.

Yeah, right. Now she's got you believing in that hocus-pocus stuff.

"Are you okay, Terra?" the woman asked. "You look a little pale."

"I'm okay. Thanks." I gave her an extra-wide smile as I set down her plate. Then I scurried back to the coffee machine to make the rounds with the coffeepot. I needed to keep busy. Just keep moving and keep the thoughts at bay.

My feet hurt when I made the final turn onto my street. My head hurt even more. My wish for keeping busy had been granted. Shortly after my schizo-thoughts moment, customers had come pouring into the café like ants at a picnic, and I had been running ever since. I didn't have a chance to talk to Lennie about getting paid, or about quitting.

So that would have to wait until tomorrow.

Now I was dog tired. Dusk was settling, and the streetlights were just starting to come on.

I heard a horn beep and turned in time to see a little white car come up the street, Cor behind the wheel. I smiled as he pulled up under the light in front of Helen's house, the branches from the weeping willow brushing the top of the car.

My car. My ticket out of here. My sign?

I started running. "You're nice and early," I called out.

"I thought you would want the car right away," he announced in a voice that, I was sure, carried all the way to Bozeman.

He laid his hand on the hood of the car as he walked around it, and as he came closer, I heard him wheezing.

"Are you okay?"

He waved my concern away. "Fine. Fine."

"How are you going to get home? I should drive you."

"No. Father Sam is picking me up. We're going bowling to-night. Now get those license plates you got the other day."

I waited a beat to make sure he caught his breath, but he flapped his hand at me in a shooing motion. I got the hint, hurried inside the house, and found the plates, surprised to see my hands trembling. A car. The North American dream of freedom.

When I brought the plates out, Cor was already kneeling at the back of the car, a toolbox opened out on the pavement in front of him. He looked ready to do major surgery.

"You need all that just to put two screws in a license plate?"

"Jack got this for me for Father's Day." Cor's large hands passed lovingly over the various screwdriver bits lined up like obedient little soldiers. "Thought I would give it a test run."

I will not think about Jack now, I told myself, banishing the image of his concern from my mind. Erasing the memory of his kiss. Pushing aside the confessional moment in his arms. *Focus on the car. The sign.*

"Can I have the plate?" Cor's gruff question pulled me back from the thoughts I wasn't thinking about Jack. I handed him the piece of thin metal, my car's entrée into the world of roads and interstates and fuel consumption.

"Anything I can do?" I asked, uncomfortable with the spectator aspect of my situation.

He shook his head. "You just sit and watch a master at work."

"Where?"

"Very funny, young lady." He chose a Phillips end for the screwdriver, fitting it in while I watched.

"I really appreciate this, you know," I said.

"Well, I wouldn't do it for just anyone, you know," he replied.

The trouble was, I did know. And the thought that he would do this for me created an unexpected lump in my throat.

"The only problem with this, though," Cor continued, wheezing as he walked to the front of the car to repeat the procedure, "is I'm afraid I'm just making it easier for you to leave." He looked sad. As if he knew.

I swallowed the lump, my solid plans teetering.

Lights swung onto the street as a large car pulled up behind us and stopped. Father Sam got out. "You ready to go, Cor?" He waved at me. "Hey, Terra. So, you've got your own car. Now you can hit the open road."

Did he know, too?

"I'll be with you in a minute," Cor said, putting the final twist on the last screw. He took his time packing up. Then, when he was done, he tossed me a sad smile. "So. We'll see you tomorrow? At the diner?"

"And why wouldn't we?" Father Sam said. "She always works that shift. Now, old man. Let's get moving."

Cor held my gaze, then came over and gave me a hug. "You're a special girl, little lamb. Don't let anyone tell you different." He handed me the keys, wrapping my fingers around them and squeezing my hand. "Here you go, girl. She's all yours."

"I have to pay you yet."

"You will. I'm sure." He patted me on the shoulder and got into Father Sam's car. I stood on the road, watching as they drove away, wishing I felt more certain about my decision.

Don't change your mind. Going once. Going twice. You're gone.

My feet kept time with the words as I hurried up the walk. I was leaving. I was leaving.

"Terra?"

The voice jumped out of the night.

Chapter Twenty-one

My heart jumped as I spun around in time to see Amelia step out from behind a tree beside the walk.

As she stepped out into the light, I saw a large smear of blood on the front of her shirt, on her sleeve. She had her hand on her arm.

"What happened? Where's Madison?" I cried. "How did this happen?" Anger coursed through me as blood seeped from her arm through her fingers. So much for Jack's talk about how much Rod cared. He should be here to see this.

"I got hurt. My arm."

"You need to have that looked at," I said. Her hand was getting redder by the minute, and I could feel my head getting woozy at the sight of the blood oozing between her fingers.

"I don't want to go to the hospital. I'll be okay. You can fix me up. It's just a cut." She pulled her hand away to reveal a four-inch gash. I winced in sympathy.

"I can't do that. You need stitches." I was no nurse, but the ragged edges of flesh told me that this had not been done with a knife. "How did this happen?" I asked, wishing I could just grab her and drag her to the hospital but knowing that, as tired as I was right now, she could probably outrun me.

She leaned against the tree, her face paper white under the streetlight. "I'm not sure." I could smell liquor on her breath, so it was a safe bet that, as the ubiquitous domestic violence reports state, alcohol was involved.

"Did you and Rod have a fight?"

Her anxious gaze flew to mine. "Yeah. A fight." She gave the information reluctantly, as if afraid to implicate her boyfriend.

"So how did you get hurt this bad? Did he hit you? Or cut you with something?"

"I tried to duck away, but I couldn't move fast enough." She winced.

I imagined twenty different ways I could hurt this man. "Is Madison with Rod now?"

She caught me with her other hand. "You have to help me get my baby back."

I tried to understand what had happened. Why was she here? Had she walked all the way after her fight with Rod? It didn't make sense.

"He said I'm a bad mother. I'm scared that Rod is taking her away."

Her comment pulled me back to her situation. "He can't. You're the mother—he's not even Madison's biological father."

"You have to help me get her back." Amelia grabbed my shirt, tugging on it.

"I'll help you; just calm down." I didn't care how much she protested, I had to get this girl to a hospital. And then I had to file a police report. Rod may have friends in high places, but he wasn't going to get away with this. Not if I could help it.

"Where are you going?"

"We need to stop the bleeding. Helen might have something." I ran to the house and up the front stairs. Helen was sitting at the kitchen table doing a crossword puzzle when I burst into her kitchen.

"What's wrong, hon?"

"Amelia Castleman is outside. She's hurt. I need to take her to the hospital, but for now I need something to stop the bleeding."

"Amelia's here?"

"Yeah. Why?"

"There's a message on my answering machine. Rod was looking for her, asking about her. He was worried."

"Did you call him?"

"Not yet."

I held up a warning hand. "Please don't call him. Amelia's got a huge cut on her arm from Rod, and she's scared to go to the hospital because she's afraid he'll find her there."

Helen frowned. "Rod hurt her?"

"Yes, he did," I said, squeezing the words past my clenched teeth.

"Do you need to use my car?" Her hazel eyes sparkled with questions I knew I would have to answer later.

"No. I've got my own." My keys were still tucked in my hand. "I just need something to stop the bleeding for now."

"I'll get a towel."

Amelia still stood outside, leaning against the tree.

Helen hurried back into the kitchen holding a couple of

fluffy pink hand towels. "The closest I have to red," she said, thrusting them at me. "Now hurry. If you need help to get her to go to the hospital, holler. She's not too trusting. Otherwise, I'd be out there helping you myself."

"Thanks, Helen." I gently tugged on my hand, the keys digging into my palm. "I should get going, though."

"You be careful. The hospital can be crazy this time of night. All the loonies decide to go out and get hammered then start driving around and get into accidents. I don't want to see you get hurt. Okay?" She sandwiched my hand between both of hers, as if to underline her comment.

"I'll be careful." Another gentle tug.

But Helen didn't let go. "Are you sure you're okay? You look a little drained."

"Just worried about Amelia."

Helen held my gaze. "You're a good girl. Don't let anyone tell you different. Not everyone would take the time for someone like Amelia."

I gave her a quick smile, gave my hand another tug, and this time she let me go.

But as I ran down the stairs her words echoed in my mind, rife with more meaning than I had head space to decipher.

An hour later I was flipping through a magazine in the emergency ward of the hospital, ignoring the crying baby beside me and the funky smell emanating from the muttering man across from me, trying to stifle my own hospital memories and my thoughts.

All my plans to leave would have to be put on hold until

I got Amelia settled. And what would that entail? How was I going to get Madison back from Rod?

I threw the magazine down in anger, remembering how Jack had defended that rat. How could he?

Restlessness clawed at me, pulling me to my feet. Why was this taking so long? The doctor said they'd be done quick. This wasn't quick. This was long. This was *Titanic* long.

I caught a glimpse of the time. Close to midnight. The pumpkin hour.

Now that I had made up my mind to leave Harland, I wanted to be gone. I wanted to be down the road, away from people who asked too many questions. People whom I had already told too much. People with whom I had become too connected. Too fond.

I couldn't stop my mind from flitting back to Cor DeWindt. How good it felt to be hugged like a daughter. Remembering that hug made me jump to memories of Jack, who hadn't hugged me like a daughter at all.

You need to get going. Get gone. Remember the plan. The longer you stay, the better chance Eric has of finding you.

Desperation clutched at me. I couldn't leave until I helped Amelia get Madison back. I'd promised her, and I knew I needed to do this. Needed to reunite mother and child. Needed to close the circle. To atone for my own sins.

The doors to the main entrance whooshed open, letting in a draft of cool evening air. I shivered and turned.

And came face-to-face with Jack, Rod right behind him.

Rod's jacket was buttoned askew, his eyes were bloodshot, and I could see the beginnings of a beard. He looked like ten miles of bad road. He looked exactly like the kind of guy who could hurt someone badly.

"Where's Amelia?" Rod asked, his eyes piercing me.

My angry gaze ticked from Rod to Jack. "How did you know?"

"My dad saw Amelia talking to you. He told me."

"Well, it didn't take you long to go running to your buddy." I spat out the words, my anger burning hot and hard.

"I didn't. He found me." Jack's eyes grazed over mine, then past me to the emergency department.

"Is Amelia okay?" Rod asked, all solicitous and caring.

He had to be kidding me. "And you care because . . ."

"Terra . . ." Jack warned.

"Amelia is lying on a bed in there, getting who knows how many stitches in her arm because of you, and you dare act as if this wasn't your fault?" My anger gained strength, my words lashed out at him. People were watching us, but I didn't care. All my attention was focused on this man who had hurt my friend.

"Terra, please listen," Jack said, reaching out to me.

I spun away, afraid that if he touched me I would lose my momentum. Just like I always did with Eric when he tried to make me look unreasonable.

"That poor girl has been living in fear of this guy. He hurts her—and now he has the nerve to show up here acting like he cares?" I turned to Rod, my anger building. "And where is Madison? Where is Amelia's little girl?"

"She's safe," Jack said quietly. "Please, you have to understand."

I turned to face him, lashing out at him as well. "No. You have to understand. Amelia is doing the best she can. She needs help, not condemnation . . ." I stopped myself in time. I'd already been down this road before. With Jack. The scenery wasn't worth the trip. I took a deep breath. Men didn't listen to hysterical women.

"Rod's been sick with worry about Amelia," Jack said. "He's been taking care of Madison all day and night. He's been phoning anyone who knows anything about her, including you."

"And somehow he found time to hurt her, too."

"What are you talking about?" Rod cried out. "What do you mean, 'hurt her'?"

Jack held up his hand to quiet his friend, then turned to me. "Amelia left Madison with a babysitter this morning and said she was going to be home at suppertime. She didn't show up. Rod hasn't seen her all day."

I thought of the message on Helen's answering machine. I thought of the alcohol I sniffed on Amelia's breath. I was no nurse, but I could see that Amelia's wound wasn't very old. In spite of my anger, my mind flashed back to the first place I had been with Amelia. And the second. The bar each time.

And Rod, who was supposed to have been in a drunken rage, according to Amelia, looked, in spite of his bloodshot eyes, fairly sober.

As the information settled, my mind cast back to other things Amelia had done and not done. Taking Madison into that sleazy bar that first day we met. I thought of the skim milk in her grocery cart, the dirty diaper and how she didn't know how to use a thermometer.

I shook my head as if to rid myself of the disloyal thoughts. Amelia was in the same situation I had been. I'd had no one to believe me or help me either.

I couldn't be wrong. I'd been here before. I'd lived Amelia's life.

Remember how Eric could be so charming. So sweet. So manipulative.

But Eric had not been the only man in my life. If I was ever going to free myself from his memory, I had to use my discretion and not judge every man I met based on my experiences with one man.

"Please, did she say how she got cut? Did she tell you anything?" Rod asked again.

I wavered at the distress in his voice, remembering Jack's concern over Amelia.

"She said that you did it."

Rod bit his lip and shook his head. Jack laid his hand on Rod's shoulder as if sympathizing with him.

"I have never hurt her or Madison," Rod said. "Ever. Amelia . . . she has a few problems. So does Madison."

"She said that you want Madison taken away from her."

"I can't take care of Madison," Rod said quietly, looking past me to the emergency ward where Amelia was still getting stitched up. "She has problems that I don't know how to deal with. And I know that Amelia hasn't taken proper care of her. But I can't be around all the time. I'm gone too much."

I felt as if my world was shifting as I tried to reconcile what he was saying with my first impressions of him. Impressions that had been reinforced by Amelia.

I knew she was a little loopy. I knew she had her problems. And Rod sounded sincere. Could I believe him?

Rod sighed and ran his hand through his hair. "I don't care what you think of me, Terra. But I do care about Madison. And Amelia."

I rubbed my forehead with my fingertips, trying to figure out what to do.

"Terra, please believe him." Jack's quiet voice slipped over my roiling thoughts. Jack was a good man. I knew that. I felt that. And it mattered to him that I believed Rod.

I held Jack's gaze, wishing I could trust my own judgment, realizing that I didn't need to. All I needed to do was trust Jack, who had given me no reason to distrust him or anything he said. In his line of work, he'd seen more domestic situations than I had. Had a larger base of knowledge.

Just trust Jack.

"I do," I whispered. "I believe him."

"Thanks," Jack said, brushing my arm with the back of his hand. A casual touch, but a gentle connection.

"I'm going to talk to a doctor. See if I can talk to her." Rod gave Jack a curt nod, then without another look at me, left me and Jack alone.

I turned to watch Rod walking toward the nurses' station, still unsure what to do.

"I should wait to bring Amelia home," I said, reluctant to pass on what I saw as my responsibility.

"Rod will do that. No matter what you think of him, he's a good man."

"I believe he is because you say he is," I said quietly.

Jack brushed a strand of hair away from my face, a gesture that grazed my heart. "Are you okay? You seem tired."

"It's late, and it's been a long, hard day."

"Do you need a ride home?"

"I drove my car here." I couldn't do anything more for Amelia tonight, so it was time to go.

"Let me at least walk you to it." He put his hand at the small of my back, gently escorting me to the doors. As they swung open, a man stumbled in, followed by two more supporting a man who sagged between them.

"Hey, Jack. What's goin' on here, huh?" the first man called out, breaking away from the group.

Jack drew in a slow breath, as if gathering patience. "What do you want, Ralph?" His cop voice was back, and I was glad I wasn't the recipient of that low-level growl.

Ralph wavered a moment, the stench of alcohol washing over us. He pointed at me, his finger weaving and bobbing. "You friends with her?" He swayed, trying to focus his bleary eyes on me. "That why you told me to drop the charges? 'Cause she's a friend?"

"I told you to drop the charges because there was a strong possibility you would lose the court case and a bunch of money." Jack didn't raise his voice, but I could hear the steel as he spoke.

As my tired mind tried to wrap itself around what Ralph and Jack were saying, Ralph poked his finger toward me. "That girl is trouble, ya know?"

Jack intercepted Ralph's hand without any change in his expression.

"She and that frien' of hers," Ralph continued, keeping his hand down this time, "that Amelia chick. She was nothing but big trouble tonight."

I was desperately trying to catch up.

Jack had convinced Ralph to drop the charges?

Ralph and Amelia had been in the same place tonight?

Was that where Amelia had gotten hurt?

"I'm sure I'll find out once I get back to work tomorrow," Jack said, placing his arm on my shoulder. "For now, you'd better get your friend some help, and then you'd better get sobered up so I don't have to charge you with a Drunk and Disorderly."

Jack gently eased me toward the door, not giving Ralph as much as a second glance.

Once we were outside, I turned, holding my hands up as conversations caught up with me and settled in my woozy brain. "Do you really think Amelia was with Ralph? Tonight? Do you think that's where she got hurt?"

Jack shrugged. "I can't draw any conclusions based on what a half-corked idiot says."

My mind skittered over previous events, comments, and my own perceptions, trying to put this all together. "Amelia took me to the Pump and Grill. That's where I met up with Ralph in the first place."

"Yeah."

"So she probably knows him."

"Probably."

"So Rod was right."

Jack just nodded.

"And this Ralph thing. Did you convince him to drop the charges?"

"I was doing him a favor." Jack rocked back on his heels, tucking his hands in the back pockets of his pants, humoring me.

"And doing me a favor."

Jack angled me a wry smile. "I had a few ulterior motives, yeah."

"Why?"

Jack sighed, put his hand on my shoulder again, and steered me toward the parking lot. "It's no big deal. He was going to lose badly, and it would have been a waste of time and money for you, too."

"For my wallet's sake I'm glad you did." I didn't look at him as I moved things to what I saw was an inevitable conclusion. "And I have my money back, which means I'm free to go."

Jack's step slowed; his hand tightened. "Go? When?"

I tried for a casual shrug, and when he dropped his hand, I felt as if I had lost something important.

Keep with the plan.

"I don't know. Soon."

"You had no intention of staying around?"

His voice had gotten hard, more gruff than usual. I thought of what Leslie had said and, for a moment, felt guilty.

How was I supposed to know this would matter to him?

I should have. We had gone on a date and it was fun. Jack didn't seem like a casual dater. Even more important—he'd kissed me. Three times. I didn't think Jack was a casual kisser either.

I kept my eyes on my car, my ticket to freedom, parked halfway down the parking lot as I stumbled through this conversation. "That was the plan."

"You had a plan? I thought you lived for the moment."

"Well, sometimes."

"So, make a new moment." He stopped and gently turned me toward him. "Make a new plan."

I weighed the wisdom of what he was saying as I felt the heat of his hands on my shoulders.

Hands that were strong and gentle at the same time.

Then I made the mistake of looking at him—at how the evening light glinted off the whiskers shadowing his chin, at the slight wave in his hair. His eyes held a secret that I wanted to discover.

And then, for the fourth time, he kissed me. Just a light

brush of cool lips over mine, then a harder brush as I melted toward him.

This wasn't fair. He wasn't playing fair.

"I guess . . . I don't have to leave right away," I said, trying to find my breath. "I could stay awhile . . . you know . . ." I let the sentence drift off, hoping he would fill in the blanks—if not verbally, then mentally.

"I know. I think that would be good," he said quietly, his voice a rumble under my hands, which had, somehow, ended up resting on his chest.

He slipped his arm over my shoulder and pulled me against him.

He finally let me go when we got to my car.

The faint crinkling at the corners of his eyes caught my attention. I couldn't decipher his expression, but I wanted to see it again.

"So, I guess I'll be around for a bit, then," I said, my voice growing soft, as if uttering the words quietly made them less tangible, easier to withdraw.

Jack brushed his knuckles across my cheek.

"You must be beat," he said, one corner of his mouth tilted up in a half-smile. "You should go home."

"Yeah. I should." I pulled the keys out of my pocket and unlocked the door, surprised to see my hands trembling. As I drove away, I could see Jack still standing in the parking lot, watching me, and I had to smile again.

I replayed the conversation Jack and I just had, trying to figure out where things had changed from my relief that I could leave to my telling him that I might not.

And as I drove I realized two things. If my car had been parked closer to the hospital, my plans might have stayed the same. It was that long walk with Jack that gave me time to think so that I was now considering staying in Harland.

I could stay awhile. Just a little while.

Chapter Twenty-two

I have to confess, for a few moments I thought you were going to duck out of the party." Leslie walked me down the porch steps to my car, birthday party kids screeching all around us, burning off the vestiges of the cake and soft drinks they'd consumed in ridiculous amounts.

Ignoring the cacophony, Leslie leaned against the hood of my little car, her sisterly smile alternately making me feel like a proper aunt and a fraud. She didn't need to know that three plans ago I was supposed to be in Chicago today.

"I'm glad I could come." I sidestepped a little boy who tore past us, trailing a balloon that a barking Sasha considered an intruder. "I think."

"You made Anneke one happy princess with that silly getup."

I heard an extra-loud screech and saw my dear niece jumping up and down on the trampoline, her tiara on her head, a cloud of pink feathers floating loose from the boa around her neck. "I'm sure that outfit won't last the evening."

"She thinks it's great. You did good, Sis. And thanks for getting Nicholas something. He's still a bit young to get this whole center-of-attention thing that makes the birthday person harder to live with than Roseanne Barr."

"At least Anneke didn't throw up like I did at my fifth birthday party."

Leslie laughed. "Thank goodness for small miracles." She didn't seem to be in a rush to get back to her kitchen table smeared with purple icing, stacks of paper plates on her counter, and a floor crunchy with potato chips.

"And how was your date with Jack last Friday?"

Ah. Now I knew the reason for the lingering. "The date was good."

Leslie angled me a skeptical look. "You go out with a guy like Jack DeWindt, and the best you can come up with is 'good'?"

"Okay. Really good. Except for the movie, which was so incredibly bad that calling it bad would be a compliment."

"Do you like him?"

I pondered the question as I relived the moments I had shared with Jack. Did I like him? A person liked the color brown, chili peppers on their hot dog, and ergonomic keyboards. Saying I liked Jack made him sound as bland as a taste test.

"Your mouth is getting all soft and pouty," Leslie said. "You do like him."

She made it sound like an accusation. Which, in turn, made me angry.

"Yeah. I do, you know. And I think he returns the sentiment."

Leslie nodded. "I'm not surprised."

"Is that a bad thing? Is it so awful that your sister has finally found a decent guy? Someone who has integrity and is decent and likes his dad and . . . and carries a Springfield .45?"

Leslie held her hand up. "No. It isn't awful. I'm glad for you."

"Look, Sis, I get the whole I'm not good enough for him . . ."

"I'm sorry if I ever made you feel that way before," she said. "I just want you to be careful. That's all."

"I know who I am, and Jack knows who I am. He was the one who put me in jail, don't forget." I took a quick breath, trying to calm myself before I said something we would both regret. "You gave me the Bible. I've been trying to read it, even though I really don't get a lot of it. But I'm trying. Give me some credit, okay?"

Leslie pushed herself away from my car. "I'm sorry. I was wrong." She pulled me close in a hug. "I am happy for you. Jack's a great guy."

"Thanks."

She gave me another squeeze and drew back, still holding me by the shoulders. "I'm not much of a Bible expert myself, but there is a group that gets together at the church Tuesday mornings for Bible study. It's very low-key, very informal and easy. I go when I can. If you're not working, you could come, too."

I tested the thought. Bible study. That was something I'd never thought I'd see myself involved in. "I'll think about it."

"Thanks, Terra." Leslie squeezed my neck. "Thanks for coming today. That meant a lot to Anneke, but it also meant a lot to me. I don't often have my own family around on these special days."

"I'm glad I came, but I'd better get going," I said. "You sure you don't need me to take some of these yahoos away?"

"I don't want to spook you. We want you around for a little while yet."

I returned her hug. "Thanks for having me. It was fun."

"You're a good auntie."

I wrapped myself in those words as I got into the car and drove out of the yard. A good auntie. I gave myself a congratulatory grin in my rearview mirror.

Nicholas knew my name and even gave me a spontaneous hug after he got his present. Dan laughed at my jokes, and Gloria had pulled me aside to tell me that Tabitha was getting involved in something called YWAM, as if I were as involved in the girl's rehabilitation as she was.

It seemed like I was finding my place in the VandeKeere family pecking order.

I cranked up the radio, laying down a funky sound track to the countryside slipping past me. The fields were like a soft green carpet as crops started to push up through the soil. I passed a farmer driving a tractor who waved to me and I recognized one of the regulars in the diner.

My cell phone rang.

"Hey there, how are you doing?"

And my good day just got better. "I'm doing fine, Jack. How about you?"

"Doing good. I was wondering if you're busy this Sunday."

"I think I'm off that day." I carefully tucked the phone under my ear as I geared down for an intersection. Was he going to ask me to come to church?

"What do you say to a picnic?"

"Hello, can you pass the sandwiches?"

His light chuckle reverberated in my ear. "Let's try that again. Would you like to go on a picnic with me on Sunday?"

I waited, wondering if church was on the agenda as well. But he added nothing to the invitation.

"Where do you want to meet?" I asked.

"I'll pick you up at your place."

I took a chance. "Or we could meet at church."

Jack was silent a moment. "Or we could," he agreed.

I never knew you could hear a smile over the phone.

"I'm on night shift until Saturday," he said, "so I probably won't see you until Sunday."

"Then I'll see you at church." I waited a moment for him to hang up, heard a throaty chuckle and then a beep as he disconnected. Flipping my cell phone shut, I tossed it onto the seat beside me. I smiled as I thought of the detour my life had taken in the past few weeks. Things were good.

Actually, things were very good.

I turned the corner and there it was. The church where I was meeting Jack.

Though I was already late, my foot came off the accelerator. What if I was making a big mistake? My blue jeans and corduroy blazer seemed pretty suitable back at home, but seemed too casual now that I faced a building with stained-glass windows and topped with a cross.

I gave my head a shake. If Jesus was willing to go looking for a lost sheep, I was sure He wouldn't fuss with what that sheep's wool looked like once He found it. Or that this particular sheep had slept in and stood a good chance of missing the first part of the service.

I angled down the rearview mirror, finger-combed my hair, licked my lips, and brushed a piece of lint off my jacket. I was as ready as I'd ever be.

This was a new adventure for me, I thought. Meeting a guy at church. I wished Leslie was here for extra moral support, but she was working so I was going solo this morning.

As I came closer to the church, I saw a man running up the steps. Thank goodness I wasn't the only latecomer. And then my cell phone rang. I pulled the phone out of my purse reminding myself to turn it off after this call. As I flipped it open, I glanced over the parking lot. It was already full.

"Hello," I said, hoping it wasn't Jack, calling to cancel.

"Well, well, you did miss me."

The blood drained out of my head, my hands, my arms. The phone wobbled and I couldn't breathe.

"Eric. How did you get this number?"

"The magic of caller ID, honey."

I fought the panic that grabbed my throat. I remembered dialing the number of the apartment by mistake. I had hung up as soon as I realized what I'd done, but obviously not fast enough. "I guess I'll have to change this number, then." *Relax. He has no clue where you are.* I spied an empty spot in front of a house a ways down the street, drove to it, and parked my car. "I don't want any more unexpected calls from you."

"Unexpected? C'mon, honey, you wound me." His voice was as smooth and charming as ever. But the easy tones sent a chill through my midsection. "Don't tell me you thought you would never see me again."

"I thought I wouldn't even hear from you again." I got out of the car, urgency hurrying my steps.

"I told you not to run away from me. I told you I would find you."

Time to end this call.

"Good-bye, Eric."

"You're breaking my heart, Terra. This abrupt good-bye after all we shared?"

"We didn't share anything, Eric."

"Then why are you still talking to me?"

Why indeed? I hurried just a little faster. The church doors were already closed, but I felt an overwhelming urge to be behind them. To find sanctuary there.

Sanctuary and Jack.

"By the way, you can stop running, honey. You'll see me soon enough."

What did he mean? I glanced around and almost dropped my phone.

A tall, heavyset figure sauntered down the empty sidewalk toward me. Black leather coat, dark jeans, and white shirt.

Eric, with his cell phone to his ear.

"See, darlin'?" his smooth voice drawled in my ear. "I told you that you couldn't run away from me. When you used the debit card in that grocery store in Harland, I knew I had found my girl."

Stupid, careless girl.

"And don't bother trying to run back to your little car. You won't get far in those boots."

In spite of his warning, I stopped and looked back to my car. He was right. I'd never get to the car before he caught me. I was trapped.

"So now what, Eric?" I asked as he came closer. "What do you propose to do?"

He was close enough for me to see a lazy smile crawl over his lips. Whiskers shadowed his lean jaw, and his hair looked like it hadn't been combed in a couple of days. A casual pass-erby could be excused for thinking he looked distraught from missing me. "I'll charge you with theft, for starters. Pulling that money out of our account? That hurts. Thank goodness I set it up so we could only pull out two hundred bucks at a time; otherwise, who knows how much you would have taken me for."

"You owed me that money, Eric. I paid the rent for the past two months." I snapped my cell phone shut.

Eric made a show of scratching his head, as if trying to gather his thoughts. We were close enough now and he shut his phone off as well. "Well, seeing as it's your name on the lease . . ." He spread his hands in a *What can I do?* gesture. "You're still a thief."

"We had an agreement when—"

"When what?" Now he was directly in front of me, block-ing my way.

"When you moved in with me." I spoke quietly. To have to say these words aloud in front of the church showed my previ-ous life for what it was. Tawdry and shallow and cheap.

Even though many of our friends had lived together, I knew it was wrong then, and I knew it even more now.

Shame washed over me as I was faced with the reality of the baggage I carried.

"If you really need that money, I can pay you back."

He put his hand under my chin, and as soon as I looked into his flat, blue eyes, I knew this had nothing to do with money. A chill slithered down my back.

"I didn't drag my sorry self all the way to this hick town

just to collect a few hundred bucks." He shook his head as if surprised at my naïveté. "This is about much, much more than that, babe. It's about you and me and what we had going. We were going to have a baby together . . ."

"That you didn't want." I pressed my lips together. Hadn't I learned? Confrontation and contradiction were not how to deal with Eric.

"That hurt, babe. How could I not want a child that we made together?"

Now I was getting creeped out. How could I have gotten involved with this guy? What had I been thinking?

I hadn't. Been thinking, that is. In the beginning, Eric had charm. He was attentive. And every time we went out, he had another gift for me. He even hinted at marriage. I was taken in by it all, jealous of my sister and her stable life. I wanted some of that stability myself. And I thought Eric was the one to help me achieve that. By the time he had moved in, I'd realized my mistake.

But then he wouldn't leave, and he wouldn't leave me alone.

Just like now.

The very single-mindedness of his trip here made my heart pound. He had warned me the first time he caught me packing my bags that if I ever left, he would find me and kill me.

What could I do?

Pray?

Wasn't I on the wrong side of the church doors for that to have any effect? Did I seriously think God would listen to someone who hadn't spent any time with Him at all?

"Were you heading there?" Eric asked, angling his head toward the church behind us. He laughed. "Do you really think those Christians want someone like you? Do you think God wants someone like you?"

I faced him down, my own insecurities fighting with what I'd been told by Jack, Cor, Leslie. My own reading of the Bible.

"I think He does. So please, move."

"Please. That's a polite touch." Eric smiled, and ice slivered through my veins.

"I'm going inside, Eric." He moved to block me.

"Get out of my way," I yelled, fear and anger propelling the words out of me.

Eric grabbed for me, and I ducked, screamed, and started running. I knew he was going to catch me, but I wasn't going to make things easy for him. He wasn't going to take me without a fight.

"Get back here, Terra. You'll be sorry . . ."

Heavy footfalls behind me, a hand grabbing at my shoulder. So close. Too close.

I twisted away, spun around. I was tired of being afraid of this man. I made another quick turn, then ran up the church steps and turned to face him.

He charged up the steps, but I had the high ground. I swung my purse and smacked him right across his face. He pulled back, and for a split second stared at me in disbelief.

I hit him again, but Eric's volatile anger kicked in. He grabbed me and hauled me down the stairs. Or tried. I hit, I kicked, I punched, I elbowed. I didn't care what happened to me. I would not go down without a fight.

And then, behind me, the church door slammed open.

"Stop right there," I heard a rough and familiar voice call out.

My foot twisted to one side, and I fell onto my knees. Eric grabbed me by both arms as he tried to haul me to my feet.

"Gotcha now——" But the rest of what he said was cut off. His hand let go of me and I fell onto my chest, my chin scraping the sidewalk. Through the sudden ringing in my brain I heard a thud, an exhalation, a few more thuds and grunts, and then Eric was screaming at someone to get his knee off his back.

"Terra, are you okay?" I heard Jack call. "Are you okay? Someone help Terra."

I dimly heard Eric yelling that he was going to sue as I tried to sit up. Then a grunt from him and silence.

Feet pounded down the steps. I caught a whiff of perfume and looked up to see Gloria, her forehead creased with concern as she helped me sit up. She gently brushed my hair away from my face, then grimaced. "You need to have that checked out."

I put my hand to my face, but she stopped me. "Don't. Your chin is all scraped up. It's bleeding."

"How is she? How's Terra?" Jack's voice held an urgency that drew my attention to him. He was kneeling on Eric's back, Eric's arms twisted up behind him. Cor was standing over them.

"Who do you think you are, huh?" Cor yelled at him. "Who do you think you are? Coming here and causing trouble for our Terra?"

"Dad. That's enough," Jack said, not moving, his hard eyes flicking my way.

"I'm okay," I said, wincing as Gloria helped me to my feet.

My neck hurt and as I turned, I saw a group of people standing at the top of the steps. Had they all seen what happened?

One of the young men came running down the stairs. "Do you need help, Jack? Can I do anything?"

Jack handed the young man his cell phone and gave him instructions, his voice brusque and businesslike as he tugged his tie off then wound it around Eric's hands with swift economical movements.

This wasn't the same Jack who had held me on the bench in the park. Not the same Jack who had cooked dinner.

This Jack was serious business, and I was glad I wasn't on the ground, under his knee.

A couple of women came down the stairs toward me. "Are you okay, Terra?"

"Oh, no, you're hurt!" the other exclaimed.

A murmur rose from the group and grew as the news passed from person to person, and soon the entire congregation of the church knew that Terra Froese, sister of Leslie VandeKeere, had just had a fight with her old boyfriend, who was subdued by Jack DeWindt.

I'd have to leave now for sure, I thought as Gloria helped me to her car. All I needed was for the *Harland Chronicle* to get wind of this debacle, and I'd never live it down.

Chapter Twenty-three

A re you sure you're okay?" Leslie dabbed the abrasion on my chin with an alcohol swab. I winced.

"Yeah. My pride took a worse beating than my face did." I gave her a wavery smile as I swung my legs onto the gurney. "At least I got a few hits in."

"So I heard," she said, a note of admiration in her voice.

"I didn't want to be afraid of him anymore."

Leslie put a bandage over my chin and gently taped it down. "I'm sure Eric has a few things to be afraid of himself. I heard that Jack was a bit rough with him."

"I hope Jack doesn't get into trouble over it."

"I doubt it." Leslie finished taping. "Well, you're good as new. Now you just have to wait for Sheriff Diener. He wants some kind of statement from you." Leslie tossed the alcohol swab into a garbage can and made a quick note on my chart. She stripped off her gloves and pitched them in the garbage as well, then gave me an encouraging smile. "Are you okay?"

The aftermath of the morning pressed down on me. "I was on my way to church, you know," I said, drawing in a shaky breath. "I was going to meet Jack there."

Leslie gently stroked my hair away from my face. "So I understand. I'm so glad. You're a good person, big sister. You really are."

"Well, not really, but thanks for saying so."

"You are. I heard what you did for Amelia."

"I didn't do anything for her."

"You were a friend to her. You stood up for her. You're the one she went to when she got hurt. That means something."

"What's going to happen with her and Madison?"

Leslie shook her head. "She finally agreed to let us run the tests on Madison, to nail down the failure to thrive issue. I'm fairly sure that Amelia, given the right support and help, will be able to take better care of Madison. Rod wants to stay involved."

"I feel a little dumb about Rod," I said quietly, picking at a broken nail. "I was so sure he was exactly like Eric. I was so sure he didn't want Madison, just like Eric didn't want that . . . our baby. But I didn't deserve . . ."

No. I shouldn't go there. I was feeling too vulnerable to bring that up.

I closed my eyes and tried to relax. Tried to fight down the relentless undertow of emotions that threatened to swamp me. I'd been feeling shaky ever since I heard Eric's voice on my phone. I couldn't get a grip on the loose ends long enough to pull it all together.

"Didn't deserve . . ." Leslie prompted.

Still I hesitated. What would she say if I told her? I had held the secret so close for so long. Would she understand?

"I've got time." As if to underline her point, the gurney squeaked as she sat down beside me. She took my hand and laid it palm up on hers. "Talk to me."

Would releasing the words so long held down change anything?

"I love you, Terra. You need to know that."

I acknowledged her gift with a nod, took a deep breath to center myself, and began. "I was going to have a baby."

The sorrow on her face made me feel bad that I hadn't told her before.

"I didn't connect with you when you were having your troubles with Nicholas because my own life was such a mess." I took a slow, shaky breath, trying vainly to find equilibrium. "I got pregnant. Eric didn't want the baby, and I wasn't sure I wanted to bring a child into that messy relationship. So he drove me to the clinic and dropped me off." I stopped there, trying to read some reaction from Leslie, but she continued holding my hand, her fingers gently stroking it, as if drawing my confession from me.

"I waited until he was gone and then started walking around, thinking. I couldn't do it. I thought maybe if I waited he would get used to the idea. Then two months later, I miscarried." Hot tears coursed down my cheeks.

"But you didn't follow through with the abortion. Losing that baby wasn't your fault."

"Maybe it was."

"What do you mean?"

I thought of what Cor had told me. That our sins were an abyss between us and God, and when confessed, they became a bridge. I needed to tell someone the story I had held close all those years. Who better than my own sister?

"I was sixteen," I began. "Just a bit younger than Tabitha is now. I was dating Corey Schroeder. We . . . we were intimate. I got pregnant."

Leslie's hand tightened.

In the background I heard the rattle of a cart being pushed down the hallway. Life moving on while for me, here in this small confessional, time moved backward.

"I was scared. I didn't know who to talk to. Mom wasn't around much, so I went to a guidance counselor at school who put me onto a social worker. This guy must have taken a bunch of sensitivity training courses because he kept telling me I was a victim, I had rights, and I had a right to take care of me. I was valuable. The whole schmear. Then he laid out the numerous ways a baby would ruin my sixteen-year-old life. How I wouldn't be able to finish school. How I would end up in a dead-end job, practically on welfare. Living Mom's life. He had me shaking. So when he suggested an abortion, it made sense. Seemed easy. So I agreed."

"He didn't give you an alternative? Adoption?"

"Not protocol, I guess." As the words rolled off my tongue, the old feelings of fear and guilt washed over me once again. The disorientation I had felt when I walked out of the clinic looking, from the outside, as if nothing had happened. But inside I had a hollowness that I'd tried ever since to fill.

"When I decided to keep this baby, I thought this was my chance to atone for what I had done. To right the wrong. Eric tried to make abortion sound so easy, but I know better. It's not like pulling a tooth. It's like pulling out your soul." I looked up at Leslie. "No one ever wants to acknowledge the side effects, you know? I've met women who have had two, three abortions and they act like nothing happened. But there's an echo of pain, guilt, and even a bit of fear that you can push down, but it never really goes away. It didn't for me. God knew I didn't deserve that baby. I did wrong. I was punished."

When I'd insisted on seeing the baby, the nurses brought me a tiny, fragile creature with underdeveloped skin that had darkened after birth, but she had eyes, lips, ears, and fingers as tiny as a grain of rice.

And when I held her, I realized that what I had previously swept from my womb was not tissue or the euphemistic product of conception.

It was a child.

And then the guilt, suppressed so long, had washed over me in a wave that threatened to pull me under.

"Life for a life, I figured. That's why I can't judge Mom. She kept us both. She kept us together. After I lost the baby, I realized I didn't deserve to have her because of what I had done before." My throat closed off as grief sluiced through me, pulling me down into the guilt and pain once again.

"Don't talk like that. God doesn't work that way." Leslie blew out a sigh. "I don't know where in the Bible the passage is, but I remember something about God not punishing us as our sins deserve. God is like a Father. He loves us so much that He gave His Son so we could live. I know I sound like the televangelists we used to poke fun at, but I know it's real. I've experienced that love. That comfort. It's there for you, too. All you have to do is just what you've done. Confess. Acknowledge that you've done wrong."

My mind slipped back to Father Sam. *Confession. Absolution.*

The words lingered, tantalizing with their promise of comfort.

"It sounds too easy."

"Forgiveness is too easy. We don't deserve how easy it is."

I closed my eyes to absorb better what Leslie was saying. And as she spoke, the tears came again. And again, I couldn't stop them.

Sorrow is not graceful, I thought as I took the tissue from Leslie's hand and started mopping up. I heard the swish of another tissue being pulled out of the box that had magically appeared on Leslie's lap, and I took it and tossed aside the soggy mess of the first one. Then I took another.

And another.

My eyes were thick and sore and my nose raw by the time I was done.

I sniffed, and finally dared to look at Leslie.

Leslie, who had endured her own storm of sorrow for a child. But she had been praying for health, for recovery, for a child she had wanted. She had gone through that dark valley with her child and come out the other side, her family intact and bound together by their experiences.

I was a ragged mess with a medical bill I had finally paid off and nothing to show for my experience. Nothing outwardly, at least.

"So what am I supposed to do now?" I asked, looking at my dear sister's tender expression.

"For now? Sheriff Diener needs to ask you a few questions, which I promise won't take long. I'm going to finish up my charting. Then I want you to come home with me. I'm taking the next few days off. Just to be with you."

Then, while I was still trying to absorb it all, I looked out the half-open door and there stood Jack, his arms folded across his brown jacket, his head bare, his eyes looking directly at me.

And from the hard set of his features, I was sure he had heard every word of my sorry tale.

"Thanks for your time, Terra," Sheriff Diener said, snapping shut his notebook. "I just have to ask Dr. Brown and Leslie a few questions and we're done here."

Jack nodded, and when Sheriff Diener left, pushed himself away from the wall and walked toward me. "How are you doing?" he asked, his voice softened with concern.

I kept my eyes on the vending machine across from me. "I'm okay." The epitome of bland. What else could I say? I had to gather up some vestige of privacy. I had just let go of secrets I'd held to myself for years, and this man, whom I barely knew, might have heard them. "So what's going to happen to Eric?"

"He'll probably get bail."

I felt a shiver of fear.

"But I'm pretty sure he won't be trying anything." He waited a beat, then crouched down in front of me. "Are you going to be okay?"

When he took my hand, his calluses rough on my skin, I tried not to read more into it than plain ordinary comfort. And though I yearned for more than that, I knew for now I didn't deserve more.

I didn't want to think that I didn't deserve him. Living with Eric had worn away enough of my self-esteem. But the reality was that I was hardly the virginal girlfriend I was sure good Christian men like him preferred.

"I'm sorry we didn't get to go on our picnic."

I was too.

And with that, he straightened, then left.

I released the breath I hadn't known I was holding. *Well, I guess that was that.*

Chapter Twenty-four

An hour later, Leslie's car crunched up the gravel drive to her home.

This was a home with a complete family. And in spite of their troubles, Dan and Leslie had stuck it out. They were established members of society with neat and tidy lives. They went to church and paid taxes. They didn't have public brawls on the church steps with ex-live-ins who had threatened to kill them.

No amount of self-talk could get rid of the feeling that I was a ragged, naked, and unworthy prodigal sister come to beg for scraps.

"Are you going to tell Dan?" I asked as Leslie parked the car.

"I'm sure he and half of Harland know about Eric already," she said.

"I meant about the rest."

Leslie turned off the engine, and as the quiet of the country pressed in on us, she sighed. "He doesn't *need* to know. But I *want* him to know. I want him to understand what you've had to deal with."

My silence must have said more than I realized because suddenly Leslie grabbed my hands in hers. "None of us deserve what we have. All of us need God's grace in our lives. All of us. And that includes Dan and me and his family."

I wished I believed her. But even as she spoke those quiet words of reassurance, I kept seeing Jack's face. Kept wondering what was going through his mind.

I got out of the car and followed Leslie up the walk to the house. The door opened on our arrival, and Dan stood silhouetted against the light. Leslie got a hug, a gentle kiss.

Then Dan let go of Leslie, walked forward, and stood in front of me. "Nice to have you here," he said, holding out his hand to me.

"Thanks, Dan." I took his hand, and then, to my surprise, he pulled me close in a rough hug. He held me for a moment, then stepped away, looking as if his manliness had somehow been compromised. In spite of the turmoil of emotions I had just dealt with, I had to smile.

Leslie led me upstairs. I showered, changed, and, ignoring the time on the clock, crawled into bed, weary and wrung out. But no sooner had I pulled the blankets around me than the door opened once again.

"You may as well come in," I said, turning over.

"You don't mind?" Leslie poked her head through the door, her expression tentative.

"Please. Come."

When she was settled on the bed, facing me, she reached over and gently stroked a strand of damp hair away from my face. "I'm so glad you can stay here for a bit."

"I'm glad too." The last words came out with a weary sigh. "I think I need to be here."

Leslie smiled. "You know, as much as I grumbled about how you came here, it was meant to be."

"Destiny?"

"Well, I was praying for you."

"So I didn't have any choice?"

"Not as much as you thought you did."

"And all the stuff that happened?"

"Who knows the mind of God?" Leslie said. Her face grew serious. "I want to tell you that I'm sorry I warned you against Jack. That wasn't fair. Wasn't my business."

"You were probably right, though. I haven't been one to stick around."

"Meaning you might be now?"

I wished I could answer her. "I don't know what I want anymore."

"You could stay awhile. Figure out what you want to do."

"I could."

"I think Jack would want you to."

"You were right, Leslie. I'm not good enough for him."

"Do you like him?"

"What is this, a junior high slumber party?"

"Do you?" Leslie repeated her question, her voice quiet. Serious.

"I'd like to."

Leslie's smile showed me I was off the hook. "That's good."

"Though I still feel unworthy."

"I have to think of something I read somewhere. Something about our spirits being restless and finding their rest in God. I've found a lot of peace in my life since I became a Christian." Leslie cocked her head to one side. "I think you came here seeking, consciously or unconsciously. I think you knew your life wasn't working. And I'd like to think that God answered my prayer by bringing you back."

"Poor little lost lamb chop," I said.

"Yeah. Poor lost Terra." She breathed out my name on a light sigh, then touched my hand. "Can I pray with you?"

I nodded, my previous objections to faith withered by the steady onslaught of words, love, and caring I had received since coming to Harland.

I had no defense and, I realized, no longer wanted one. My resistance had been an unthinking absorption of my mother's thoughts and opinions. I had never read or experienced enough to form my own.

But here in Harland, I had experienced God as tangible. As real. And I wanted to bridge that chasm and get to know Him for myself.

"You need to close your eyes," Leslie instructed. "Then you won't get distracted."

When I did, she began.

"Dear Lord, thank You that Terra came here. Thank You for what she showed me. For what she told me. Please, heal her pain, Lord. Fill the emptiness in her life with Your love. Help her see that she can find rest for her weary soul in You."

I felt like a distant cousin being presented to the patriarch of a family. Unworthy and unrecognized.

Yet, as she prayed, a gentle peace suffused me, washing away the stress of the evening, softening the pain I had unearthed. I felt carried. Like the lost lamb Cor had said I was.

Then she said, "In Jesus' name, amen," and squeezed my hands, and I dared to open my eyes.

"That's it?" I asked.

Leslie smiled. "For now." She stroked my cheek, then bent over and kissed me lightly on the forehead. "You just rest."

I smiled at her as my mind grew fuzzy, waited until the door clicked shut behind her, then rolled over onto my side and let sleep's sticky fingers draw me down.

Sasha sighed, dropped her head onto her paws, and lifted her eyes, as if double-checking to see if maybe, this time, I would leave the shelter of this poplar tree on the crest of the hill and go wandering as we'd done yesterday.

I liked sitting under this tree. I liked how the leaves rustled when the wind picked up, laying down a gentle foundation of sound on which to gather my scattered thoughts.

I'd found the tree the day before in my uncharted rambles around the pastures and fields of Dan and Leslie's farm. I had a perfect view of fields laid out below me with swaths of alternating brown and green. Summer fallow and crops, Dan had told me. The patterns of dryland farming.

Shadows of the puffy clouds in the endless sky above chased one another silently across the valley, and all around, serene and quiet, lay the jagged purple edge of mountains. Like a border of lace on a tablecloth.

Sasha sighed a doggy sigh, then closed her eyes, giving up on me. I opened the Bible that Leslie had given me and turned to one of the psalms she had recommended.

Psalm 130.

"A song of ascents." Whatever that meant.

I took a deep breath and started reading out loud, my voice muted, lost in the vast space surrounding me. "'Out of the depths I cry to you, O Lord; O Lord, hear my voice. Let your ears be attentive to my cry for mercy.'" I took a moment to let the words settle into my soul. To let them speak for me. I wondered if God could pick the sound out of the millions of voices that cried out to Him every day. Leslie said He could and He did.

"'If you, O Lord, kept a record of sins, O Lord, who could stand?'" I liked the sound of that word prefacing the question. *If.* Keeping a record of sins was not a foregone conclusion. Were my own sins lost? Unrecorded? "'But with you there is forgiveness; therefore you are feared.'" I didn't understand that part, but I clung to the forgiveness portion of the psalm. I still felt I had much to be forgiven for. But since I had come to Harland, I'd also felt the first glimmerings of hope and of rec-onciliation. As I worked alongside Leslie through the rhythms of her day as wife and mother, I felt a gentle peace suffuse a life that had seen little of it in the past few months.

Sasha lifted her head, then jumped to her feet, her tail wag-ging, looking down the cow trail we had followed to get here.

I wondered if Leslie had followed me, but as I turned around with a happy smile of welcome, my heart forgot its next beat.

Jack strode up the trail toward me, his hands tucked in the pockets of his blue jeans, his eyes on the ground ahead of him. He looked up as Sasha bounded toward him. As he reached out to pet her, his gaze caught and held mine.

"Hey there," he said, his rough voice resonating in the thick quiet his presence created. "Leslie said I could find you here. I hope you don't mind."

I shook my head, embarrassingly tongue-tied.

"Dad and I brought your car."

"How is your dad?"

"He's fine. Wondering when you're coming back to listen to some more bad jokes and serve him coffee at the café. He and Father Sam miss you. Some of the other patrons have been making up new names for the menu items."

"That'll be interesting." I was missed. *Imagine that.*

"Thought you might also want to know about Eric," he said, still petting Sasha, who leaned against his leg, soaking up the extra attention. "Can I . . . ?" He gestured toward the ground beside me. I moved over as he sat down.

"You won't have to show up at the trial if you don't want to," Jack said. "There were enough witnesses."

"The wheels of justice seemed to turn quicker for Eric than for me. I had to wait longer for a trial."

Jack scratched Sasha behind the ears. "Well, there were a few extenuating circumstances with you and Ralph."

"How so?"

Jack shrugged. "I figured I could get Ralph to drop the charges, so I just told the judge that things were pending yet. And I was right."

"I don't know if I thanked you properly for that."

Jack's gaze caught and held mine. "There's time." The faint promise in those words kindled a glow of hope.

"Good to know."

"I also talked to Rod. Amelia has agreed to in-home care, and Rod has agreed that he needs to get out of her life for a while. So she can sort things out."

"They were living together, but that didn't bother you?"

"It did. I'm not going to lie."

I winced from the deflected blow, but I had no right to be upset.

Jack had standards, and I knew I fell short of them. *Reality check, missy.*

"Amelia also agreed to have medical assessment tests done on Madison and to get a nutritionist involved."

"I'm so glad. That baby needs some extra care."

"She's getting it." He leaned forward, his elbows resting on his knees as he looked out over the fields. Finally he looked sidelong at me. "Did you get past Deuteronomy?"

I held up the Bible, still open to Psalm 130. "Leslie gave me some suggestions. Should be an interesting trip. Probably the only one I'll be taking for awhile."

Jack leaned back against the tree.

"So that means you're not taking my dad's old car and heading down the open road?"

I shook my head, running my thumb down the gilt edge of the page. "I was thinking of staying before you asked me to."

"I'm glad."

I turned to face him. "Why?"

He fixed me with a clear, unwavering gaze. "Because I like you. And I want to get to know you better."

Long seconds ticked between us as I absorbed the promise in his words.

"In spite of the messy life you got to hear about the other day in the hospital?"

Through the thin knit of my T-shirt I felt the warmth of his hand on my shoulder. "I heard the story of a young girl who didn't have the support and guidance she needed. A girl whose only mistake was to believe the advice of people who didn't care as much for her as they should have. I heard about a woman who was abused and working with wrong information."

"What I should have done was talk to someone else."

"Who?"

I had no answer. His hand tightened, then turned me to

face him. "What you did when you were young was a mistake. But what you did for Amelia was an atonement, Terra." He sat up, slipped his hand to the back of my neck, and let his fingers linger a moment, sending shivers up my neck. "You showed me how a Christian should behave."

His words were like rain on parched ground. I hardly dared believe that this upstanding, caring man was sitting beside me, his deep voice filling empty spaces in my life while his hand caressed my neck.

"Did you mean what you said about staying around?"

"Yeah. Don't have anywhere else to go and no reason to go there. Why?"

"My dad told me I was too cautious, and much as I hated to admit it, he was right. I've always been so careful about who I dated. I was waiting for something, some connection that never happened. Then you came whirling into town, and for the first time in a long time, I met a girl I found fascinating. So I decided to take a chance, and I was hoping you'd be willing to do the same. To take a chance to let us get to know each other better. See where it goes."

I sat immobile, hardly daring to believe what he was saying. "I've got a lot to learn," I said quietly, unsure of how to progress. "And a lot of other baggage comes with me. Other sins. Other mistakes."

Jack gently took the Bible from my unresisting hands. He paged through the book one-handed, then started reading.

" 'He does not treat us as our sins deserve or repay us according to our iniquities. For as high as the heavens are above the earth, so great is his love for those who fear him; as far as the east is from the west, so far has he removed our transgressions from us.' " Jack smiled at me, the crinkles I was getting to know well forming at the corners of his eyes. "I guess that pretty much tells you what can happen to those mistakes and that baggage."

"As high as the heavens are above the earth." Above us, white clouds drifted aimlessly, blown by a wind I couldn't feel. I thought of my first view of Harland. Of the endless blue sky. "That's a long ways." Then, looking back at Jack, I took a chance, as he had recommended, and reached out with both hands and cupped his face. "I guess someone willing to hitch-hike the roads of Harland County, work with Mathilde, and try to read the Bible for the first time in her life should be able to take a chance with a policeman."

Jack's smile held all the promises of tomorrow.

His kiss was the seal on today.

Reading Group Guide

1. Terra has been living footloose and so-called fancy free. What are the advantages of a lifestyle like that? The disadvantages?

2. Terra carried a burden of guilt that took time for her to acknowledge. Why do you think she hid it? What were some of the things she felt guilty about? What are some of the things she should have felt guilty about?

3. Father Sam spoke of confession being a bridge to God. Do you agree? Why?

4. Many women are caught in situations that are destructive and abusive. How do you think this happens?

5. Terra originally planned to stay with her sister, Leslie, only for a short while. Why do you think she wanted to keep moving? What made her want to stay?

6. Why do you think the story line of Leslie and Terra's mother wasn't resolved? How do you see that playing out? What are some possibilities for this situation that are realistic?

7. Terra befriended a young woman who was struggling. Could you identify with Terra's point of view of the situation? Have you ever made a wrong call on a situation based on your own experiences? If so, how did you resolve it?

8. Why do you think Terra assumed God would not forgive what she had done?

9. In this second book a recurring character, Tabitha, shows up again, making yet another set of mistakes. Why does it take some people a couple of times to learn a lesson? How do you think this was mirrored in Terra's life?

10. There are a couple of themes running through this book. What do you think one of them is?

About the Author

Carolyne was originally a city girl transplanted to the country when she married her dear husband, Richard. Thankfully the move took. While raising four children and a number of foster children, as well as assorted chickens, dogs, cats, and cows, Carolyne's résumé gained a few unique entries. Besides the usual challenges and joys of wife and motherhood, she found out how to grow a garden, can produce, bake, sew, pickle, and preserve. She learned how to sort pigs; handle cows; cant logs at their small sawmill; drive a tractor, an ATV, a snow machine; ride a horse; and train a colt. Through all of this, she came to appreciate the open spaces of the countryside, the pace of life away from the city, and the fellowship in the Christian community she and her family became a part of. She is most thankful, however, to be able to express her faith in God through the books and stories she writes.

For more information about her books, past and current, stop by her Web site at www.carolyneaarsen.com, or her blog at www.carolyneaarsen.blogspot.com and drop her a comment or a letter.

If you enjoyed
All in One Place . . .

The Only Best Place

A thriving career. A big-city life. A move
that could change her dreams forever.

Leslie VandeKeere had a good life:
a happy family, a great career (even if
it did pull her away from home), and
all the energy of urban living. But she
finds herself miles away from the city
she knows and loves when her husband
moves her and the kids back to his boyhood home in Montana,
to help his mother work the struggling family farm. Being
a farmer's wife was definitely *not* in Leslie's plan, and now
she finds herself dealing with dirty cows, giant machinery,
eccentric neighbors, and an extended family she doesn't quite
fit into. When her husband begins to hint that the move might
be permanent, Leslie must decide—can she really handle this
much fresh air?

Available now at a bookstore near you!